September Girl

To Mary Beth
Enjoy!
Kathryn Leigh Scott

September Girl

a novel

KATHRYN LEIGH SCOTT

Cumberland Press
New York

Available in trade paperback and e-book
Trade paperback ISBN: 978-0-9862459-7-8

Cumberland Press, New York, New York

For author contact and press inquiries, e-mail
cumberlandpressbooks@gmail.com. To order signed copies, visit
kathrynleighscott.com.

Also by Kathryn Leigh Scott

FICTION

Meg Barnes Novels
Down and Out in Beverly Heels
Jinxed

Dark Passages

NONFICTION

Last Dance at the Savoy
The Happy Hours
Now With You, Now Without
A Welcome Respite
The Bunny Years
Dark Shadows: Return to Collinwood
Dark Shadows Memories
Dark Shadows Almanac
The Dark Shadows Companion
Lobby Cards: The Classic Films
Lobby Cards: The Classic Comedies

FOR NICKIE,

AND MY DEAREST DEPARTED FRIEND, BRIAN

Chapter 1

FELIX STREAKED ACROSS MY PATH, his ebony fur bristling in the wintry blast from the open door. Jake, a step behind, bumped against me as the cat leapt to his customary perch in the bay window of the restaurant.

"Tonight of all nights!" I leaned into Jake. "You think it's an omen?"

"Always. That's his job, Livvie. But I've appeased him by ordering their best Bordeaux." Jake had already called ahead to have Alain, the chef and owner, decant a bottle of St. Estephe.

Felix, his work done, lay curled in cat-like indifference on a well-worn cushion. But on a night when tidings of disaster ruled the universe, a black feline crossing my tracks left a sense of foreboding hard to shake. I slipped off my coat and took comfort in the fragrant warmth of the restaurant.

If Jake and I were to enjoy a last meal on earth, there was no place better than our favorite corner table at Le Chat Noir, a family-owned bistro in Greenwich Village. That was our plan for the eve of the new millennium, January 1, 2000, the day that life as we'd lived it would abruptly change, if not end altogether. For the better part of a year, dire Y2K warnings predicted computers would malfunction, causing airplanes to fall from the sky, trains to collide, banks to fail and nuclear reactors to spew radioactive fallout, obliterating all life on the planet.

Jake, a journalism professor and former senior editor at a major news magazine, had cast a dubious eye on the wild projections of Y2K havoc that prompted otherwise sane people to accumulate a two-month supply of cash, bottled water, medicine, tinned food and generators, but he'd backed up his computer's hard drive just in case. As a freelance travel writer, I'd pitched a tongue-in-cheek piece on avoiding trips over the New Year's holiday, particularly those involving air travel, that saw print as a hoary checklist of emergency supplies to pack and an admonition to keep an eye on breaking news: first reports of Y2K disasters would probably come from New Zealand.

"Then what?" Jake grunted incredulously when I showed him my published travel feature. "Duck and cover?"

"My editor's two cents' worth, but at least I got her to take out the part about filling a bathtub with drinking water."

I'd backed up my hard drive, too, and took the added precaution of printing out a draft of a book due to my publisher the following week. *September Girl*, a novel about a woman who finds unexpected romance later in life, was a significant departure from my lighthearted mystery series featuring a travel writer who solved crimes, primarily murder, in scenic locales. I was nervous enough about the book's reception, but the specter of losing all I'd written and having to begin again was a stomach-churning nightmare I couldn't face.

I also sensibly invested in a box of Maison du Chocolat and a fine vintage champagne to see us through the doomsday forecast. Meanwhile, a bottle of red accompanying slow-cooked comfort food—braised short ribs for Jake, coq au vin for me and a plate of profiteroles to share—in a restaurant that had remained unchanged since before JFK was elected was an ideal way to spend the century's waning hours. After dinner, we walked home to my old garden apartment, now our pied-à-terre in New York. Wrapped in each other's arms, we stood in the snow-covered backyard toasting the New Year at the stroke of midnight. If earth survived the dawn of the new millennium with no disruption, we'd drive back to our home in Connecticut the following morning and life would go on.

It did. On New Year's Day, the coffeemaker worked, the *New York Times* was on the doorstep and the young couple in the apartment next door welcomed home Justin, their first born, a brown-eyed baby boy with a pair of robust lungs. We returned to our cottage in the wooded fields of rural Connecticut and life went on, at least for a little while longer.

What we could not have anticipated was a warm summer day in late May, not quite six months into the year 2000, when Jake would look at me in surprise before collapsing on the tennis court. That's when everything we'd been led to believe might collide, fall out of the sky, break down and stop, did.

The new millennium, rather than hurtling me into the future, unexpectedly sent me straight to a reckoning with my past.

Chapter 2

LATE ONE DRIZZLY JUNE MORNING, I sat at Jake's desk in the wood-paneled attic looking out the window at the tennis court, my gaze riveted on the sagging, rain-soaked net I could no longer bear to go near. Rumbling thunder unleashed a rainsquall that slashed across the court, the wind whipping the net into jerky frenzy. I grimly willed the straining net to rip free from its cords and blow far away. I didn't want to be reminded of the sunny morning when Jake had reached for the towel and collapsed, his fingers tangling in the webbing as he fell. If he were to choose a place to die a quick, sudden death, his beloved tennis court would've ranked as a fitting spot—just not so soon, his look of surprise had said.

I'd spent the morning responding to bereavement notes in longhand on thick cards with a narrow black border. Wearing one of his flannel work shirts, I thanked the multitudes my husband had loved and befriended, who had sent flowers and condolence cards. I read scores of well-composed, artfully written personal tributes to a gifted editor who had nurtured so many writers.

It was the card from Robert Yardley, a photographer Jake had worked with on an assignment in Northern Ireland, that was the most unexpected, flooding me with memories of my early career as a picture researcher at a news magazine. I'd met Robert years before I knew my husband, and I'd never told Jake the details of a fraught romance that ended badly. There'd been no need to. So why did I feel guilty now?

Unsure how to personally respond, I'd set the card aside, intending to move on with others. And yet here I still sat, pen in hand, anger welling up. Widow's Rage, I told myself, part of the grieving process. But it was Robert I fixated on, his card expressing "heartfelt sympathy" provoking memories of all that remained unresolved between us. It wasn't until I'd met Jake that I'd felt able to come to terms with that part of my life. And now Jake was gone.

Jake and I bought the cottage on a whim shortly after we married, justifying the purchase as an affordable weekend getaway in close proximity to a commuter line. The main selling point was the quirky, hand-built fieldstone-and-timber house that seemed to wrap itself around us the moment we walked through the door. The acre and a half of land also afforded space for a tennis court, an extravagance Jake, an avid player, coveted. The house he dubbed Willow Creek became the lodestone pulling him back between postings abroad, the "someday place" where he'd eventually settle. He was a bear of a man, tall, burly and agile, who made five-year plans, charting our course and organizing our lives with little regard for fate playing a hand.

How long did I sit transfixed, my brain unspooling images of Jake on the court while my coffee grew cold in a mug on his desk? My hand still held a pen, but I'd written nothing. Nor could I even recall to whom I was supposed to be writing. In the room's deafening silence, my ears thrummed with the beat of my heart, an eerily pulsing sound like a tennis ball in play; *thwack-pock, thwack-pock.*

This wouldn't do! I pushed back the chair, eyes brimming with fresh tears. Every card I opened, every letter I read, swept me into the past, reminding me the life I'd shared with Jake was over.

That afternoon I turned the key in the lock of our home in Connecticut and caught a train to New York. I'd lease Willow Creek until I could bear to return. The house was suffused with Jake's spirit, too full of his ideas for our future to make me comfortable in a present without him.

Back in the city, aching with loneliness and missing Jake terribly, I found reminders of him lurking everywhere— bathroom cabinet, clothes hamper, his bedside table— discovering things that made me laugh, weep and wonder if he was letting me know he was still with me in spirit.

I began looking for signs of him on my walks through the Village, finding pennies on the pavement that I imbued with celestial significance. I sensed Jake's presence while sitting on familiar benches and in coffeehouses we'd frequented, missing him all the more. Going home alone after dinner with friends was so depressing I preferred staying in. I barely noticed how reclusive I was becoming.

One morning I passed Le Chat Noir, a restaurant I'd avoided since Jake's death, unable to imagine occupying our corner table without him, only to discover the place permanently shuttered, vacancy notices plastered on the door. *When? Why?* Stunned, its death-like loss incomprehensible, I peered through windows nearly opaque in grime and dust. Ochre walls were stripped of sconces and garnet silk lampshades. Gone, too, were the vintage New Wave cinema prints collected by the owner's wife.

I glanced down at the window seat, not expecting to see

the worn cushion caked in cat fur that Felix had often occupied. *Whither Felix?* A framed, hand-lettered placard explained all. After forty years, Alain and Beatriz, and presumably Felix, had packed it in and moved to Naples, Florida. It was hard to imagine Beatriz, plump in one of her signature black silk dresses, and frenzied Alain in his toque and apron, strolling a beach in shorts and tank tops.

I stood for long minutes in the growing shadows, numbed with the shock of loss. I should have stopped by sooner. Had I known Le Chat Noir was closing, would I have come in for a last supper of *moules frites*? Or sat at the bar drinking in memories of wonderful meals? Why hadn't I?

For that matter, if I'd had a glimmer of foreknowledge that day in May, would I have said no to another set of tennis? Why didn't I see what was happening and do something about it? Could I have recognized the signs—*what signs?*—and called 911 before Jake collapsed?

"What do I do now," I whispered, staring at the furry spot Felix had once occupied. "What next?"

On a Saturday afternoon, following long hours spent immersed in a final proof of *September Girl*, I reached the last page and had a sudden craving for a cheeseburger. Still shaking off twin sensations of apprehension and relief at seeing my words set in type—not quite ready to let the book go and desperate to be done with it—I set out for a late lunch.

On my way back home, I stopped in front of what had once been Mulligan's, a rundown tavern serving famously good burgers that I'd frequented decades ago. My thoughts shifted swiftly to Robert Yardley. The building's original ironwork and distinctive leaded windows were intact, but it was now a Brazilian tapas restaurant with tables out front under a colorful awning. Just down the street, a crooked brick-and-timber building was another reminder of Robert. Originally a nineteenth-century butcher shop, he'd converted the two-story structure into a live-in photography studio in the early 1960s.

A flash of movement caught my eye and I glimpsed a slim, dark-haired woman emerge from the building carrying a cardboard box. She balanced the carton on her hip while unlocking the rear passenger door of a sedan, then shoved the box inside, brushed her hands on her jeans and walked swiftly back in what struck me as a thirty-second clip of myself. She could be me, as I once was, blue-jeaned, my chestnut hair in a ponytail, going in and out of Robert's studio.

I walked to the middle of the block, shading my eyes against the glare of late afternoon. The door opened and the woman emerged again carrying two smaller cartons. She glanced at me on her way to the car.

"You the realtor?" she called out, not breaking stride.

I shook my head and crossed the street, stepping onto the curb as she shut the car door. "No, but I know this house from a long time ago. You live here?"

"Nope, just clearing out." She turned away, then looked back at me, gray eyes wary. "Don't tell me you knew my uncle?"

"Norm Jurgens is your uncle?"

"Was. He died a month ago. A stroke, but he had everything wrong with him you can think of." She glared at the front door and blew out her cheeks. "Sorry, but if you were a friend of his, too bad. He's gone and none too soon."

"Okay, got it. Condolences aren't in order." She shot me a look, catching my smile. "I knew Norm a long time ago. We weren't friends."

"My family couldn't stand him." She was older than I'd thought, perhaps early thirties, and looked tired. "Sorry to unload on you, but dealing with Norm's crap is *not* what I want to be doing. Ma saddled me with it."

"Want me to give you a hand?" At her look of surprise, I plunged ahead. "I know. I don't know why I suggested it, but . . . actually, I used to know someone who lived here a long time ago."

"Got it. So you want to see inside, right?" She took in my summer-white pants and blue linen shirt. "The place is a dump, so . . ." She turned and nudged the door open with her knee. "Enter at your own risk. The electricity is turned off. No A/C. No light, but I opened the back windows."

I nodded my thanks and stepped inside, apprehensive about seeing the studio not only as it was now, but as I remembered it decades ago. I half listened to Norm's niece— ". . . took over someone else's lease, but that ran out years ago. He was a sitting tenant they couldn't get rid of"—as I took in the old brick walls and thick ceiling beams.

"Sounds like Norm," I murmured.

The iron steps of the spiral staircase were piled high with debris, evidence that Norm's infirmities had prevented him from using the sleeping loft. I glanced at a jumble of bedding heaped on an old couch I recognized. Next to it, a TV tray overflowed with medications. I quickly looked away, gazing back up at the loft where I'd spent so many nights. Dust motes danced in the gloom of the grime-pocked skylight, once a bright window to streaming sun, rain and falling snow.

"Fixed up, it could be nice. It's a listed building, so there's not much they can do to the exterior. But they'll gut the inside and rent it for an arm and a leg. People go for this kind of thing. Me, I like things more regular looking."

"It used to be a photo studio," I said. "The man who lived here before Norm stripped the walls down to brick and put in the skylight himself."

"So I heard." She stopped wrapping a teapot and looked at me. "You're talking about Robert Yardley, right? He and my uncle were friends. You knew him?"

"A long time ago." I turned toward the kitchen area and looked up at the beam where I'd once hung a spider plant. "I was working as a picture researcher back then."

"Is he still alive? My uncle was so jealous of him. Thought he should've had Yardley's career. That's a hoot."

"He's alive. I heard from him not long ago." I looked out the back window to the garden, weed choked with barbed wire atop a chain link fence, remembering I'd put off responding to Robert's condolence card. "Actually, your uncle Norm was a pretty good photographer, too, but... times changed. He didn't."

"I think most of his work is over there." She nodded toward stacks of file cartons. "Ma said to junk it all, but I'll take whatever fits in the trunk. You never know if it's worth something, right?"

Was she asking me? I glanced at the boxes, knowing what I would find inside. Plastic sheets with color transparencies, contact sheets clipped to glassine-encased negative strips and bulky folders stuffed with black-and-white prints that were faded and curling with age. Back in the sixties, photojournalists like Norm and Robert covered civil rights marches, wars, political campaigns and various Kennedys at play in Hyannisport, or later, their funerals. The bulk of those mid-century archives, abandoned in musty basements and garages, had ended up in a landfill. "I couldn't say. Depends."

"Yeah, not like family pictures you want to keep." She finished wrapping a vase. "Go ahead, look around. I came across some stuff of Yardley's my uncle stashed in a closet. Feel free to take what you want. Whatever is left goes into a dumpster on Monday." She picked up the carton and headed for the door. "I'll be here at least another hour or so."

I took her at her word. While she busied herself packing up family knickknacks to haul out to her car, I rummaged through the hall closet, setting aside a shopping bag bulging with old press credentials, correspondence and documents in tattered envelopes that I'd sort through later. I couldn't leave without seeing the whole place, so I managed to work my way up the debris-clogged steps to the sleeping loft. My skin prickled as I drew nearer to the space I'd once shared with Robert.

Aside from clutter on the landing, the slope-ceilinged loft appeared largely untouched, an indication Norm had long ago abandoned the idea of hoisting his bulk up there to sleep. I recognized the throw rug and even the coverlet on the low platform bed. Had everything been left as it was? I'd packed up my few personal items on my last morning there, but I remembered items I'd purposely hidden for Robert to find.

Not really expecting they would still be in place, I reached to the back of a shallow drawer in a small bedside table, pushing aside scraps of paper, pens and a tin of cough drops. My breath caught as I retrieved a plastic wallet holding snapshots of Robert and me on a tropical beach, mugging for a camera set on a timer. He, tanned and long limbed in cutoffs, held a kayak aloft. Wearing a scant bikini, my dark, curly hair wind whipped, I stood next to him, grinning and waving paddles. I turned the pages, knowing that if the photo album was still in the drawer, something else I'd left behind would be there, too.

I reached in again and felt the heart-shaped contours of a stone I'd picked up on the beach the afternoon the pictures were taken. I pulled the blood-red stone from the drawer and held it tightly, its warmth throbbing in my palm, then slipped the stone and photo album into my pocket. Robert had packed up in a hurry, too, leaving behind personal items as well as household furnishings. To my knowledge, he'd never returned to the studio, probably never knowing I'd placed a heart-shaped stone and an album of memories in a bedside drawer in the hope we'd reunite.

Light was fading as I made my way back down the stairs. Norm's niece had wedged the front door open, a shaft of pale light spilling into the darkening studio.

"That's it, the car's full. I'm about ready to go."

"Me, too. Thanks so much for letting me look around."

"Hey, glad of the company. Don't forget your stuff."

I picked up the shopping bag and took a last look around, noticing that his niece had taken all but one of the boxes with Norm's photos. I walked with her to her car, thanking her again.

"You won't thank me for the bed bugs," she said, laughing. "By the way, I came across this." She handed me a post-card. "It's only six years old. Honestly, I don't think ol' Norm threw anything away."

I watched her drive off, then stood under a street lamp turning the postcard over. On the front was a picture of the main street of Robert's hometown in West Virginia, a place I'd visited years ago. He'd written on the back: *Hey, Norm, Glad I could help you out. No need to pay me back. Hope you'll be on your feet again soon. We're all fine down here. Take care, buddy. Robbie.*

We're all fine down here? Who was "we?" I turned the card over, then back again, looking for some explanation. The words, printed in his precise all-caps, were clear enough, but still—didn't he live alone? His aunt, the formidable Dorah Ellerbe, had passed away years ago. He'd never wanted to marry or have kids. That much he'd made clear. Maybe he had a dog.

I started to walk home, then stopped and flipped open my cell phone, punching in a landline number long ago committed to memory. I listened to the ring tones, silently counting. I was about to hang up when he answered, his voice low and hesitant. My heart pounding, I slipped into using his nickname the moment I heard him speak.

"Robbie? Hey, it's me. You won't believe why I'm calling—"

"Livvie? That you, gal? Where are you?"

"Here, outside your old studio in the Village. I just found out Norm died," I blurted. "Did you know?"

Norm hadn't warranted a *Times* obit, so his death was news to Robert. I told him about the clutter and the niece hauling away most of Norm's photographs, but didn't mention I'd salvaged some of Robert's belongings, too. I joked that if he wanted anything, I'd scrounge in the dumpster for him on Monday.

"Not on your life." He laughed, then grew serious. "How's it with you? I was sorry to read about Jake."

"Thank you. I got your card, but just haven't had a chance to write back yet. I'm fine, doing okay. You still on your own down there?"

"Yeah. Hanging in. Nothing much new. You still writing?"

"Yes. I've got a novel coming out and a book tour in the autumn. It'll be good to hit the road again. It's been a while."

"Well, if you're in this neck of the woods, stop by."

"Really?" Was he asking to see me again? It wasn't a chance I'd pass up. "You mean it? Actually, I think I'll be down your way in September. It'd be nice to catch up. I'll send you my itinerary as soon as I get it."

"September? Yeah, do that. I'll be here."

I was barely breathing when we hung up. I sucked in humid night air, trying to calm myself as I parsed each word we'd exchanged. I walked in a daze, arriving home without recalling how I got there, my mind churning memories of Robbie. Our brief chat had been amiable and surprisingly casual considering we hadn't spoken in years. Old buddies catching up, that sort of thing; not former lovers who'd parted in rancor.

And he'd invited me to visit... hadn't he? *Stop by*, he'd said. *I'll be here.*

He'd indicated he was on his own. There was no "we," so why not?

Chapter 3

SEPTEMBER GIRL WAS OFF THE PRESSES, ready to be shipped to bookstores for, appropriately enough, a September pub date. Jake had encouraged me to write the novel, even suggesting its title. I was sorry he wouldn't be with me for the launch of the book, a story inspired by our "second chance" romance.

"Thank God, not a memoir!" Jake had said after reading my first draft. "But close enough."

"True," I said, laughing, "and the love affair goes on."

I'd jumped at Norm's niece's offer to take what I wanted, but kept putting off examining whatever loot was in the shopping bag I'd brought home from Robert's old studio. The bag remained just inside my front door, intact, the manila envelopes unopened. The never-ending widow's work that involved going through files, sorting out drawers and closets, took precedence. It was time to start fresh without a closetful of Jake's suits, shirts and shoes. Despite serial bouts of tears, I dealt with the past in practical terms. His hairbrush stayed put on the bureau; the rest went to a local Goodwill shop.

In the weeks that followed, waves of emotion still overtook me when least expected, but they weren't all about Jake. The visit to Robert's studio, finding the snapshots and heart-shaped stone, had lifted a lid on raw memories. Delving into personal letters, journals and news clippings I'd long ago packed away refreshed my fading recollections. I realized I was grieving for a lost part of myself, too, one I'd concealed from everyone, including Jake.

Whatever subliminal thoughts had drawn me back to Robert's Greenwich Village studio, I now felt an urgency to visit him at his boyhood home in Weymouth, West Virginia. Vivid as certain recollections were of what I'd experienced there, that period had been too fleeting, too insular, to reliably remember. With a Northerner's urban perspective, I'd perceived his hometown at the time as a quaint Southern backwater, a place where women didn't wear black unless widowed, food was steeped in sugar and vowels dragged on for hours. Unfair, of course, but it was an unfair time in my life. I needed to revisit the scene of the crime, so to speak—and perhaps finally reckon with all that had happened there.

With my book tour as an excuse, I sent Robert my itinerary and boldly accepted his invitation to visit during a break in my travels. His reply was swift and warm, which made my knees buckle at the thought of following through on my visit. But it also prompted me to look through the shopping bag just inside my front door.

I systematically separated everything into piles mentally labeled: Toss, Keep, Bring to Robert. Junk mail and debris went into the Toss sack. The Keep pile consisted of correspondence, office memos and expense receipts composing a timeline that happened to coincide with our breakup. The Bring to Robert items consisted of mementoes I would pack in my suitcase for him.

One item, a matchbook from Mulligan's, had spilled out of a manila envelope and dropped to the bottom of the bag. I nearly threw it in the Toss sack, but stopped to flip it open—then gaped in astonishment.

A diamond ring glittered from behind a row of tall red match heads.

My head swirling, I pictured myself back in Mulligan's, once "our place" decades ago. Had one of their matchbooks, new and unused, been a hiding place for a diamond ring meant to surprise me? Surely it wasn't intended for someone else—not way back when this ring, tucked into a matchbook, was dropped into a manila envelope among travel receipts for a trip we'd taken together. Why had it been left there, abandoned and forgotten?

I imagined steaks and red wine at a corner table with a checkered cloth and a candle dripping wax. Afterward, coffee and Calvados with my single after-dinner cigarette lit by Robbie, who didn't smoke. I pictured him slyly striking a match, its bright flame revealing the gleam of the ring—but that scene had never taken place. Why not?

How different my life would be if it had. I glanced at the shabby Eames chair near the French doors, Jake's place to sit with his stocking feet planted on a matching leather footstool that would never have existed if—I shivered and hurried to close the French doors, locking them and drawing the curtains. I shut out nightfall, the cries of the baby fighting off bedtime next door and a terrible emptiness that numbed my mind. *What if* without Jake was a life I couldn't imagine.

I gazed at the ring, a cluster of small diamonds in a beautiful vintage setting. It wasn't a traditional engagement ring, but had Robert meant it to be . . . and then changed his mind? Seeing Robert again was now necessary. I needed to know the truth.

Chapter 4

FOUR CITIES AND A BLUR of media events and book signings later, I rushed to an airport for the start of my weekend with Robert. After the frantic pace of trying to stay on schedule for appearances, time slowed to a crawl once I boarded. My flight landed early. There was no wait on the tarmac, and my valet-checked carry-on, tangerine-colored so it's easy to spot, was the first bag delivered to the gangway.

More than once I'd come close to canceling my stop in Weymouth, but couldn't chicken out on this chance to face the past—and Robert. I was glad he had no cell phone, that I wasn't compelled to alert him I was early.

My heart thumped an extra beat, pumping a battalion of butterflies into my chest. A glass of chilled white wine suddenly struck me as a therapeutic necessity and speed-walked straight to a sports bar on the far side of the terminal. The last time I'd been here, the gleaming terminal was a cavernous shed with linoleum floors and sparrows twittering in the eaves. I thought of the young woman I was back then and the hopes and dreams I'd carried within me, long before I arrived in New York.

When I'd told Robbie I had a book tour coming up, I'd said that it would be "good to hit the road again," and could almost hear him smile in response. We both thrived on travel, particularly work related; it was how you really got to know a place. From the beginning, stories I wrote always had to do with *going places.*

Scuffed, with one sprung lock and a cracked mirror glued to the inside lid—that was the old brown leather traveling case my Danish grandmother gave me to play with in a game I called just that: Going Places. It held my doll, a hairbrush, ribbons, cookies and whatever I thought I might need. Dress-up games, for me, generally involved packing to go somewhere. It wasn't surprising that travel writing eventually became a staple of my freelance work and a necessary source of income for a number of years.

Yet I didn't take my first trip on an airplane until I graduated from college and moved to New York. My entire family, including an aunt and grandparents, walked me to the gate and waved as I crossed the tarmac to board my flight. I wore high heels, seamed stockings and a worsted wool suit in a shade of mustard popular that year. I'd left behind my grandmother's old traveling case, but in my white-gloved hand, I carried a portable Olympic typewriter, a graduation gift from my grandparents.

My letters home had been particularly revealing, reminding me of the headstrong young woman I'd been even in college. I'd broken up with my boyfriend, Malcolm, after graduation when he returned to Wisconsin to go into his father's furniture business (their motto: *Five floors of fine furniture*). It wasn't a relationship meant to endure and we'd both known it, which made the breakup easier. But my father was disappointed that I'd turned my back on what looked to be a secure future.

"You can't write in Wisconsin? You need some kind of special air?"

In fact, I did. I catapulted to New York and fell in love with the city the moment my feet touched the pavement and I looked up at glittering canyon walls of glass and steel. Those heady first days were thrilling. I walked everywhere, breathing in the smells of street food I had to taste. My ears became attuned to strange, exotic accents of people I wanted to get to know. The streets throbbed with energy, the rush of a populace on the move—was everyone late for an appointment?

I slept on a couch in a friend of a friend's apartment for a couple of nights and immediately signed up with Kelly Girls as a temp secretary. With a cheese sandwich wrapped in wax paper in my handbag, I set off daily to work as a replacement typist in various Midtown office buildings, earning roughly sixty-five dollars a week. I loved the constant shift from one office environment to another, meeting new people and getting to know the city. I also liked to type and was pretty good. Since no one was ever happy to see an office temp show up in the morning to slow things down, I took pleasure in dazzling everyone. I was determined to make my mark—even as "the speedy typist that turned up last Wednesday."

I moved into an Upper East Side apartment after spotting a notice thumbtacked to a grubby message board in a corner deli. I barely had money to cover a month's rent and deposit, but after vetting me over a glass of cheap Chianti, my three new roommates invited me to move in that night. I was back within an hour, lugging a suitcase, a grocery carton full of books and my portable typewriter.

I paid a quarter of the rent on the two-bedroom, two-bath sublet leased by a woman none of us ever met, but whose furnishings we all detested. We threw colorful batik cloths over an avocado-green couch, draped scarves on the lampshades and stashed an orange corduroy beanbag chair behind a folding bamboo screen. Prior to my arrival, the elephant-ear plant had died of thirst, but its skeletal remains still protruded from a chipped pink-and-charcoal-gray planter no one knew what to do with.

According to one of my roommates, the leaseholder was an actress who'd been on a soap opera and moved to Hollywood to try her luck in the movies. The hall closet, supposedly off limits to us, was packed with stuffed garment bags and personal items that had been pretty much picked over by a succession of uncaring sublessees, all using the place as a way station before moving on as fast as possible. A new job, a boyfriend, even a raise were all reasons for an abrupt departure, and explained the high turnover rate.

Cindy, tall and wraith thin, with a butter-smooth Louisiana accent, was a salesgirl at Bonwit Teller's on Fifth Avenue. She roomed with Barbara, a big-bosomed receptionist from Delaware, who worked in a Wall Street law firm. I was stuck in the smaller of the two bedrooms with Patty, blond and plump. Like me, she was from the Midwest and worked as a temp secretary. As the newest recruit, my bed was the farthest from the window. There wasn't much of a view, anyway. Both bedrooms looked out on an airshaft and the back end of another building. I was entitled to half the space in a narrow closet with accordion doors that no longer clicked shut and the bottom drawer of a low cabinet that separated our single beds.

I was lucky I'd found a place I could afford, but hated everything about the white brick-clad building with its sterile lobby and long, ugly hallways that smelled of fatigue and disappointment. Life in a career-girl gulag was tolerable as long as everyone took turns emptying the garbage, didn't use the last of anyone's milk or hog the bathrooms. What I hated most was the lack of privacy, and I often retreated to the basement laundry room to write in the evenings.

One night when I returned very late to the darkened apartment, I found a penciled warning taped to the bedroom door and heard amorous sounds of my roommate in bed with her new boyfriend. Stuart was plump like Patty, but some ten years her senior and able to take her in yellow taxis to good restaurants, two luxuries unimaginable to me. I curled up on the couch until he left, figuring she, too, would be moving out soon and I'd at least get the bed by the window.

I wasn't a virgin, thanks to Malcolm, and empathized with her. More than that, she mentioned that she'd met her boyfriend, an associate editor at a big news magazine, while temping as a secretary. That's all I needed to hear. I happily slept on the couch whenever asked and nurtured a friendly relationship with the couple.

It paid off when Patty's boyfriend mentioned there was an opening for a researcher. I typed my skimpy CV on a sheet of good bond and gave it to Stuart, who noted that while I'd graduated with honors, my degree wasn't from Bryn Mawr or Smith, the colleges most of the female researchers had attended. "It's sorta doubtful," he said, "but we'll see."

Still, I was called in for an interview and arrived at the magazine wearing white gloves and navy pumps, grateful to find Stuart waiting at the ground-floor reception desk to escort me. I stepped carefully on the thick carpet, mindful that one of my pumps, missing its button of a heel, was worn to the metal. I did not need to trip and fall on my face during a fast-paced march to what I hoped was my future. Along the way, I learned that Stuart's social connections carried more weight than his middling position on the masthead—and that he was married, a bit of information he made clear I was not to mention to Patty.

Muffin Hanley, the personnel director, was a brittle, stylish woman in her thirties, occupying a spacious office with a piece of beautifully framed cubist artwork hanging on the wall. She seemed to have a special regard for Stuart and little interest in me once we were left on our own. She barely looked at my résumé, but asked me where I shopped.

"Lord and Taylor, mostly. Bonwit's, Saks," I rattled off. Indeed, I shopped in those stores but didn't buy anything. My gabardine suit was a relic bought in Milwaukee on a college weekend trip. Gimbels' basement, where I'd bought my pumps, was more my speed.

Muffin looked at my shoes and seemed to sense that might be the case. "Really," she muttered, her jaw in well-bred lockdown. "We'll be in touch."

Three nail-biting days later I was offered a job—as an office girl, not a researcher. I'd earn less than my salary as a Kelly Girl temp, but I jumped at the offer. I'd spent barely an hour in the magazine's shiny new office building, but I hungered to work in that sleek, open space with teak and chrome furnishings and steel-framed windows that looked out on Manhattan from a dizzying height.

In college, I'd dreamed of finding employment with a publishing house or a glamorous fashion magazine, but working for a news magazine, even as an office girl, felt vital and relevant. I loved the clattering teletype machines spewing scrolls of wire service text that often meant breaking news, rewrites and another late night. I was enthralled listening to behind-the-scenes anecdotes about the powerful and famous, and hearing off-the-cuff remarks by editors that would end up in print days later.

I was thrilled, over the moon, ecstatic—and then I met Robert.

Chapter 5

CLING-WRAPPED IN THE LINGERING HEAT of a dying autumn day, I stood under the eaves of the arrivals terminal, shifting from foot to foot as long minutes ticked by with no sign of Robert. Had he gotten the date wrong? The time? To quell mounting anxiety, I took deep breaths of moist, sultry air and exhaled slowly, to little effect.

I'd last seen Robert years ago when Jake and I ran into him in Midtown Manhattan and chatted briefly. Oddly, that chance encounter was the first time I was aware the two had worked together before Jake and I met. It had been decades since Robbie and I were intimate—how awkward could this be? A gruesome thought struck me—did he fear I'd come to Weymouth with the intent of picking up where we'd left off, and he couldn't face it? *Ridiculous!* A second time around was not what I had in mind. Still, I'd practically invited myself. Had he misunderstood? Would he show up at all?

As if this rat's wheel of angst weren't agonizing enough, I also had an inexplicable desire for a cigarette. I hadn't smoked since my days at the magazine, but a kid in cutoffs standing at the curb was puffing away, the muggy air wafting tantalizing fumes in my direction. I watched the thin curl of smoke loop and thin, rising in a bent halo above the kid's spiky hair, and recalled the days when a thick, gray fug clouded every diner and cocktail lounge, a bygone time when people lit up while eating, drinking and sitting at their desks, when sharing a cigarette was a ritual after making love, if not a signal to fore-play. I didn't crave nicotine so much as the era it evoked—my youth and those thrilling early days at the magazine.

I'd signed on as an office girl in a state of rapture, immersing myself in the company's employee "bible" drafted in the mag-azine's trademark staccato journalese. I figured Copy Desk would be my next step up and imagined myself jamming a thick wad of bond and carbon paper through the rollers of my typewriter to produce a "draft typed twelvefold with top copy and eleven flimsies," dazzling everyone. I bought a new dark-blue knit sheath with white piping on sale at Lord & Taylor that cost every penny of my savings, leaving me barely enough for carfare home and a tuna sandwich my first day on the job. I was shown the coat closet, stashed my handbag in a desk drawer and set about learning the ropes.

My initiation into the culture of the fabled twenty-seventh floor began my first Friday night, the weekly's closing deadline. All hands were expected to remain on deck until the issue set sail, generally well after midnight. Before the effects of a martini lunch could wear off, a liquor trolley was rolled into a central area known as the bullpen, where, ironically, mostly women worked. The free and easy camaraderie esca-lated to full-blown party mode as drinks flowed and the night wore on. I attracted considerable attention as the new girl, but I'd worked in enough offices to be adept at dodging even the most persistent advances.

Among the benefits of working late on closing night was a three-course dinner served in the conference room by uniformed waiters from the four-star restaurant in the building—and any employee who worked past ten o'clock could request a ride home in a chauffeur-driven limo. I'd clearly entered Heaven, or as close as I could get to it on the twenty-seventh floor.

An office girl's job was basically delivering something from someone to someone else whenever asked. I was initially assigned to a researcher in the World section, who was one of the magazine's oldest employees. Brígh (a Gaelic name pronounced *Bree*) Donnelly had been with the company since well before World War II, much of that time as a senior researcher. A tough, scrawny woman with burnt-ginger hair, stick-thin limbs and a hard, round belly, she was an unapologetic, high-functioning drunk, who was predictably one of the last to leave the building on Friday nights.

In the days when the magazine's generous expense accounts fueled three-martini lunches, Brígh could (often did) drink the big boys under the table. A smoker and not-so-secret drinker, her desk was a toxic zone that held an industrial-size ashtray and a lipstick-stained white coffee mug that did not contain coffee. She was precise. She smoked four cigarettes an hour after a doctor told her to cut down, and timed each to the quarter hour without having to check the clock. Gin with a splash of tonic water was her tipple of choice from nine a.m. until one o'clock. After a lunch of martinis, she sipped straight gin until she tottered out of the office at the end of a workday.

From the moment I met her, I adored Brígh, who had the wit of Dorothy Parker and must have longed to have her storied career, as well as a seat at the celebrated Algonquin

Round Table. Not long after I started working, I confided to Brígh that I wanted to be a writer myself.

"Of course, dearie, but you're not likely to get your chance here. I never did—never will."

This was hardly news to me. The magazine's policies were unshakable: Men wrote, women researched. Women were assigned cubicles. Men occupied offices that had a door and windows. If this wasn't clear enough in practice, the guidelines were virtually spelled out in the company manual. Researchers were referred to with feminine pronouns, editors and writers in masculine equivalents.

One day Brígh asked to see something I'd written. I gave her a copy of a short story that had won a place in a literary review my senior year in college. I was quite proud of it and handed over my original manuscript.

The following day I found she'd left the papers face down on a corner of my desk. I turned them over, horrified to discover my neatly typed manuscript covered in red pencil markups. Minutes later she summoned me to her cubicle. I stood staring at my shoes, my face burning, as she instructed me to pick up a folder that had been set aside for her at the clip desk.

Before dismissing me, she said, "By the way, you show promise. Good work on that piece."

"But you ... I mean, you ..." I blubbered, mortified by welling tears.

"Butchered it? No, go take a look. No need to embroider. Just tell your story."

She was right, of course. My writing at the time was of the "unfurling fronds of fern" variety. Without taking undue advantage, I began slipping Brígh other pieces and learned more about writing from her than I had in four years of college.

A side benefit is that I caught a small glimpse of her life outside office hours. She left a marked-up manuscript on the corner of my desk one morning that had a circular red stain in the middle of the second page. A wavering line from the stain to a note in the margin read: *BROUILLY 1963*, a clue she most likely switched from gin to red wine during the evening hours when she worked at home.

On a frigid November afternoon, only months into my new job, I barreled down a hallway toward Brígh's cubicle, telex in hand. A tall, lanky man swung around a corner, halting me in my tracks. Without a glance in my direction, he slung a duffel bag, metal camera case and leather grip on the carpet and jammed a key into the lock on an unmarked office door I'd assumed was a storage room. He wore a sheepskin jacket, collar up, with a scarf wound around his neck—and had a deep suntan. *A suntan in November?* I couldn't take my eyes off him.

"That for me?" He nodded at the telex clutched in my hand.

"No, sir," I said, startled he was even aware I was standing at his elbow.

"Wait, you're new?" He looked at me, a glimmer of humor in his eyes. "You know where you're going?"

"Yes. Yes, sir."

"Sir, again?" He smiled and stuck out his hand, winking at me. "Robert Yardley. Call me Robbie."

"Olivia." I grasped his hand, the quick, warm grip rocketing longing to the pit of my stomach. "Olivia Hammond. Call me Livvie."

"Oh-o—o-livvie it is. Stop by later and we'll talk. I gotta get some film to the lab."

"Yes, sure. Nice to meet you."

I unhitched my hand from his, my entire arm prickling with the sensation of his touch. I scuttled down the hallway, feeling limp. I almost forgot I had a telex to deliver to Brígh until I saw her eyeing me. She hadn't missed a thing.

"You want to give me that while it's still today's news?"

"Sure, sorry." I walked the few feet to her cubicle, my hand hanging like a dead thing, and gave her the telex.

"Easy, girl." She stubbed out her cigarette and reached for her coffee cup, her eyes on me the entire time. "Take a few deep breaths and it will pass."

I pretended I had no idea what she was referring to, but I did. "Could I take my break now?"

"You've seen the Second Coming, have you?" She rolled her eyes. "The blood-dimmed tide is loosed."

Chapter 6

HEADLIGHTS FLASHED AT THE TOP of the arrivals ramp. I shielded my eyes and squinted into the high-beam flare. A black SUV appeared, turn signals winking flirtatiously. I thought it might be Robert, but in an SUV? I hadn't imagined him in that sort of vehicle—an old Porsche, maybe, or even a vintage Jeep.

The SUV pulled slowly toward the passenger loading area, the car's headlights dipping in a wobbly curtsy at the bottom of the entrance ramp. The car jolted to a momentary stop, then slowly made its way to the passenger-loading area. The driver hunkered forward, hands gripping the top of the steering wheel, as though he were navigating through a dense blizzard instead of a balmy moonlit night.

With a sharp intake of breath, I recognized Robert as the grizzled warrior behind the wheel. I watched him drive the length of the loading zone, eyes peering through oversized aviator glasses, trying to single me out among the few stragglers still waiting to be picked up. He was not as I remembered him from our chance meeting a few years earlier. I glimpsed him now as a stranger might, someone who didn't know him at all and would wonder if he was safe behind the wheel.

Still, Robert's driving hadn't caused my quick inhalation;

it was a sudden rush of the sort I'd felt decades ago when I first laid eyes on him. I stepped out of the shadows of the cement pillar. Tugging my wheelie behind me, I waved my arm in a wide arc.

"Hey, Robert! Over here!"

He saw me and waved back. Without warning, the shiny black car shot forward. My gut seized as the car lunged toward me, its headlights blinding me. The tires mounted the curb. I stumbled back, screaming, "Stop! Stop!"

The skinny kid in cutoffs tossed his cigarette and scrambled out of the way as Robert reversed the car back onto the pavement. Had he even seen the kid? The SUV shuddered to a stop, rocking on its chassis. I watched the passenger window slowly yawn open. Robert's voice, low with a resonating burr, sounded maddeningly calm.

"Hey, there, Livvie, that you? C'mon, get in."

His hair was steel gray, but his signature shaggy cut was the same, a thick shock falling across his forehead. As though I'd willed him to do it, his hand reached up and brushed it back, the gesture as familiar as the sight of the hair tumbling right back down onto his forehead. His cheeks were more hollowed, the eyebrows just as bushy but now salt-and-pepper. A scrappy cotton scarf, a faded blue one I was sure I recognized, was knotted around his neck above a collarless shirt. I could almost smell a musky lime scent; his alone, and one that wasn't bottled.

"Were you aiming for me," I said, "or just being overly exuberant?"

"Guess I'm glad to see you," he drawled as I opened the door. "This your way of greeting me after all this time?"

"You almost ran me over!"

"Now, why would I do that? C'mon, get in, Mizz Olivia, time's a-wastin'."

I shook my head, my hand holding the car door open while I considered my options. "Brand new car?"

"Had it for a while. You want to admire it or climb in?"

"How about I drive?"

"You let your hair grow out since I saw you last."

"It's been longer. I think I better drive."

"You say that to every guy picking you up?"

"It's just that you're really late. Maybe you stopped at a bar for Dutch courage?" I knew he hadn't been drinking. He'd never been a drinker, but I was scavenging for a cutting retort. I missed by a mile. He let me know it.

"Now, why would I need to do that?" He lifted his eyebrows, a teasing smirk on his lips. "C'mon, you can do better. I want your good stuff."

"How about a tradeoff? Hand over the keys and I'll keep you entertained."

His smile spread into a grin. "I like you blond. You having more fun?"

I slammed the car door closed, my temper rising. He was getting the best of me, as he always managed to do. "You know, this isn't working out too well. I'll take a taxi."

He rocked back against the seat, laughing. "Well, you'll just want to hold up your hand and one of those big yellow Checker cabs will be along any day, now."

I reached in my pocket for my cell phone. "Maybe we can make it happen a little quicker."

"Give it a break, Livvie." He leaned over and opened the car door. "I think you need a hand with that case of yours."

I didn't answer. My eyes were on his lanky frame climbing out of the SUV. The rugged style was there, manly but from another era—Robert Redford, not his younger doppelgänger, Brad Pitt.

I swung my wheelie around and joined him at the rear end of the SUV. He was punching a black key fob with his thumb.

"What're you doing?"

"Whad'ya think? Trying to get this damn thing to open."

"Let me try."

He ignored me. I stood back watching him jab his thumb on the unresponsive piece of technology in his hand. That's when I noticed he had a camera hanging on his shoulder. He was rarely without one, but I was still surprised he'd slung it on just to open the trunk. For Robert, it had to be an involuntary action akin to breathing.

"Maybe you oughta just stow your bag in the back seat. I don't think this trunk is going to open."

"It has to." I reached for the key, my hand sliding over his, plucking it from his fingers. The fob fell into my palm, still warm, the intimacy of my fingers touching his rocking through me with an unexpected pang. I jiggled the fob in the hollow of my hand as though it were too hot to handle.

"That's not how it works. You have to press it."

"I know, I know. Hang on."

I peered at the tiny symbols on the miniature buttons. They were impossible to distinguish in the dark. I slid my thumb across the surface and pressed down, taking my chances. We both flinched as the alarm triggered blasts from the horn. Headlights flared on-off-on-off in time to the blaring noise. I jammed my thumb back down, shutting it off midblast.

"If that's the best you can do, hand it back."

He reached for the fob, but I pressed down again and heard a quiet click. We stood back watching the hatch glide up as if by magic. I dropped the key fob in my pocket, not about to relinquish it. I collapsed the handle on my wheelie and swung it into the trunk.

"Okay, let's go."

"That all the luggage you've got?"

"I travel light, remember? Something I may have picked up from you."

When Robert wasn't on assignment, burdened with camera cases, he'd required nothing more than a small carry-on to see him through days on the road. Traveling light was a trait we shared.

I reached in my pocket and pressed the fob. The hatch closed with a soft click. I quickly moved around to the left and slid behind the wheel. "C'mon, hop in."

By the time Robert climbed into the passenger seat, I'd pulled the door closed and fastened my seat belt. I adjusted the mirrors, getting familiar with the dashboard. The odometer registered only sixty-three miles.

"Nice car, Robbie." I slipped back into using his nickname, relieved he hadn't put up more of a fuss that I was driving. "How long have you had it?"

"A couple of months, I guess."

"And never opened the trunk before?"

"No need."

I pressed the ignition, then glanced at Robert. He was looking at me, clearly amused. "What? Are you thinking what I'm thinking?"

"Nothing changes, does it, Livvie?"

"With us? No, I guess not." I turned to face him. "I thought things might be a little awkward after all this time, but I didn't figure we'd be hollering at each other right off the bat."

"Yeah, I know." He sighed, the sound ending in a low chuckle. "Maybe it's easier that way. Anyway, we missed the part where I say, 'Good to see you again. Welcome to town.'"

"Good to see you, too. Thanks for inviting me and—actually, I think I might've invited myself."

"That's okay. So why'd you want to come?"

"Like I told you, I'm on a book tour and I thought—well, why not?"

"It's been a while, that's all. A lot of water—"

"A lot of bridges, too. Why don't we talk later." I put the car in gear and pulled away from the curb. "This time of night, we should make it to your place in well under an hour."

"Hold up a sec. Go past the first ramp and take the second exit off to the left—"

"But Weymouth's to the right."

"We're not going to the house."

"You want to get a bite to eat first?"

"Sure, but we're still not going to the house. I figured we'd stay in a motel down the road here."

"Excuse me? What's that all about?"

"Two rooms. I'm paying. No need to get excited."

"That's not what I meant." I stopped the car and pulled the hand brake. "Why not your house? I thought I'd be staying with you. I mean, in your guest room. You invited me, didn't you?"

"Storm damage. Place is a mess. Roof leaked and soaked into the walls. I had to get the power turned off. The contractor says he's tied up until next week." He gave me a sad clown smile. "Nothing I can do about it."

"What a shame. I'm so sorry. When did it happen?"

"Couple days ago."

"Why didn't you call and tell me?"

"Didn't want to upset you."

"I'm not upset, but you should've said something. Where are you staying?"

"Nowhere yet. I didn't have to move out until today."

"Too bad. I wish I'd known." I sucked in breath, exhaling slowly.

"You look upset. I didn't think it would be a big deal."

"Sorry. It's just . . . not what I expected. Actually, it is upsetting."

"Nothing I can do." He raised his hands, palms up.

"You said that." With a quick yank, I released the hand brake. The SUV rocked as I veered a little too sharply into the exit lane. "Where should we eat?"

"Up to you." He shrugged, indicating my choice was of no consequence to him. "There's a waffle place down the road. Pretty good eatin'—"

I threw him a look. "Actual food, please."

"Your tender palate's just going to have to make do, girl. No fancy New York grub down here, remember?"

"You can cut the clodhopper talk. You've eaten as much fancy food in fancy places in the world as I have, okay?"

"Just sayin' it's all down-home cooking around here. Most places close up by now."

I glanced at the dashboard. "It's just after nine o'clock."

"Like I say. So why don't you just pull into the first place with a light in the window."

The only place still lit up was the waffle house, which turned out to be locally owned, not part of a chain, but still the sort of place that slathered whipped cream thick as soapsuds on anything lying flat on a plate. The waitress, hearty and wholesome, took some pleasure in telling me they didn't serve wine.

"This is a nice family restaurant," she said, her hands splayed on ample hips. "I can getcha some sweet ol' iced tea."

"Thanks, just coffee and a mushroom omelet, no hash browns, please."

Robert decided against the waffle extravaganzas and ordered a short stack he bathed in butter and ersatz maple syrup. I gritted my teeth as he poured four packets of sugar into his iced tea.

"So, how are you feeling these days?" I said.

"Can't complain. Plumbing and heating's holding up. I can still make it around the block and back. I gotta say you're looking fit."

"Thanks. I work out. Walk everywhere, like we do in New York."

I took a bite of omelet, which was pretty good, and gave myself time to think. He'd managed to turn the tables on me, but I shouldn't have let it get to me. I'd promised myself I wouldn't. Yet how did he always get the upper hand—even at this stage of the game?

Pretending interest in the gingham-and-wagon-wheel décor, I glanced at our images in the mirrored paneling, noting that the interrogation-room lighting did neither of us any favors. I looked tired, with faded makeup and hair limp on my shoulders. Robert's craggy good looks were merely craggier, but his eyes were glazed and red. He blinked and rubbed them in a manner I knew well from our years together.

"You still have to use drops?"

"Yeah, but the pressure's good. It's pollen that's the problem."

"It's affecting your work?"

"Not much. I'm finishing up an annual report for a local outfit and photographing some historical homes for a brochure. Maybe you want to drive out to Spaulding with me tomorrow while I grab a few shots. Hang out."

"Sure, I've done that before." I smiled at the offer, having served as "camera caddy" on a good many of Robert's shoots in our early years together. "My time's yours. Besides, I'd like to get a feel for this neck of the woods."

"Glad to hear it." His face relaxed and he grinned around a mouthful of pancake. "We had some good times, Livvie. I was thinking about that earlier on the drive down here. Remember when the old Fiat gave up the ghost in Bucks County? We must've hiked five miles of back roads lugging camera cases."

"How could I forget trying to hitch a ride with all that gear? I'm not sure I'd call it one of the good times."

"What the hell." He laughed. "Cost us some shoe leather."

"Right, and my blisters had blisters." I picked at crusts of toast, avoiding Robbie's gaze. I pictured the roadside motel next to a chicken farm where we stayed that night, the two of us soaking in an old claw-foot bathtub together. It was one of our best times, but still I made a point of not meeting his eyes and acknowledging it.

"Hey, I'm glad to hear you're still working," I said.

"No problem. I can see better through a viewfinder than these damn eyeglasses."

"Really? What about driving?"

"I can drive. No problem, except maybe at night."

"What about your license? I know they sometimes make you take a road test when you've got eye problems."

"You think I'd drive without a license?"

Hell, yes! "No, of course not. That would be crazy."

"Look, if it's some kind of big deal to you, I'll let you drive tomorrow. Happy?"

Relieved. "Sure. Fine with me. Whatever you want."

He sipped his coffee and crumpled a paper napkin to his lips. "Say, you think we might've got off to a prickly start here?"

I nodded. "Sorry about that. Just tired. It's my fault."

"No, I was late—"

"And tried to run me over—but hey! What's a little thing like that between old friends." I smiled. "Good to see you again."

"You too." He cocked his head. "And you're lookin' darn good."

I laughed. "Two rooms tonight, remember?"

"Don't worry." He shoved his plate aside. "You seem to be doing okay. I'm glad. I was a little concerned about you after Jake. I'm sorry."

"Thanks. I'm fine now."

"Still, I know it's hard. Want to talk about it?"

"Not now." My chest constricted as I swallowed back tears with a sip of coffee. "Go back to flirting, okay?"

"Sure, if I haven't lost the hang of it." He settled back, scratching his stubbly chin, the beginnings of a yawn turning into a lopsided smile. "Seriously, I'm kinda glad you stopped by here, Livvie."

"Kinda glad?" The words, not really a question, fell from my lips and hung between us. Somewhere a chair scraped back. A cash register *ching*ed and a pneumatic door wheezed open and shut. "I'm kinda glad, too. It's time we had a good talk, you know? Set things straight."

The lopsided smile faded. He hitched himself up and pulled a wallet out of his pocket. "I think it's time we got some rooms for the night. Ready?"

The down-home warmth had dropped from his voice, his manner turning abrupt. He tucked bills under his plate for a tip and got up from the table. It was a chill reminder of how Robert set parameters. In this case, they didn't include staying in his house or talking about a past he didn't want dredged up. I'd set my own goalposts and would have to bide my time to reach them.

I took a last sip of coffee and followed him to the door. His shoulders were straight, his gait familiar. From the back, he still looked like the man who'd walked ahead of me down the dirt road in Bucks County, his shoulders loaded with camera gear. I remembered the rest of that night, too, after we climbed out of the claw-foot bathtub. The bed had a creaky iron bedstead that bumped against the pasteboard-thin walls and made us laugh. At sunrise we were awakened by a crowing rooster—then made love again before falling back to sleep.

Chapter 7

MY EYES BLINKED OPEN TO A ROOM awash in sepia light streaming through oilcloth roller blinds. The sash was raised high. A braided string attached to a crocheted loop swayed above the sill in a gentle breeze. At least the windows opened, an amenity long banished from most hotels.

Robert had neglected to make reservations anywhere, which hadn't come as a surprise. After stops at two motels that had no vacancies, a clerk helpfully directed us to a two-story white frame guesthouse off the main road. A tired-looking middle-aged woman, a threadbare chenille wrapper thrown around her nightdress, greeted us at the door of the Liddicote Bed & Breakfast. She'd already been alerted by the motel clerk and had our rooms ready; thirty-seven dollars each, breakfast included.

Our evening ended cordially with a cheerful "G'night, sleep well." No hugs. I left Robbie at the door to his room and went to mine one floor up.

It rankled that I wasn't waking up in the guest room at Robbie's house. Was it really so severely rain damaged or, as I suspected, did he simply not want me there? I'd had my own misgivings about revisiting the house, but it was also a large part of why I'd made the trip. I needed to see it again.

Once plans were made, the dates set, I'd fallen asleep

night after night in New York imagining myself in the old
four-poster bed in Robbie's guest room, propped amid pillows
piled against a scrollwork headboard. Did the room still have
flower-sprigged wallpaper? I hoped there were still two rocking chairs on the wide veranda and a sycamore tree in the
front yard. In the weeks after I'd invited myself to visit, I
couldn't stop dwelling on moments from our past and playing
out imagined scenarios of what it would be like seeing him
again. I'd even pictured the two of us in the cool of the evening, sitting in the rockers, engaged in a heart-to-heart talk I'd
figured we were both ready to have. Whatever I may have envisioned, it didn't include the Liddicotes' bed-and-breakfast on
the edge of town. Then again, when had I ever been able to
second guess Robert?

My travel writer instincts kicked in as I assessed my
room, noting lovely vintage wedding-cake moldings framing a
ceiling with a mirrored light fixture that would have been
more at home in a disco. The house was old, but not historic,
and had been done up as a serviceable bed-and-breakfast. No
frills. To its credit, there were no water pitchers in flowered
bowls that no one used or pointed messages on needlepoint
pillows, such as *Press button for maid. If no one answers, do it
yourself.* I'd seen enough of those in my travels, and they usually portended weak coffee and stale muesli for breakfast.

In place of showiness, there was basic comfort, the plain,
unfussy sort familiar from my girlhood summers at a Northern Minnesota lake cabin: bureau, chair, lamp and a framed
print of Millet's *The Gleaners* hanging over the bed. There was
no television or minibar, and that suited me fine. I'd been
staying in enough upscale, though not grand, hotels on my
book tour. I had no need here for an electric iron, blow-dryer

or illuminated magnifying mirror, all necessary when I had TV appearances and book signings scheduled. After days of crowded airports and city traffic, the peaceful setting was welcome.

I swung my legs out of bed, savoring the fresh, cool air and sounds of chirping birds. I yawned and gave the window-shade cord a quick tug, then shrank back as the roll shuddered to the top in a frenzied clatter and crashed noisily to the floor.

I looked out the window. Robert sat hunched over a newspaper at the sunny end of a backyard picnic table, a coffee mug and half-eaten donut within reach. He was wearing the shirt from yesterday, the scarf tied around his neck. His elbows were spread wide, his nose in close proximity to the newspaper folded in his hands. Even when his eyesight was fairly good, he'd read as though devouring the page. Apparently the clattering window shade hadn't disturbed him. He didn't look up.

With the unfurled shade splayed at my feet, I weighed my options—to rehang, or not? I stepped over it and headed for the shower, a bathtub affair with a clear plastic curtain and a vintage sunflower-sized showerhead. Minutes later I was toweling off and finger-combing my hair. My wardrobe choice was easy for the road trip ahead: Pants, shirt and sandals, sunglasses jammed atop my still-damp hair. Shoving my laptop into a canvas shoulder bag, I headed downstairs.

On my way to the kitchen, I stopped at the open door to Robert's room, pin-neat, the bed made. It was characteristic of him to leave a place undisturbed; "as it was," he'd say, not wanting to intrude or leave his mark on anything that didn't belong to him. As a photojournalist, covering space launches, political campaigns, wars or natural disasters, he saw it as his mission to chronicle a moment in time *as it was.*

Mrs. Liddicote suddenly appeared at my elbow, a bundle of folded linens tucked under her arm.

"Morning," she said, peering into Robert's room. "Checkout's at noon, but I see you're both packed up. Bread by the toaster. Cornflakes on the table next to a thermos of coffee. Milk's in the fridge." She moved briskly into Robert's room.

"That's fine. I'm good with toast and coffee. I'd also like to pay for both our rooms. You take credit cards?"

"The gentleman already squared it away. Take it up with him." She threw back the coverlet and ripped sheets off the bed. "You know, it's just double work to unmake a bed. Sheets have to be changed. You might tell your friend that for future reference."

I watched her windmill linens in her arms before tossing them into a pile on the floor. I decided not to mention the displaced roller blind in my room. At least I hadn't made my bed and created even more work for her.

Robert was still engrossed in his newspaper when I joined him in the garden. I set my coffee mug next to his on the picnic table and eyed the remains of a powdered-sugar donut left on the saucer.

"I see you charmed Mrs. Liddicote. All I found was a loaf of sliced white bread. Where was she hiding these babies? I haven't had one in years."

Before I could break off a piece of donut, Robbie snatched the saucer out of my reach. "It's petrified rock. I don't know what the half-life is, but I'd say this one's prehistoric."

"That good," I said with a laugh, sitting down on the bench opposite him. "At least the bed was comfortable. But I can pay for my own lodging, you know. You didn't need to do that."

"I said I would. I feel bad about you not being able to stay at the house. You know, it's not something I could help."

"I know. God's work. Anyway, your eyes look better today."

"Pollen count's down." Folding his arms across his chest, he studied me as though looking for the best angle. "I like you barefaced."

"Really? You used to like me just—" I stopped myself, a grin aching to break free. "Never mind."

"Bare-assed?" He laughed. "So who's flirting now? But I bet you still look good, you know—"

"Bare. Yeah, got it. Enough."

"I didn't get to the legs yet. No one looked better in a miniskirt than you."

"Stop, okay? This much adulation can't be good for the soul."

"Your soul, of course. I was just getting around to it."

We gazed at each other with comfortable ease, the banter part of our old game. In that moment, I didn't know what he might be seeing, but possibly some shred of my soul. I saw someone who could still make my heart melt. How could that be? Despite our rocky history and neither of us being young, what caused the pheromones to kick in after so many years?

He smiled, obviously enjoying his own thoughts. I smiled back, fixating on the way his eyebrows sloped, a downward trajectory that made him look vulnerable, when, in my experience, he was essentially impervious. He was certainly the most enigmatic creature I'd ever come across.

"So, how long have you got?" he said.

"Here? With you?" Flustered, I tried to corral free-ranging thoughts. "A couple days. I need to catch a flight out Monday to make a connection to ... um, I can't remember, another ... I'll have to check my itinerary. I mean, it's all a blur these days ... racing down some moving walkway to make a connection in what looks like a shopping mall ... and a glass of wine! If you get fouled up with weather or a mechanical delay and park yourself in a cocktail lounge, it's big bucks ... although I did get a whole chapter written on my laptop in Houston one night when I missed the last flight out, fueled on some terrible down-market plonk that cost an arm and a leg, but ... sorry, what? Oh ... Monday. I've got until Monday." I stopped abruptly, my heart thumping. "How long have you got?"

"Me?" He yawned and stretched his arms behind his head. "Free as a bird. Nothing planned. No flights to catch. It's been a long time since I had to get somewhere."

I nodded, maybe too vigorously, recalling a time when air travel was freewheeling, exciting, and Robert always had to get somewhere. This was a man who at one time knew every commercial flight schedule throughout Africa, Europe and the Far East so he could ship film from a war zone or summit meeting to make a deadline. In a long ago, predigital age, a plane equipped with a photo lab and an editorial staff flew Robert and his film from a political convention to the printer in Chicago to beat the roll of the presses for a cover story. I was on board that particular flight, a member of the picture department at a time when our relationship was still secret.

I caught myself and took a deep breath of sweet morning air, trying to staunch the flow of other recollections of that trip and our stolen hours together on company time. "Right. Okay. Then I'm all yours."

"Really?"

"I mean, until Monday."

Our eyes met again, this time with less ease. Rattled by a memory of the two of us joining the "mile-high club" on that chartered flight to Chicago, I abruptly stood. "I'm going in for more coffee. You want some?"

"Sure. I'll give the weapons-grade donuts a pass. Maybe some toast?"

"Coming up."

I took his cup and headed across the lawn, damp curls batting my cheeks with each step. I knew he was watching me. Light-headed, my ears drumming, I focused on the screen door and reaching shelter inside the kitchen just ahead. I was determined not to fall under his thrall again. It wasn't why I'd come.

I popped bread in the toaster. Poured coffee. I dipped a spoon into the sugar bowl four times and stirred his coffee, focusing my thoughts on the house he didn't want me to visit. The easy banter and mild flirtation meant there was still rapport between us. I counted on it, determined to change his mind about a trip to Weymouth and a visit to his house on Orchard Street, where so much had happened.

For the next hour I wrote. Robert read. We shared the picnic table, he with his newspaper and me tapping on my laptop, as easily as we'd always shared space since our early days in New York. Even in his small Greenwich Village studio, we'd managed to find our own quiet space without getting in each other's way.

There, amid the brick walls of the derelict butcher shop, thick pieces of iron hardware, from which meat hooks had once hung, were still embedded in the dark wood beams. He'd fitted brackets into two of the metal ceiling devices to hold rolls of background paper. There was a cabinet filled with cameras and lenses, a rack holding tripods and a corner unit in which lighting equipment and other materials were stored on metal shelves. Two file cabinets supported a plank that served as a worktable with a light box. The vegetable crisper in the old Hotpoint refrigerator was packed with Polaroid film. Two shelves held neatly stacked yellow Kodachrome boxes. The kitchen and bathroom, tucked away in an alcove, had the appearance of afterthoughts.

My clothes were not hung in his closet, because I didn't live there. I didn't have a key. But I did have my own cup in the bathroom in which to store a toothbrush, and a shoebox stuffed with toiletries that I kept tucked under his bed. I was a frequent overnight visitor and spent most weekends with Robert. I still paid a quarter of the rent on my official "home," the two-bedroom, two-bath uptown Manhattan apartment I shared with three roommates.

As comfortably as Robbie and I traveled together and shared space, we'd never actually lived together. His home had never been my home, even though I'd spent more than two weeks there as the guest of his Aunt Dorah. Still, was it really an act of God that had stripped me of houseguest privileges?

Chapter 8

"READY TO GO?" ROBERT WAS ON HIS FEET, the newspaper folded under his arm, his camera slung on his shoulder. "We can grab lunch in Spaulding if we leave now."

"Just waiting for you. I already put our bags in the trunk." I shut down my laptop midsentence, a phrase left dangling. I was having a hard time concentrating. "Finished with the paper?"

"Yesterday's. Takes me a while to read these days."

"That's okay. We've got plenty of time." Before I realized it, I'd slipped my arm through his, hugging my laptop to my chest as we walked toward the car. "We can always turn on the news so you can hear how everything turned out yesterday."

He laughed. The old news junkie had always been glued to a transistor radio or a headline feed wherever he could find it, but now appeared content reading yesterday's news. During the 1964 Harlem riots, following the death of a fifteen-year-old black boy shot by a cop, Robbie had hooked up a police scanner to keep on top of the breaking story. By the time I met him a year later, the scanner had become an addiction, an impossible-to-ignore intrusion blaring nonstop bad news. Hearing sirens screaming through the streets was disruptive enough, but knowing where they were headed and why was even more alarming. I found the bulletins so distressing that Robbie turned the scanner off whenever I was there.

It was midmorning by the time we set out for Spaulding, the warm autumn day sunny and bright. Robbie didn't quibble when I slid behind the wheel. He climbed in on the passenger side, pushed the seat back and crossed his legs.

"Head back the way we came and go up the ramp just past the underpass. I'll take over whenever you get tired."

"It's roughly two hours, right? I can handle it. I never get to drive in New York, so it's a treat."

I was overstating my enthusiasm for driving, but it beat sitting on the edge of my seat gripping the door handle with Robert behind the wheel. He'd once been an excellent driver, taking precision driving courses back in the days when he covered Formula One racing, photographing Stirling Moss, Graham Hill and the young James Hunt. I'd loved watching Robbie drive, his arms straight to the wheel, relaxed and focused as he shifted through gears. He'd always leaned toward British sports cars, owning MGBs and a rebuilt Singer, before he acquired the ill-fated Fiat that sputtered to a final stop during our weekend drive in Bucks County.

I pulled onto a service road as Robert pressed buttons on the radio. An all-news station blared, a reporter's voice urgent, authoritative. The president was making a surprise visit to the Middle East. I recalled Robbie's story of photographing President Dwight D. Eisenhower during a whistle-stop campaign in Weymouth, then bicycling to the newspaper office to deliver the spool of film still in his box camera. He was fourteen years old. It was hard to reconcile the effects of aging on Robert, who'd once been so vital, always in the thick of things. I glanced at him reclining in his seat, the lenses in his aviator glasses dark against the sunlight.

"Do you ever hear from the old gang?"

"All dead. Like Norm." Robbie said, sounding cheerful. "Gone. Pfffft."

"C'mon! All of them?"

"Charlie. George—that was hard. Denny, a month ago. And Eddie got fat."

"Sorry to hear it."

"Who would've thought it? He lives on a houseboat down in Louisiana, sucking up bourbon and crawfish."

"I mean, I'm sorry everyone's dying."

"That's life. No one gets out alive. Remember how Eddie and I did the march out of Selma with King back in sixty-five? We walked backward, shooting pictures the whole way to Montgomery. We called Eddie 'jackrabbit' because he could sprint faster than any of us to get a good shot."

"I remember his wife, June. She was practically a den mother to the rest of us."

I smiled thinking of June, the spirited wife of a longtime press photographer, who was a driving force in the clique of wives and girlfriends that used to hang out together when the guys were on assignment. I was a member of that ever-evolving group of women during the tumultuous sixties.

"Hey, just remembered . . . I've got something for you." I reached into my shoulder bag wedged in the space between us and yanked out a chain dangling with press credentials. "You left these behind at Norm's place."

I heard an intake of breath, then a low whistle. "Holy Moses, these go way back."

"Truman, at least." I laughed. "Maybe even Lincoln."

"Could be."

We laughed again, then lapsed into silence as Robert fingered the laminated credentials in his lap, each with a sober mug shot of his youthful face. I stole another glance, my eyes sweeping from his weathered profile to his image on a long-expired press badge, and remembered our first meeting and the black-and-white photo of Ike waving from a train caboose that I saw pinned to the wall of his office.

Just past five o'clock, later that same Tuesday afternoon in November, I saw Robert strolling from the elevator. He'd shed the heavy sheepskin jacket and was wearing a work shirt and khakis, the scarf knotted around his neck. Before turning into his office, he glanced down the hall, saw me and cocked his head toward the open door.

I nodded back and walked toward Robert's office. His eyes were on me the entire time, sizing me up. But then I was doing the same and liked what I saw. His hair was dark and shaggy, his eyes smoky blue, a shade deeper than his shirt. He stepped aside so I could enter the room, but stood close enough to the doorway that I could breathe in his warmth and the musky lime scent.

He left the door open, which was just as well as the space was cramped. The room had the feel of an oversight, a narrow slice of space sharing a strip of window from the adjoining office.

"Barely enough room to have a complete thought," he said, a line he'd probably used many times before. "But I'm not here all that often."

I smiled, liking his casual, self-deprecating manner. I

looked down at the metal suitcase open on the floor, with cameras and lenses wedged into thick gray foam cutouts.

"Where've you been?"

"Venezuela. Got in this morning."

"I guess that accounts for the tan. Lucky you."

"Ever been there?"

"Not yet."

"Good answer." He smiled. "You will, one of these days."

I nodded and continued looking around, giving him time to take me in and—I hoped—remember me. I glanced at the news photo of Ike, pinned to a bulletin board, his grin broad, arms thrust high in a victory salute.

"Do you think Nixon will make a comeback and run again?"

"Chances are. Is that what you want to see happen?"

"I'm guessing Humphrey will run. I'd like to see him win. He's from my home state."

"Ja, Minne-soh-ta," he said, affecting the tiresome Scandinavian accent everyone but Minnesotans find amusing. I didn't laugh and he noticed. "So that's why you don't sound like the other researchers around here. They all talk like their molars are stuck together. No fancy boarding schools for you, I'll bet."

I shook my head, not wanting to betray any more than I already had. Despite graduating near the top of my class, I was painfully aware that almost everyone working on the editorial floor had attended an Ivy League school. "Where are you from?"

"West Virginia."

"Grits and cornpone country," I drawled. "But y'all don't sound like it."

"I got it knocked out of me at Ohio State."

"So you're not Ivy League, either!" I blurted.

"Did I say I was?" He laughed and shoved the door closed with his foot. "But don't let it get around."

"I promise." I perched on the edge of the desk, swinging my feet, feeling more than a little reckless.

"You smoke?"

"No," I lied. The way he asked let me know he probably didn't smoke and didn't like people who did. If I had to open my purse, I hoped he wouldn't see the pack of Kents. I'd bought the cigarettes largely for show because of the elegant package, but lit up only when I had lunch with girls from the office.

"Drink?"

"Not really." The legal drinking age in Minnesota was twenty-one. I'd had my first cocktail a week after arriving in New York, a grasshopper that tasted like whipped-cream mouthwash. I was still getting used to the taste of Scotch, a fancy whisky my parents associated with Episcopalians, which was the booze of choice in the office. I drank it diluted in nine parts water. "Some. A little."

"Then I don't know that you're long for this job." He pulled a face, his voice a lament. "Too bad, because you're a breath of fresh air around here. Literally."

"I can be tempted." I uncrossed my ankles and leaned back, my arms braced on the desk. "Especially if it's in the line of work."

He laughed. "The place is also crawling with letches. Don't get tempted into thinking that's part of your job. Got a boyfriend?"

That's when the lights went out. There was a fragment of silence, then I sensed him moving closer.

"I didn't turn them off on purpose," he whispered, "but as it is—"

His lips brushed mine, a fleeting kiss that electrified me. He reached behind me and flicked the wall switch on, off, on—but the room remained dark.

"The bulb," I whispered, not moving.

"I'm fresh out," he said, leaning in for another kiss, a lingering one that left me breathless. I raised my arms to his shoulders, hungry for more.

There was a muffled shout from the hallway, followed by the thump of feet, some laughter and more shouts. We pulled back, our arms still embracing each other. The room was pitched in darkness. We both turned to the sliver of window, dark now, without sparkles of light shining in the windows of neighboring buildings or the glow of neon signs illuminating the night sky. It was very dark.

"That's more than a fuse," Robert mumbled, opening the door.

The hall was dark, too, with sudden flashes of light as people struck matches and held lighters above their heads. Somewhere someone shouted, "My God, there are no lights on in New York City!"

"Perfect timing," Robert whispered, turning back to me. I laughed, shaking my hair onto my shoulders, content to remain sitting on the desk with Robert's legs hugging my knees.

Still holding each other close, we peered into the hallway. The chatter, laughter and expletives grew louder. Shadowy figures clung to the walls, bumping into each other as they moved outward from the central common area into the offices with windows. The cries got louder.

"It's dark!"

"There's no light anywhere out there!"

"My God, what's happening? This is freaky!"

"Aliens! The end of the world!" a woman shrieked, then burst into laughter.

"You never know," a male voice responded calmly. "Which of you girls has the key to the cabinet? We need to get the emergency supplies."

Robert grabbed a transistor radio from a desk drawer, flicked it on and held it to his ear. "Not that I'm all that anxious for the lights to come back on," he said softly, "but it shouldn't be taking this long."

Feeling the first twinge of concern, I swung my feet to the floor and peered out the window. A full moon was rising in the night sky, its pale light frosty behind the hazy darkness of nearby buildings. Far below, a frayed string of headlights, barely moving, dragged raggedly through the streets.

A voice rang out in the hall. "Hey, wait, this is serious. Anyone got candles? Who's got flashlights?"

"Okay, I've got the key. Could you shine your lighter over here?"

"Wait, how do I get home?" It was a man's voice, sounding panicked. "Could someone please call maintenance? Adele? Muffin? Somebody? How do I get out of here? I've got a train to catch!"

Above it all, a deep voice barked, "Hey, everyone, we're still working, okay? Let's pull together here!"

"You kidding me?" Someone laughed. "I can't even see my typewriter!"

"It's a power outage all the way up to Massachusetts," Robert said, setting the pocket-size radio on the desk.

Feedback from other transistor radios blared in the hallway, melding in a dissonant urgency of newscasters' voices. New Jersey still had power, but regions from New York to Ontario, Canada, were plunged in darkness.

Robert reached for a canvas bag, its zipper open, and pulled out a flashlight. He flicked it on and handed it to me. "I've got another one here somewhere, hang on."

I directed the beam on him while he fumbled through a leather bag on the floor. He pulled out two penlights, then grabbed cameras, slinging the straps around his neck. He opened another bag, scooping handfuls of film canisters into the pockets of the sheepskin jacket hanging on the back of the door. A chain festooned with laminated press credentials flapped against his shirt.

"Where's your coat? Get your coat and come back here. Hurry."

Following the beam of my flashlight, I made my way to the coat closet in an alcove off the bullpen. People huddled in groups in the corridor, some already with drinks in hand. I pulled my yellow polo coat off the hanger, stuffed my woolly hat in the pocket and grabbed my handbag. As an afterthought, I kicked off my good pumps and slipped my feet into the old brown leather penny loafers I wore when it rained.

Enough matches and lighters were in use to make moving around less tricky for everyone. Joey, one of the copy boys, was passing out orange grease pencils, lit and sputtering, to anyone without matches or lighters.

In a flicker of spiraling smoke, I saw Brígh raise a cigarette to her lips and inhale.

"Are you okay?" I asked, stopping at her cubicle. "Need anything?"

"Bliss," she breathed. "Utter bliss."

Her knobby feet were crossed at the ankles on her desk, her skirt riding up past her garters and the tops of her stockings. A bottle of Chivas Regal stood open on the desk, its cork resting next to a tumbler filled with amber liquid.

"Seemed to call for a good whisky." Her voice sounded like a drool. "I don't usually allow myself to indulge."

The route back to Robert's office was congested, with people crowding into the common area. As I passed by, a woman with a key to the locked storage cabinet labeled *Atomic Crisis Closet* pulled open the door. There was a round of raucous laughter as someone held a lit grease pencil to a hand-printed sign: IF THERE'S AN ATOMIC ATTACK, YOU'LL ONLY NEED BOOZE. The emergency storeroom held shelves full of liquor, but no candles, matches or flashlights.

By the time I reached Robert, he was already in the hallway wearing his sheepskin jacket, the assortment of cameras and press badges dangling around his neck. He thrust a leather bag at me. "You mind?"

"Not at all." I slid the strap of the camera bag over my shoulder and followed him, my flashlight beam backing up his.

He darted past a cluster of people and turned the knob on a corner office. I gulped, knowing it was the managing editor's office. Robert made a beeline for the windows.

"Close the door. Turn off your flashlight," he said, and began shooting frame after frame.

I stood back, my heart racing, listening to the soft *whirr-clicks* of the shutter, my eyes fastening on the panorama Robert must be seeing through the viewfinder.

In the vast darkness, a chalky full moon hovered in the far distance, the nearby skyscrapers silhouetted in sharp relief. A single pinpoint of light flashed, a match struck in the darkness in one of the buildings, glittering like an errant star that had tumbled out of the sky.

But my eyes were mostly on Robert, moving almost stealthily along the perimeter of the windows, pausing briefly, *whirr-click*, *whirr-click*, then moving on. I could taste him on my lips and still feel the afterglow of his body pressed to mine.

Whatever was going on outside those windows twenty-seven floors below, my only thought was: *I want him. Now.*

He turned to me, snapping the lens cap on his camera. "Ready? Button up, we're hiking down the stairs. You good with that?"

"You bet. Let's go."

Chapter 9

AT A JUNCTION AN HOUR OUTSIDE of Spaulding, Robert suggested taking a scenic route off the Interstate. The two-lane county road wound into marshland rimmed with beech and river birch, their leaves turning garnet and bronze. Rays of sun glanced off silvery curls of bark. Birds swooped over glistening patches of water. I wasn't surprised when Robbie insisted I pull off the road. The picturesque cove, with its filtered light and autumn colors, called to him. He was determined to photograph it.

I eased to the side of the road, but parking on the soft shoulder of the narrow country road was hazardous. A stream of cars sped by, each one shaking the SUV as it hurtled past.

"Wait, Robbie. Don't open the door yet."

But he already had, his eyes on flocks of birds, not the traffic that had backed up behind us.

"For God's sake, watch it!"

He didn't. Standing with the car door ajar, he slung a camera on his shoulder and patted his trouser pocket. "You got the keys?"

"Of course I've got the key. Could you please get out of the road?"

He took his time, impervious to honking horns and cars arcing around him. When the whoosh of a van passing too close almost blew him over, he grabbed the edge of the car door to steady himself.

"Robbie, move! You're going to get run over!"

I held my breath as he closed the door and wobbled unsteadily at the edge of the macadam. Trying to secure his footing in the loose gravel on the narrow shoulder, he slapped his hand hard against the roof of the SUV for support, making me jump. He looked around and, in a heart-stopping moment, appeared ready to dodge between speeding vehicles to get to the marshland on the far side of the road.

I leaped out of the SUV, shouting, "Robbie, this way! It's too dangerous to cross over."

"You're right. Light's better over there, anyway."

I took his elbow and we started down the mushy incline. He pulled away when we reached level ground.

"I don't need you holding me up, you know."

"Sorry, I was afraid I might slip."

"Really?" he scoffed. "And you thought I'd keep you on your feet?"

I laughed, shrugging off my clumsy subterfuge, reminding myself that this was the sort of thing he did all the time on his own. He didn't need me looking out for him, although that had once been my job as a picture researcher. I stood on a rock and watched him plow into marsh grass, sidestepping now and again as muddy water oozed up around the rubber soles of his canvas shoes.

He hunched down and trained his camera on a flock of birds flying low, his feet sinking deeper into the wetlands. I looked away, focusing instead on stands of feathery grasses swaying in the wake of flapping wings, and the twitters, chirps and musky smells of the soggy marshland. Still, I brooded about Robert. Did he have another pair of shoes with him? Clean khakis in case he fell in the mud? *Stop!* His shoes and pants were *his* concern.

Still. I looked back at Robert, now some distance away, hunched forward shooting frame after silent frame with a commonplace digital camera that hadn't even existed when I first met him.

Robert had a Leica and two Nikons on straps around his neck the night we edged down twenty-seven flights of stairs during the Great Northeast Blackout of 1965. I followed in his footsteps, both of us holding flashlights and gripping the handrail as we joined the spiraling trail of evacuees. There was an eager, boisterous camaraderie in the stairwell that grew noisier as others joined us at each floor, many passing along news bulletins they picked up on their transistor radios.

Railroad lines from Grand Central Terminal and Pennsylvania Station were out of service. Airplanes couldn't land and were diverted to other airports. The subway was shut down. People were being herded out of stalled subway cars and through tunnels to safety. Droves of commuters were hiking home across the Brooklyn and Queensboro Bridges. Emergency crews had broken through the walls of elevator shafts in the Pan Am building to free trapped passengers. Hospitals switched on emergency generators to complete surgeries already in progress when the power shut down.

By the time we reached the last few floors before the lobby level, the steps were choked with office workers, some of whom had walked down more than forty flights. I held on to a corner of Robbie's jacket, not wanting to lose him in the crush when we stepped onto the street.

The darkness was eerie, with gaping blackness north of us where Central Park should be. People loomed up out of the shadows, holding lighters at arm's length. Headlights glimmered in bright arcs on the traffic-clogged streets, limning darkened street lamps and overhead traffic signals.

Robert reached for my hand as we weaved between car bumpers crowding the crosswalk, heading downtown. "You, okay? Stick close."

I squeezed his hand and trotted along, trying to keep up with his long strides. Along the way we popped into saloons and cocktail lounges, not to drink, but so Robert could grab shots of patrons huddled at crowded bars, smoky candlelight illuminating scenes of conviviality. The tinny sounds of transistor radios punctuated the din of talk and laughter.

But there were also tense, fearful faces on people hovering at curbs, anxiously waiting to squeeze aboard one of the jam-packed buses crawling along the avenues. At almost every intersection, civilians dressed in work clothes and business suits had stepped in to direct traffic.

The Theater District's Great White Way was dark, the marquees ghostly. We made our way down Broadway to the murky environs of Times Square, where a lone policeman was trying to keep order in the congested crossroads.

Robbie photographed a homeless man, accustomed to dark nights and no place to go, placidly sharing a shadowed doorway with a grim-faced businessman checking his watch by the flame of his cigarette lighter.

By the time we headed east and reached Grand Central Terminal, stranded passengers were already staking out space on the grimy marble floors and stairways, and huddling against kiosks and the walls of ticket windows. The boards were black, the clock faces frozen at 5:28. Uniformed National Guardsmen were on hand, with a flood of people surging through the doors. I kept my eyes on Robert, stepping carefully around those sprawled and squatting on the floor, my coat clutched around my shoulder bag and Robert's leather camera case.

Avoiding the pitch-dark, less populated streets, we walked to the Bowery, stopping for cold coffee and ready-made sandwiches in a candlelit deli along the way. The migration home was still in operation for many people trekking across the Brooklyn Bridge.

When we finally reached the desolate harbor area, I whooped in surprise at the sight of the Statue of Liberty—her torch miraculously lit! Exhilarated, bursting with pride, I hugged Robert as tears ran down my cheeks. What a glorious view! With the world around her plunged in darkness, Lady Liberty had found a way to keep her beacon shining in New York's harbor.

I leaned against a railing, listening to updates on the transistor radio, while Robert mounted a concrete bulwark and tottered on its edge to frame the best angle. According to a news report, power for the Liberty torch came from New Jersey, which wasn't affected by the outage. The neighboring state was on a different power grid than the one that had darkened nine other states and three Canadian provinces.

I relayed the information to Robert, then jotted it down in my notebook with everything else I'd seen and heard that night. While he took photographs, I crammed page after page with quotes and caption material.

In the early hours of the morning, flashing press credentials and identifying me as a reporter, Robert got us on board a harbor patrol boat. Pulling my woolly hat low on my ears against the frigid ocean breeze, I leaned into Robert as the boat chugged deeper into the harbor to swing around Liberty Island. Across swells of inky water, the full moon was a giant white sphere looming over Manhattan's blackened skyline, a view that became another of Robert's iconic photographs from that night.

We stayed aboard the patrol boat until dawn, when smudgy gray light burst into streaks of magenta behind a still-darkened skyline. Power had been restored to Brooklyn and parts of Queens and the Bronx, but not yet Manhattan. By best estimates, some thirty million people had been left without electricity from dusk to dawn.

Robert and I walked along Canal Street in the first blush of morning light, his arm across my shoulders, my hip bumping his thigh with every tired step. My eyes felt gritty, my voice hoarse, but I was energized by the night's adventures—and thrilled to be in Robert's company. Laughing and teasing, we bantered like old buddies. I'd fallen for him in a way that gave me a dizzy, ringing sensation every time he looked at me.

"Wait here," he said, positioning me next to a battered wooden gate hanging on its hinges. Behind it, a narrow cobblestoned alleyway glistened with morning dew. He stepped back, raising his camera. "Look to your left and stay just as you are."

I heard a soft *whirr-click*, then another, the ringing sensation sweeping over me once again. I held still until he finished shooting and then looked at him, our eyes meeting. He came closer, sliding the strap of his camera onto his shoulder, and kissed me.

"G'morning, sunshine," he whispered, nuzzling my neck. "You're looking awfully good after a night on the town."

His breath tickled my ear, sending flutters to my belly. I turned my face, my lips brushing the stubble on his cheek, and pressed closer. My hand burrowed inside his jacket, feeling the warmth of his body, the beat of his heart.

His hands slid down the back of my coat, tightening on my hips. "If a taxi came along, I could put you in it and send you home, or—"

"Or?"

"Take you to my place for bacon and eggs."

"I'm starving," I said in a rush, my warm breath forming a frosty puff in the morning chill. "Really. Sounds good."

He laughed. "So, it's breakfast you want." He squeezed my hand and looked around for a taxi. "Good. That's what I had in mind, too."

But there were no cabs. The streets were empty except for a beer delivery truck rumbling up Canal Street. Robert waved his arm. The driver, wearing a Giant's cap and a toothy smile, pulled up and offered us a lift. We squeezed in next to him and headed uptown. The streets were quiet the whole way, with locked metal grilles pulled across storefronts.

The lights were still out when we arrived at Robbie's place in the West Village.

He flicked the switch on and off before ushering me into the ground-floor studio. In the half-light gloom filtering in from semi-open shutters, I took in the raw brick walls, steel shelving and wide-plank wood floors, registering the spare, masculine décor of a man who lived without a woman. There was nothing to water, polish, plump up or iron. I'd never seen anything like it.

"This is where you live?"

"And work." He set his cameras on a bench near the door and pulled off his jacket.

I moved farther into the room and unbuttoned my coat. "But where do you sleep?"

"You're asking to see my bedroom?" He grinned and pulled me toward him. "Happy to show you, if you'd like."

My stomach lurched, the floor seeming to shift under my feet. "Thanks," I mumbled. "Maybe some coffee?"

"Sure." He kissed me lightly, then held my face in his hands and kissed me again. "As promised, eggs and bacon coming up."

I stuffed my hat into my pocket. "I should probably freshen up first."

He took my coat and hung it on a peg near the door. "Towels are on the shelf. Poke around in the medicine cabinet and help yourself to new toothbrush. Holler if you can't find something." He handed me a flashlight. "You'll need this."

"Thanks."

I flicked it on. A beam flashed across a wall of framed black-and-white photographs of the Beatles clowning on a hotel balcony, a windblown John F. Kennedy sailing and a solemn Martin Luther King Jr. stepping off the Pettus Bridge on the recent Selma-to-Montgomery march. Below these images, I caught the glint of a silver picture frame perched on a bare butcher-block counter. I shined light on a pastel-tinted photograph of an older woman with coiffed blue-gray hair and a tight smile that turned up at the corners as though instructed to do so.

"Your mother?"

"My aunt Dorah. The old bat's making her semiannual pilgrimage to New York, so I took her picture out of mothballs."

"She stays with you? Here?"

"God, no!" Robert laughed and headed to the kitchen. "She takes the train up twice a year and generally stays four days at the Plaza. She's got her routine. Shopping. Matinees. Gin rickeys at Sardi's."

"She sounds like fun."

I heard a snort from the kitchen. "She packs in another four days over Easter. I generally end up buying her a hat."

"You take in the Easter parade, too."

I lifted the picture for a closer look at Aunt Dorah. She looked like someone fully in charge of herself and probably everyone around her. Elegant cheekbones and arched brows gave her an air of imperiousness. Her nubby wool suit had the look of Chanel and was worn with a double strand of pearls that dipped just below the hollow of her throat.

"Are you close to her?"

"She and my uncle raised me."

"I see." I glanced at Robert. "That means—"

"She's all I have left." His tone was flat, not inviting more comment. "You like your eggs scrambled?"

"My favorite." I set the frame back on the countertop. "I'll give you a hand in a minute."

I closed the door to the bathroom and took in the blue-and-white-tiled space, spotless and clutter-free. I waved the flashlight around, shining it on a dark-blue robe hung on a peg behind the door. A wooden shelf was neatly stacked with matching towels and washcloths.

Then I turned toward the mirror and gasped at my sorry reflection. My hair was matted from my hat, my eyes dark pools in a pale, drawn face. I groaned at the thought of what I must look like in the photos Robert had taken of me less than an hour earlier.

I unwrapped one of the cello-wrapped blue toothbrushes I found in the medicine cabinet and brushed my teeth. By the time I'd washed up and run damp fingers through my hair to restore some curl, the smell of bacon permeated the apartment.

"Anything I can do to help?"

"There's still no electricity, so the toaster's not working. At least I have a gas stove. I'll be back in a minute to scramble eggs."

I poured myself filtered coffee and took a look around. The kitchen was tucked into a corner of the studio. Pots and pans hung from hooks on a metal rack over the sink. Stoneware plates, bowls and mugs were stacked on a tray on top of the refrigerator. When I opened it to get milk for my coffee, I was surprised to see shelves packed with boxes of film.

Robert returned minutes later, barefoot and wearing a clean shirt. He was lean, his shoulders strong, and his faded jeans hugged narrow hips. I sat down at a round table next to a small barred window that looked out on a weed-choked backyard, and watched him scramble eggs.

"Is this your breakfast specialty?"

"Who said eggs and bacon were just for breakfast?" He set a heaping plate of eggs and crisp bacon in front of me. "The best things are good anytime you want them."

I smiled. "I couldn't agree more."

Our knees touching under the table, we lingered over

coffee. His hand reached for mine as I put down my empty cup. He stood and, in a move so swift it took my breath away, scooped me out of my chair and swung me around into the studio.

As he set me back on my feet, I saw that Aunt Dorah's picture had been turned to the wall. Moments later we climbed up to the sleeping loft, satisfying another hunger.

Chapter 10

WE BOUGHT NEW SHOES FOR ROBERT in Spaulding. After settling on brown leather Rockport's, he left his soggy canvas shoes with the clerk to discard.

"Got something to show you," he said when we were back on the street. "They've hung some of my mug shots down at the courthouse."

The "mug shots" turned out to be an exhibition of Robert's photographs in a sky-lit anteroom of the courthouse that served as a civic art gallery. *Regular People* was a remarkable display of decades-spanning black-and-white photographs Robert had taken of ordinary people "as they were" in everyday settings, doing nothing more than being themselves.

Each image revealed a stunning, closely observed moment of human life. An elderly woman wearing a threadbare coat gazed forlornly into a butcher shop window. A girl in a sprawling line of grade-schoolers looked warily at a nurse who was about to jab a needle in her arm. A middle-aged woman, a small bunch of garden flowers in hand, stood pensively among headstones in a cemetery. A gangly kid on a bike looked over his shoulder at a pretty girl as he passed a bus stop. A soldier, with a duffel bag at his feet, sat in a train station eying a travel poster of a surfer cresting a wave.

Midway through the gallery, I stopped abruptly in front

of a picture of a young woman wearing a polo coat and penny loafers, standing in front of a sagging wooden gate. Her woolly hat framed a face luminous in hazy morning light. It was a picture of me in the chilly, cobblestoned alley, looking expectant, eyes brimming with wonder, the morning after the Great Northeastern Blackout.

For the first time I was seeing myself as he'd seen me through a viewfinder that morning, not footsore and bedraggled, but as a dream-filled young woman on a great adventure. I also saw the face of a young woman tremulously in love. He must have seen that, too.

I knew he was somewhere watching me. I moved on to the next picture, resisting the urge to turn and look at him, not trusting my own reaction at seeing his. He had to know the memories it would stir of a time when our romance was new and fresh, still secret. If this was his way of opening a door to revisit our past, I didn't want to risk having it slammed shut again. *Tiptoe, my girl*, as Brígh would have cautioned me long ago.

I didn't meet his aunt Dorah on her pre-Thanksgiving trip to New York in 1965. Robert and I had met only weeks before that visit and were just getting to know each other. It was too soon to start meeting each other's family members, although I couldn't help but be curious about the woman he'd referred to as an "old bat." I knew one evening he would take her to a preview performance of *Man of La Mancha* on Broadway, and another night they'd dine together in the Rainbow Room. After she left, Robert went away on an assignment.

I had to work and couldn't afford a trip back home for

Thanksgiving, the first big holiday I'd spent away from my family. I'd given no thought to how I would spend the day, other than savoring the pleasure of having the apartment completely to myself. My roommates would all be out of town.

Late on Wednesday afternoon, Brígh called me to her desk. She was already pretty crocked and would be tottering out of the office shortly. "Where do you stand when it comes to Turkey?"

Since Brígh worked the World desk and the country had been in the news lately, I hesitated. "Uh, I know they had elections recently—"

"The bird," she said, "in terms of Thanksgiving dinner."

"Oh. I like it well enough. I seldom eat turkey any other time of the year."

"It's dry, disgusting stuff and I don't care that the Pilgrims scarfed it down, buckshot and all. I always fancy a good lobster at Thanksgiving. I have it on good authority the Pilgrims did, too. Want to join me tomorrow evening? My treat?"

"I'd love to, thanks!"

"Good, you're on. There's a decent seafood place on Fifty-Sixth Street that'll be open." She tore the top page off her notepad and handed it to me. "Book a table for seven o'clock. My name. They know me."

Brígh was already settled in the booth when I arrived at five minutes to seven. When she saw me enter the dining room, she lifted an old-fashioned glass, clinking ice. She took a long sip as I slid onto the banquette beside her. A velvet jacket with an ermine collar rested on her scrawny shoulders. She'd whipped her thinning hair into a sphere of burnt-ginger dandelion fluff and attached a small black velvet bow above a puff of bangs. With her chalk-white face and slash of crimson lipstick, she looked glamorous, if not a little scary.

"What'll ya have, darlin'? And by the way, Happy Thanksgiving."

"Thanks. Happy Thanksgiving to you. I guess I'll have lobster."

"We'll both have lobster. I mean to drink, dearie. If you're not into the hard stuff, why don't we start you off with a glass of champagne?"

She ordered French champagne that didn't taste like the sticky ginger-ale variety usually served at weddings I'd been to. I loved it, and between us we polished off the bottle over dinner. I also realized there was more to this meal than just providing an elderly lady with a drinking companion on a lonely holiday—although there was that, too. Brígh's agenda included proffering advice on office politics and romance, which seemed to be one and the same thing. Brígh liked to talk and I was happy to listen to her droll warnings.

"You need to be brought up to speed. I see you at the Friday night shindigs and you handle yourself pretty well, but there are a few pitfalls you won't see on your own. First off, if a man says his wife doesn't understand him, there's a good reason for it. You won't, either. Second, if he says he and his wife have 'an understanding,' tell him that's nice, but he doesn't have one with you. Third, if he lives a commuter trip away and the trains aren't running, don't let him sleep on your couch. That's not where he'll want to sleep. Besides, the company will reimburse him for a hotel room."

Throughout the first course of squash soup, which Brígh barely tasted, and through most of the ordeal of eating lobster, she gave me a run down on who was sleeping with whom, why, how and what the outcome was or likely would be. Seeing me struggle with the lobster and its accompanying tools, she leaned over and gave me instructions on cracking its claws.

"Never had one before?"

"Never. But you probably never had walleyed pike, either."

"No, but I may have slept with his brother. Did you say Wally?"

I snorted with laughter, almost drowning in my champagne. If nothing else, I was a good audience and well on my way to becoming tipsy. Brígh sat back against the leather banquette, a satisfied smile on her face. She barely touched her lobster.

"They'll bag it up for me. My cat can't get enough of it."

Over crème brûlée, another first for me, Brígh finally brought up Robert. By then she'd ordered Grand Marnier for both of us. I was beginning to feel unwell.

"Ah, silence tells the tale," she said when I didn't answer at once.

"There's not much to say, really. It's been—what?—a little over two weeks since the blackout. I haven't seen much of him since then." I was already in love, but knew better than to admit it. "But I like him. Quite a lot."

"He's a bit of a loner, you'll see."

She leaned back against the banquette again, looking even smaller and more pinched, regarding me with eyes glassy as marbles. She licked her lips slowly, as though savoring the liqueur.

"There's some as will wine and dine you, then cast you off, but at least you come out of it with a lovely trinket or two.

Those are the easy ones. But beware the one who makes no show of himself, promises nothing and steals your heart. They're the killers."

I nodded, though it was hard to think of Robert in that light. Brígh was as drunk as I'd ever seen her, but I didn't want to say anything that she might remember in the morning.

"You're a good girl," she said at last, her voice a slur that no amount of careful enunciation could cover. "Not drinking that?" She eyed my liqueur glass. Without waiting for a response, she stretched out her thin arm, bent her claw-like fingers around the stem and reeled the glass carefully to her lips. She drank the rest of my Grand Marnier in one swooping gulp.

I felt more than just a little unwell. I needed air. I needed to go home. "Thank you for dinner, Brígh. This doesn't have to be your treat. Could I share the bill with you?"

She waved her fingers vaguely in front of her face. "On my tab. All taken care of already."

"Well, thank you very much." I was glad I'd offered and glad she'd declined. I could only imagine the size of the bill. I started to edge out of the booth. "How are you getting home?"

"We'll go by cab, of course. Your arm, please."

I helped her up from the banquette and held her elbow as we slowly made our way through a virtually empty fish restaurant that made no concession to serving turkey, even on Thanksgiving. The maître d', who had already ordered a taxi, helped her with her jacket and walked us out to a waiting car. He gave the driver an address on Central Park West and wished us a Happy Thanksgiving.

Once we were settled in the back seat of the taxi, Brígh put her handbag in my lap. "Please take a ten-dollar bill from my wallet to pay the driver. He'll drop me first."

Her head lolled to her shoulder and she leaned against the door. As we whisked up the avenue past Central Park, I heard a gentle whiffling sound and knew Brígh was asleep. She looked like a child, huddled in her velvet and ermine, the bow askew in her fluffy little-girl hair.

We pulled around in front of a grand building several blocks north of Columbus Circle. A doorman wearing white gloves hurried out. He opened the door, nodded to me, then scooped Brígh up and carried her into the building. Her black satin court shoes dangled on her toes; the "doggy" bag with lobster for her cat swung on her arm.

I sat stunned for a moment until the cabbie asked, "Where to next, miss?"

"Across the park, please."

I gave him my address, then covered my face in my hands trying to stop my head from swirling. The drive through Central Park was a silent, frosty blur. Dazed and unsteady, I stepped out of the taxi, having given the driver the crisp ten-dollar bill. It was nearly three times the fare, but it was also Thanksgiving.

If Brígh remembered anything of what she'd said that evening, she did not bring it up when I saw her at the office. I thanked her again for dinner.

"Lovely you could join me," she said. "We'll do it again another time."

I wasn't eager to take her up on that vague invitation, but also mindful not to show it. She'd become my champion in the office and I couldn't risk losing her favor. I also genuinely liked Brígh and appreciated her eccentricities. I didn't dwell on her comments about Robert, but it did occur to me to wonder how many other young women she'd counseled about him.

There was no sign any particular women on the staff pined for him, nor was he the subject of gossip, as were some of the writers and editors I worked with every day. Flirtatious jesting was the norm for office banter, but Robert didn't make lascivious remarks that made a woman feel queasy.

I knew the pitfalls of office romances. I'd come across researchers sobbing in the restroom over a broken affair and seen office girls bleakly waiting for a last-minute summons to have drinks at O'Reilly's. That was not going to happen to me.

Aside from Brígh, no one in the office knew I was seeing Robert. As often as we spent nights and weekends together in his studio, I made no presumptions about the following night or weekend. I left nothing hanging in his closet. I didn't ask for a key. I didn't encroach. But then it wasn't a one-way street because Robert made no presumptions with me. We lived entirely in the present. No plans, no talk of the future—not even a day ahead.

I understood that with his job, a phone call could mean that he might turn the key in his door and be gone for a week, a month, perhaps longer. I sensed that even without the peripatetic profession he'd chosen, it was his nature not to think ahead or make commitments. Living in the moment with Robert also meant romance with no routine, no expectations, no schedules to fulfill—a welcome tradeoff in a burgeoning relationship.

Unfortunately, I slipped up when I arrived one Saturday afternoon with a spider plant. It was meant as a gift, a thank you for one of our first trips together, a weekend drive to the Hudson Valley. I also brought a bag of groceries with the intention of making dinner for Robert, who always paid the check when we went to restaurants.

When I saw the plant in its woven macramé hanger in a florist shop, it had struck me as the ideal gift for Robert's minimalist tastes. The lush plant, with it's long stalks of clustering flowers, would not take up counter space and would be perfect hanging under the skylight. I couldn't wait to see Robert's face when I presented it to him.

I arrived at his door grinning with anticipation. When he saw the plant, his mouth sagged. He reached for the bag of groceries and I was left holding the heavy plant by its macramé harness. I'd made a terrible miscalculation. It was a gift that required tending. It had to be watered. It couldn't look after itself when he was gone.

"It comes with its own hook," I said lamely. "I was thinking it could hang over the table and get plenty of light."

"I guess so," he said dubiously. "Thanks, Livvie. I don't know what to say."

"Well, I hope you like it. I couldn't think what else to give you."

Ignoring the spider plant, he wrapped his arms around me. "You didn't have to give me anything. You're all I need."

Why hadn't I thought to give him a set of kitchen towels? Or a cactus?

Chapter 11

I FINISHED VIEWING THE EXHIBIT and turned to look for Robbie. He was leaning against the doorframe, his eyes on his Rockports, either still admiring his new shoes or avoiding looking at me as I approached.

"Your photographs are wonderful. I hadn't seen most of them before, including the one of me. Thanks for somehow making me look good that morning."

He looked up, regarding me with a crooked smile. "Glad you like it. If you want it, it's yours after the exhibit is over. Frame and all."

"Thank you, I'd love it." I slipped my arm through his as we walked down the courthouse steps. "How about if I buy you lunch?" I asked, indicating an outdoor café across the street. "As a thank you."

We sat at a corner table under a wide awning, my thoughts straying back to the morning after the blackout. I remembered the gate, the glistening cobblestones and the dizzy, ringing feeling when I looked at Robert. Why had he never shown me that photograph?

I was about to ask, when a waitress set down two sweaty glasses of ice water and a couple of menus. "Check out the croissant specials, folks. Back in a minute."

Robert made a face. "They're doing the damnedest things

to croissants these days, have you noticed? They'll be stuffing catfish into 'em next."

I laughed. "I know, but no croissant will ever taste like the first one I had in Paris in sixty-six. Remember that weekend? You were on assignment—"

"Covering de Gaulle. He was pulling France out of NATO—"

"And I came over for a long weekend—"

"Not that long. Thirty-six hours, tarmac to tarmac—"

"You picked me up at dawn in that old yellow *deux chevaux* that shouldn't have been allowed on the road—"

"Belonged to the bureau chief. I was trying to impress you—"

"The onion soup impressed me, and Les Halles with the sun coming up and the market full of crêpes and buttery croissants—"

"That's all that impressed you?" Robert beetled his eyebrows and nudged his shoulder against mine. "Just groceries?"

"Of course not!" I nudged him back. "I remember hours in bed with you at that Left Bank hotel before—voilà, escargots! I loved them even after you told me what I was eating. And mopping up the garlic butter with baguette was heaven. *Vin rouge* and *l'entrecôte* to follow. Walking along the Seine, lights sparkling. Armagnac."

"And?"

"More Armagnac." We looked at each other, Robert nudging me once again.

"That, too, of course. Most of the night, as I remember."

"Funny, I was thinking of de Gaulle," Robert teased. "He figured into that weekend, if you recall. I dropped you at the airport and had to race to join the press flight to Moscow."

"General de Gaulle? Funny, I only remember the Armagnac," I teased back.

I remembered every moment of Robert's surprise invitation to join him in Paris that April. I hadn't seen him in close to three weeks. His crackly transatlantic phone call alone, the first I'd ever received, was thrilling.

"I miss you, Livvie. Gotta see you, baby—"

"Me, too. When are you getting back?"

"Don't know. I think you'll have to come here."

"What! I can't. I'm working."

"Just for the weekend. Did you get your passport yet?"

"Yes, but—"

"I've already arranged a ticket. Just call Air France—"

"You guys ready to order?" The jarring voice of the waitress spun me back from Paris. She shifted her weight from one foot to the other, her shadow falling across the table. How long had she been standing there? I handed her my menu.

"I'll have the tuna salad croissant."

"Make mine the chicken salad croissant. And some more water, please. No, wait," Robert said. "Make it a beer. I'm not driving."

"Cool. One Bud coming up, mister." She took his menu and sauntered off.

"Actually, a glass of wine sounds good." Robert gave me a look. "Okay, okay, I know. I'm driving."

"Get used to it, girl. We're living in a time of seat belts and helmets," Robbie said, patting my knee. "No Gitanes. No Armagnac. No gluten."

"Say it ain't so!" I made a face. "If that croissant comes gluten-free, we're leaving."

He chuckled, then cleared his throat. With his hand still

on my knee, he squeezed it. "So, once again, why did you come here?"

"What? You already asked me that."

"It's been a long time. You came a long way to see me. What's up?"

"Like I said, it was an easy stopover. A chance to get together again seemed too good to pass up." I glanced at him quickly, our eyes meeting in the same instant. "Actually, after showing me that exhibit this morning, I get the feeling you might be reaching out to me."

"How do you figure that?" He looked surprised.

I laughed. "Seriously? C'mon, you told me that if I was in your neck of the woods I should drop by, remember? Turns out I am, just in time to see my lovely mug shot in your exhibit."

"So, here you are." He cocked an eyebrow. "All this because Norm kicked the bucket. Maybe you wanted to see if I was still ticking?"

"Well, it set me thinking back to when we were together and . . ." I caught myself. Mimicking Robbie, I cocked an eyebrow. "Anyway, how *are* you feeling?"

"Fine. I'm not going to die."

"Great, that sets you apart from the rest of us."

He rocked back in his chair. "Good one. So you're checking in on me before I check out, is that it?"

"Don't say that." The words stuck in my throat. "Please, don't talk like that, it's too—"

"Sorry, didn't mean to upset you. Are you okay?"

"I'm fine. Fine, damn it!" Except that tears suddenly flooded my eyes, the hot-and-gushing variety I couldn't stop. I jammed my dark glasses on my face and let the tears fall.

The waitress glanced over. I raised my empty glass. She sloshed water sideways out of a pitcher into both our glasses.

"Thanks. Please bring me a glass of white wine with his beer."

I turned to Robert, who looked stricken. "Sorry, it just happens. Widow tears come in unexpected waves. It's not something I can help. Or I would, believe me." I mopped my face with my napkin.

His hand slid onto my knee. "Let 'em rip. Nothing wrong with a good gully washer now and then."

"To be honest, I did want to see you again. To talk and ... you know, for all sorts of reasons. Norm's death just gave me an opening." Tears still flowed, but my voice was steady. "I can't help thinking back to everything that happened. Maybe I did want to make it down here to see you before it was too late. You never know." I blotted my cheeks with my napkin. "So, how *are* you doing?"

"You already asked me that." He screwed up his face and pulled at his cheeks, making his sad-clown face. I hit his shoulder with the back of my hand and laughed. He grinned. "Fine. I'm doing better than you, it appears."

I blew my nose and balled up the napkin. "The tears don't come as much as they used to. I'm okay, getting better."

The waitress delivered our salad-stuffed croissants, large and soggy, a slice of orange and a wedge of watermelon on the side, along with beer and a glass of wine.

I reached for my wine. "It's okay. One glass. I'll have coffee afterward. Besides, we'll be in town most of the afternoon taking pictures."

"Fine by me. We can even stay the night here." He raised his glass. "To Spaulding."

"To Spaulding." I clinked my wine to his Bud. "Besides, we'll always have Paris."

"Even better." He smiled and took a swig of beer. "To Paris."

I sipped the chilled house white as my thoughts strayed again to our long-ago weekend in Paris—a tiny room in a Left Bank hotel, the sound of laughter floating up from a sidewalk café down the street, tangled sheets, moist, slippery sex and the backward letters of the neon sign reflected in the casement windows, rocking and jittering in spasms of liquid color as we made love—yet, where was I yesterday? Atlanta? Charlotte?

"Not bad," Robbie said, taking a bite of his sandwich. "I hear someone's mutated a croissant with a donut—or is it a bagel? They oughta do it with a hush puppy, just for laughs. A 'cruppy.'"

"Or a waffle. Call it a 'croiffle.'" I was still thinking about our night in Paris, replaying it with the taste of wine on my lips.

We'd parted in the morning after a frantic taxi ride to Orly airport and a kiss that couldn't linger as we said goodbye. I boarded the flight back to New York, sad and tearful. I didn't want the weekend to end. I'd caught my Paris-bound flight late on a Friday night after the magazine closed, leaving straight from work with nothing more than a small canvas bag on my shoulder. For a long time afterward I imagined that the smells of Paris clung to the small zippered bag in which Robert had tucked two surprise gifts, a bottle of Chanel No. 5 and an Hermès scarf I didn't find until I was on my flight home.

I wore both to the office in the morning. No one knew I'd

been to Paris—except, as it turned out, Brígh. I'd barely hung my coat in the closet before I heard her gravely voice.

"Trysting afar, my dear?"

I whirled around, surprised. "How did you find out?"

"I have my sources. How do you think he managed to catch the press flight to Moscow? That's my beat, you know."

Blushing, but not unhappy to be found out, I reached in my handbag for the miniature bottle of Armagnac from the Air France flight and set it on her desk.

"Salud!"

"Ooooh-la-la," she chortled. "Breakfast."

Brígh and I had become even closer after I was bumped up to a position as a full-fledged researcher. I was sure she had something to do with the promotion. Several weeks after the blackout was a cover story, she'd walked out of the managing editor's office, giving me a thumbs-up as she approached my cubicle.

"You did yourself a huge favor turning in all that caption material," she whispered. "You even managed to get some photo releases. Good girl! You skipped the clip desk on your way up the ladder, my dear. Stay tuned."

My new job became official later that day. But I owed the promotion to Robert, most of all. If he hadn't handed me a notebook and asked me to tag along with him, I would probably have spent the night of the blackout on the 27th floor dodging inebriated groping. And I wouldn't have become a picture researcher only months after being hired as an office girl.

Even though I'd been assigned to the photo department, Robert and I managed to keep our budding romance under wraps for several months—not easy in an office environment where ferreting out news was everyone's occupation. I spent most weekends at his studio or on overnight jaunts out of the city. Yet, Robert was generally on assignment and seldom in the office. We avoided meeting in O'Reilly's Saloon, everyone's favorite watering hole on the ground floor.

But throughout the day of my return from Paris, I felt Brígh's eyes tracking me, regarding me with speculation. Late in the afternoon, when jet lag was closing in and the residual euphoria of my two-day trip was wearing off, she caught me yawning at my desk.

"Your candle burns at both ends; it will not last the night."

"But, ah . . . it gives a lovely light!" I yawned again.

"Well, something like that, anyway. At least you picked yourself someone here who's single. *Very* single." She tipped her head and murmured, "Beware, and tiptoe softly, my girl."

Chapter 12

AFTER LUNCH, ROBERT WENT TO WORK photographing the picturesque bandstand that served as the logo for Spaulding's Historical District. I stood off to the side, Robbie's camera bag on my shoulder, wary of casting a long shadow in the shifting afternoon light. He changed lenses and slowly circled the old whitewashed bandstand, a charming gingerbread concoction built in 1908.

As captivating as the scene was, with golden sun flaring off the tip of its weathervane, my eyes were on Robert. He was favoring his right leg, an occasional lurch noticeable when he moved sideways. We'd walked too much, climbed stairs and been on our feet most of the afternoon. Fatigue had set in, but choosing when to quit for the day would have to be up to him. He'd always looked after himself. He pressed his own pants, packed his own bag and even cut his own hair using scissors and a pocket mirror. His thick, choppy shag was his trademark.

"Robbie always liked doing for himself," Aunt Dorah once told me. "There's no point in getting in the way of it. He was like that even as a little boy."

It wasn't until Easter of 1966, the week after I returned from Paris, that I met Aunt Dorah. Robert had arrived from Moscow in time to be on hand for her visit, but warned me he'd be busy entertaining her. It was unlikely he and I would be able to get together, and he didn't suggest that I might join them.

Her telephone call early one morning came as a surprise.

"I think Robbie's trying to keep you a secret, my dear. That's just like my boy and it won't do at all!"

Her cultured drawl had a vague thirties-movie-star inflection that reminded me of Claudette Colbert. She suggested I meet her at the Plaza Hotel, where she was staying for two more days. "If you can break away, we'll have lunch in the Palm Court. I'd so like to meet you!"

"Of course I'd like to meet you, too." I swallowed hard, wondering if Robert had put her up to this. How else had she got the number to the apartment telephone, one I shared with roommates and rarely gave out? "But I don't think Robbie will be able to join us. I think he's in Washington, D.C., today on assignment."

"Precisely. I'll be rattling around on my own, so it's a good excuse to see you. Will one o'clock suit you? If so, I'll book a table."

"Perfect, one o'clock. Thanks so much for the invitation."

It took me a moment to unscramble my thoughts. She hadn't said Robert knew about her plan to have lunch with me, and I didn't want to ask. But why wouldn't it be all right even if he hadn't personally arranged it? In any case, I'd accepted, and lunch with Aunt Dorah at the Palm Court demanded a change of clothes. I hurried back to my closet, unzipping my gray flannel skirt as I ran. The only suitable choice in my scant wardrobe was the navy knit with white piping and navy pumps.

Arriving windblown and out of breath, I'd counted on having a few minutes in the elegant ladies' powder room at the Plaza before meeting Aunt Dorah. But waiting for me just inside the entrance was a stylish middle-aged woman immaculately turned out in a pale cream-colored suit, pearls and Chanel-style pumps. I knew it was Dorah Ellerbe. She recognized me, too, and held out a white-gloved hand.

"Right on the dot! How lovely to meet you, Olivia. I'm Dorah Ellerbe. Please call me Dorah."

"So good to meet you, too. Thanks so much for inviting me."

I took her hand. I was not wearing gloves. My handbag did not match my shoes. I patted my wind-whipped hair and followed her across the lobby to the Palm Court, hoping I didn't have a run in my stocking.

We followed the maître d' to a round table near a bower of spring flowers and sat on spindly gold chairs facing each other. The thick linen tablecloth skirted itself around my knees. The maître d' flicked a creamy linen napkin in her lap, then mine. I gulped water to settle my nerves.

"You've been here before, I'm sure," she said.

"The Plaza, yes. But not the Palm Court." The closest I'd come were stops in the powder room after walks in Central Park. "It's lovely."

"Indeed," she said, as the maître d' handed us menus. "And so are you."

"Thank you. But how did you recognize me?"

"I saw your picture, of course. I was at Robbie's apartment yesterday, just tidying up a bit."

"Really? Where?"

"My dear, girl," she said, eyes twinkling, "I know where Robbie keeps things. Nothing much is secret from me."

My stomach took an elevator ride. I sipped more water, imagining Aunt Dorah on her hands and knees up in the sleeping loft, checking out my shoebox under the bed. My God, what had she found? I took a quick mental inventory of the toiletries I'd stashed, my face beginning to burn.

Robert had also taken photographs of me in the Paris hotel room, risqué pictures I hadn't yet seen and hoped she hadn't, either. I gripped the menu, trying to recover.

"Well, there's a beautiful portrait of you in his studio—"

"Years old! It's a photograph of the oil painting hanging in my living room. I think he drags it out when he knows I'm coming to visit."

"Of course not!" I laughed a bit recklessly, knowing her picture, frame and all, would go back in a drawer the moment she left for the train station. I opened the menu, although I already knew what I was going to have—whatever she was having. "You're enjoying your trip?"

"Wonderful, but of course I never see enough of Robbie. We're very close. I often wish he'd stayed nearer to home, but for him it's always been a case of wanderlust. You know, faraway places, faraway things. I'm not sure he'll ever settle down, really. Home life isn't his cup of tea. Now, do you know what you'd like?"

"What would you recommend?"

"It's all tasty, but I'm going to go with the coquilles Saint-Jacques."

"Perfect, that's what I was thinking, too."

I had no idea what it was, but this lunch was not about

food. Aunt Dorah ordered for both of us, including tall glasses of iced tea with mint sprigs that were delivered on a silver tray.

"What about your family, my dear? I take it you're not from here?"

"No, Minnesota, in a little town in the Iron Range. My father's a mining engineer. My mother's a school librarian. I have an older brother, married with kids, who teaches math and science. We have a lake cabin, so I'll try to get out there in the summer to see them."

"Well, isn't that lovely. I hope they can make it here to visit you one day. There's nowhere quite like New York, I say."

"You're so right," I agreed, nodding vigorously, knowing that any family member visiting me and seeing my bed facing an airshaft would not be a lovely thing. They would not understand why I'd forsaken pine forests and vast expanses of clear lake water for subways and soot. They considered the city a place of deprivation. My father sent grocery ads, circling prices for cauliflower and ground beef because I'd made the mistake of enclosing a neighborhood supermarket flyer with a letter home. My mother, who lived to organize wedding receptions at the church, would be horrified by the cost of a cup of coffee in a New York diner.

"Now, tell me how you and Robbie met."

She leaned back, hands folded in her lap. I guessed her age to be close to sixty, with silvery-blue hair and cheeks that balled into dainty round peaches when she smiled.

"We met at the office. We sort of bumped into each other and then started working together. It went from there."

"An office romance!" She crinkled her eyes, sounding delighted. "Now, I'm not trying to ferret out things you don't want to reveal. Robbie would be furious with me!"

"I don't think anyone at the office really knows. We've only been seeing each other a short time."

"But you must spend lots of time together since you've become a picture researcher."

"That's fairly recent. Did Robert tell you about that?"

"My dear, I subscribe. I read the masthead!" She sipped her tea, looking pleased with herself. "Meeting on the job, isn't it always the way? That's how I met Robbie's uncle. He was a doctor. I was working in hospital administration. Lloyd just swept me off my feet. Such a darling man, rest his soul. Robbie couldn't have hoped for a better father figure."

"Robert mentioned he was raised by you and your husband." I dipped my fork into a lumpy mixture served in a seashell, not at all sure what I'd find under the crusty topping. "How delicious!"

"Yes, they always do it nicely here." She tapped the corners of her mouth with her napkin, crinkling her eyes again. "Little Robbie came to us when he was just a toddler. Sadly, his mother was a bit of a party girl, not at all cut out for motherhood. He won't speak of it, of course. He barely knew her, which was probably just as well."

"What happened to her?"

"She came to a tragic end, not surprisingly. Killed in a car wreck when Robbie was in grammar school. She'd taken it in her head to come visit us, although I'd told her not to bother. She wrapped her car around a telephone pole only blocks away. Drink involved, of course. Getting up her courage to see us, no doubt."

"Poor Robert!" I put my fork down, imagining him waiting for his mother, only to lose her forever. "It must have been horrible for him."

"Indeed, but then he had us. He barely knew her. All for the best."

Startled by her indifference, I stared as she plucked a cloverleaf roll from the breadbasket. She carefully buttered a wedge and took a bite, chewing slowly.

"You're not eating."

"Sorry, I'm thinking of Robert. What a devastating thing to happen."

"Of course, but life goes on. There was much about his mother that he never knew. Sorry to say this about my own sister, but all of it unsavory. He was a lucky little boy to have us. Lloyd gave him his first camera and loved him as the son he always wanted. We gave the boy a stable home and put him through school. I think he'll always be grateful for that."

She sipped her tea, holding a finger crooked as a signal she had more to say. Regarding me carefully, she took her time settling her cup on the table before continuing. "He's very dear to me, as you can imagine. And I tend to be rather protective where he's concerned. I hope I haven't overstepped in letting this all slip out."

"Of course not. I'm glad you told me."

"Good, then let's keep this between ourselves. There's no need to mention our little get-together. I know my Robbie. He's so private." She twinkled, leaning in to whisper, "Though I don't know he'll try keeping you a secret from me much longer!"

"So he doesn't know we're having lunch?"

"Heavens, no!" She laughed. "Just us girls. But I had a hunch he was sweet on you and I couldn't wait to meet you. Now, I've divulged such a lot, you must tell me about yourself. Where did you go to college, may I ask?"

I filled her in, keeping it brief.

"How wonderful getting to know you!" she exclaimed. "You strike me as very modern and career-minded. Don't ever give up your dreams, my dear. Or your livelihood."

I twisted the napkin in my lap, wishing Dorah hadn't cornered me into agreeing to keep our lunch a secret. Through a fruit tart and coffee, Aunt Dorah turned the conversation to theater, concerts and a saleswoman at Bergdorf's who "always sets aside special little items for me." By the time the check arrived, she'd run through one charming anecdote after another about her various stays at the Plaza Hotel.

"Everyone knows me here, so I'm well taken care of. I once left my negligee hanging in the bathroom and they sent it back to me with a lovely lavender sachet tucked in the folds." She looked wistful. "How I should have loved entertaining my own little Eloise here. What fun!"

She walked with me across the lobby to the revolving door and pressed her cheek to mine. "You're so sweet! We must do this again."

"Yes, soon," I agreed, hoping next time Robert would be joining us.

She handed me an engraved card. "Keep this, my dear. If anything comes up, you can always turn to me."

On my walk back to the office, I tucked Aunt Dorah's card into my handbag, mentally composing a thank-you note I would mail that afternoon. When I got off the elevator, I was so lost in thought I passed Brígh's desk without greeting her. She whistled, the shrill kind little boys somehow learn and girls don't.

"You mad at me?"

"Sorry, no. My mind was elsewhere."

"You're all dressed up." She leaned on her elbow, cupping her chin in her hand. "Someone wining and dining you at the Twenty-One Club, I hope?"

"No, the Plaza." I laughed. "Do you have to know everything? Always?"

"I live for it. Sit. Who? What did you eat, not that it matters?"

I shoved aside some files and perched on the corner of her desk. "The Palm Court. Coquilles Saint-Jacques. Yummy."

"And?"

I lowered my voice. "Robert's aunt is in town and called me this morning. She asked me to lunch, but I'm not supposed to say anything to him."

"Ah, Dorah Ellerbe." Brígh sat back in her chair, looking thoughtful. "Interesting, my dear. I didn't see that coming, but I knew she was in town. So, she's checking you out and keeping it mum. You okay with that?"

My stomach jumped. "Not really, but I'm sure she means well."

"One can hope. I met her some time ago. Knows how to present herself, I'll say that. Hope you didn't give too much away."

"There isn't much to say." I exhaled, not realizing I'd been holding my breath. "Besides, she did the talking, mostly about Robert—"

"Trying to warn you off, I'm sure." Brígh turned back to her desk. "Keep it all under your hat, that's my advice. Meanwhile, back to work, dearie."

I didn't see Robert until the following Friday night, arriving at his apartment late after the magazine closed. He greeted me at the door with a warm embrace. The lights were low, except over the worktable. The window shutters were closed and John Coltrane was playing on the hi-fi.

"How about a glass of wine? You look beat."

"I am. I'd love a glass, if you'll join me." I tossed my sweater on the back of a chair. The light box was illuminated and the worktable littered with transparencies. "Still working?"

"Only until you got here."

I glanced at the butcher-block counter. "So, Aunt Dorah is back in mothballs?"

He handed me a glass of Chablis, then poured one for himself. "Safe in a drawer until the old bat's back in town. What'd you think of her?"

"Aunt Dorah?"

"She said the two of you had lunch together." He touched his glass to mine. "How'd it go?"

"It was nice. But I didn't expect her call."

"She likes her little surprises. I hope she didn't throw you off too much."

"Not at all. But how did she get my number?"

"Probably went through my address book. She thinks nothing of pawing through things when she comes around here. I should never have given her a key." He laughed. "When I was a kid, nothing was safe. My uncle built me a tree house and she'd climb up and check that out, too. But she means well. She did a lot for me."

"I'm sure."

I curled up on the couch, Robert settling in next to me. He drew me close, his arm across my shoulders. I looked around, imagining his aunt rifling through his drawers and cupboards.

"She told me not to tell you about our get-together. She said you'd be furious."

"I'm not." He kissed me lightly, running his finger down my cheek. "You would've met her eventually. She's a good person but likes to take charge, you know?"

"I know. Besides, I would've told you about our lunch. You beat me to it."

"I know that."

I was glad Robbie had brought it up first and that I hadn't been put to the test. But why had she made me promise to say nothing, then told him herself?

Chapter 13

ROBERT CROUCHED TO FRAME A SHOT. The glint of late-afternoon sun that had found the weathervane burnished his thick silvery hair a deep copper.

I slid my digital camera from my pocket and snapped a picture just as Robert turned toward me. I took another, catching his look of surprise as he faced me. A stream of light flaring through treetops washed his skin clear of age, wiping away the creases on his brow. The aviator glasses dangled on a lariat around his neck, his shirt clinging to his chest in the muggy heat.

I snapped another picture as he stood gazing at me. Frozen on the screen was the embodiment of the man I'd fallen in love with decades ago—and couldn't deny still aroused feelings of a sort that surprised me.

I took one last shot before pressing the video button. He walked toward me. Shifting light restored shadows and folds, each footfall seemingly marking the years between then and now. I turned off the video and held up my arms. He walked into my embrace, holding me close. With his body relaxed against mine, tension I hadn't been aware of drained away.

I shifted my head, finding the soft cushion in the recess of his shoulder, the beat of his heart resounding in my ear. It could have been a lover's embrace, but it was too familiar, a hug between pals of long-standing that could have taken place at the airport, but hadn't. Now it felt appropriate, a sweet memory of what once was.

He kneaded his fingers in the space between my shoulder blades and murmured, "That's it, all done."

"Tired?"

"Pooped. Let's call it a day."

"Should we find rooms for the night?"

"We've got time." He laughed softly. "But there was a time—"

"We couldn't wait, I remember." I laughed, too. "That vineyard outside Dijon? At dusk, on that cart, with grape pickers heading back only a few rows away—what were we thinking?"

"We weren't." He squeezed my ribs. "Can't let thinking get in the way."

I nodded, then rolled my forehead gently on his chest, recalling the feel of the rough boards on my back and the musky tang of sweet red grapes embedded in the freshly emptied cart. I'd lifted my hips as Robert released the drawstring on my cotton pants and pulled them down, moaning softly as he eased himself inside me.

Above him, a lowering sun in a vast coppery sky had flamed on the horizon. The busload of holiday grape pickers, who'd paid for the privilege of spending a day working in the vineyards, straggled back for a rustic package-tour dinner, their voices a distant burble. Later, Robert would finish photographing the harvest festivities for the magazine, but in that stolen piece of time in a long, arduous day, it was just him and me and the subtle rock of the cart, its creak rhythmic in the stillness of a fiery sunset.

Robert took my hand and we walked a few feet toward a shady area under a tree near the bandstand. His leg was seizing up. He needed my support. I remained standing, gripping his arm as he eased himself to the grass. I sat down next to him, linking my arms around my knees.

"How're you doing?"

"Good for another inning or two. Just need a breather." He stretched out his legs, massaging his right thigh before lying back in the grass. "Feels good," he sighed.

I lifted his head onto my lap. "How's that?"

"Even better." He closed his eyes and crossed his arms on his chest. "If I snooze, don't wake me."

As he dozed off, I propped myself in the warm grass and looked through the pictures I'd snapped. One photo in particular reminded me of a shot of Robert I'd taken on the Serengeti plain when we were working on a cover story about East Africa. My new boss, Don Anderson, the magazine's senior editor on color projects, had suggested a travel story on the growing popularity of photo safaris. Robert was given the plum assignment of shooting a color feature about travel to East African game reserves.

He'd already been in Kenya for a week when the reporter, Jason Woodruff, and I met him at the New Stanley Hotel in Nairobi. The plan was for Jason to tour game parks with us for five days before splitting off on his own to join a family on safari. I would stay another two weeks with Robert in Kenya and Tanzania.

Jason and I arrived in Nairobi in mid-July at a time of political unrest following the assassination of a tribal leader the previous day. The streets were quiet and many shops had shuttered early. But that evening, despite palpable tension in the air, the three of us walked from our hotel to a nearby French restaurant Robert recommended. The place had an old-world charm, with low beamed ceilings and tables set close together, but there were few diners. A portly maître d' with a broad smile, who seemed to have struck a rapport with Robert from previous visits that week, seated us at a table toward the back of the restaurant.

We'd barely ordered dinner when we heard popping sounds and commotion in the street. As shouts and crackling noises grew louder, Robert looked at Jason. "We'd better check it out."

"Yeah, might explain why this place is damn near empty," Jason said, getting up.

I stood, too, and reached for my shoulder bag. "Let's go."

Robert was already on his feet, grabbing his camera case. "You stay here, Livvie. Hold down the fort."

"And do what? Clean muskets?"

"Just stay safe. We'll be back in a minute." The two men rushed for the door.

I started to follow, but the maître d' hurried over, blocking my path. "You stay, please, miss. We wait to bring soup."

"What's going on out there?"

"Nothing, miss. All okay." But there was fear in his eyes, a sheen of sweat glistening on his face.

I gripped the strap of my shoulder bag and tried to push ahead. "I want to see for myself."

"No, miss. Over there." He touched my elbow and pointed toward the kitchen. "Safer that way."

Weaving around empty tables, we made our way to the

swinging doors of the kitchen. Pushing past a huddle of cooks and waiters, we went out a back door into a small fenced-in dirt yard with a vegetable garden. White netting, covering bamboo poles supporting runner beans and tomato vines, looked ghostly in the twilight. Red flares streamed in the darkening sky above the high fence. Shouts, screams and popping sounds, like fireworks, grew louder. The smell of rotten eggs permeated the sultry air.

A young waiter joined the maître d' and me, handing us dampened napkins. I pressed one to my face, cupping it over my stinging nostrils. Tears flooded my eyes.

The waiter stooped down and led us to a vantage point at the far end of the garden. We kneeled in the dirt, peering through cracks in the rough-hewn fence at the mayhem only yards away in the street.

I pulled a notebook from my bag. "Okay, can you tell me what's going on out there? Who are they? What're they shouting?"

Sometime later, Jason and Robert returned, both rubbing their eyes. I was already seated at the table. I signaled the waiter for a round of drinks.

"Are you guys okay?"

"Tear gas," Jason said. "Lucky you didn't get caught in it."

"But I did." I slapped my notebook on the table.

"You were out there?" Robert looked at my reddened eyes, his voice sharp. "I told you to stay in here."

"We're working. It's my job to stay on top of what's going on."

"This isn't our story."

"But we're here. You took pictures, right? Jason, you're filing this, I assume?" I flipped my notebook open. "Well, here's background on the slain minister's brother, who led the retaliation. I also spoke to the police patrol. The burial's tomorrow and they expect another protest. And just for the record, I'm not here to hold down a fort and mind my skirts while waiting for the soup to be served."

Robert nodded. "Point well taken."

"Of course," Jason said, his eyes darting between Robert and me. "Still, for her own safety—"

Robert shot him a look. "No, she's right."

By then, most of the magazine's staff knew that Robert and I were seeing each other, but I didn't want to be viewed by Jason as Robert's tag-along girlfriend. Nor could I permit Robert's chivalry to hold me back from doing my job. I'd worked hard researching the safari story, my biggest assignment to date. I'd also booked us into separate rooms throughout the trip.

Our drinks arrived and we raised glasses to the success of our venture. People drifted into the restaurant and the place was packed by the time we left. On our way back to the hotel, Robert kicked a tear-gas canister into the gutter. We stopped in the bar for a nightcap. I left them having a second round and went up to my room. I waited in bed, expecting a tap on the door. After an hour, I put my book down and switched off the lamp. I'd made my point, but never said we couldn't visit each other's forts.

On Robert's recommendation, I'd chartered a Beechcraft Queen Air owned and operated by Nils Swensen, a golden-haired, ruddy-faced fourth-generation Kenyan. Robert had already covered game reserves near Nairobi during his first week, so we set off the following day for Mount Kenya National Park in the Central Highlands, the homeland of the Kikuyu people. Jason, a trim, compact man several years older than Robert, had flown combat in Korea and was looking forward to time in the cockpit. Robert was a licensed pilot, qualified to fly twin-engine aircraft. Nils laughed and said he was fine "sitting with his feet up on a busman's holiday," giving Jason and Robert a chance to log flight hours.

On Jason's first landing, he had to buzz the remote airstrip twice to clear it of zebra. At four a.m. the following morning, we were in a Land Rover photographing a pride of lions feeding on a wildebeest. From there, we went to Aberdare National Park and stayed in Treetops Lodge, famous as the hotel where Princess Elizabeth stayed the night she learned of her father's death and assumed the throne of England. Drinking Pimm's Cups from one of several lookout posts, we watched wildlife gather at the watering hole near the lodge. Amboseli and Lake Nakuru National Parks came next, where I photographed great flocks of flamingos using Robert's old Nikkormat, entrusted to me on loan for the duration of the trip.

Jason left us before Robert and I went on to Maasai Mara National Reserve and the Serengeti in bordering Tanzania. The three of us had settled into an easy comradeship by then. While Robert and I maintained our professional working relationship, we also felt comfortable being affectionate with each other in the evenings, unwinding from our long predawn-to-dusk days.

On our first night after Jason's departure, Robbie and I stayed in a tented encampment photographing a group safari. Lying tightly curled together on a narrow cot, the fading embers of a campfire glowing through the flaps of our tent, I whispered words I'd known were true since I'd first met him.

"I love you."

His face, ruddy in the glow of the firelight, shifted back into shadow. At the same time, I heard his breath catch and felt his hand under my head move slightly. The hesitation was minimal, only a hair's breadth before I heard him whisper:

"I love you, too, you know."

I didn't know. He'd never said it. The words had slipped out of me before I could catch myself, but they were true. Why shouldn't I have said them first? Still, had my words caught him by surprise? Had he responded only because it would otherwise have been awkward—unchivalrous?

He kissed me tenderly and we made love, falling asleep in each other's arms.

In the morning when I awakened, Robbie was lying in his own cot, looking at me. "I like being with you." His eyes were solemn, his voice quiet. "We've had some good times together."

"'Had'?" I raised myself up. "I like being with you, too. I'd like the good times to continue and always be with you."

"You never know what's down the road." He raked a hand through his hair. "Things are good so far—"

"Damn good! What's wrong with keeping it that way and making a future together?"

"I don't know that it's a good idea. Not if we're going to keep working together."

"Wait a minute, if this is about what I said in Nairobi—"

"You're not someone to stay behind and hold down the fort. You were right to say it. For that matter, I wouldn't want you to be. I'm not someone who needs that."

"You don't want to be tied down? Or are you saying it wouldn't work because of the magazine? Because if that's the case, I could work somewhere else."

"You think that would make a difference? Why spoil a good thing?"

"I didn't think I was."

Somehow I managed to smile. He looked grave. How had we got into this? Clearly I'd pushed things too far. Had he been lying awake most of the night waiting to set me straight? I shivered under the loose sheet, naked but for Robbie's borrowed tee shirt. I sank back down on the pillow, my insides turning over.

"I love you," I whispered, risking the words that had probably started it all.

"I love you, too, Livvie." His voice was firm, his look tender. He swung his legs off the cot. "How about some coffee?"

I nodded, unsure of my voice.

He dug his legs into khaki shorts, then picked up his topsiders, turned them over and shook them before jamming them on his feet. "Back in a minute."

I closed my eyes, feeling sick. I turned my face into my pillow to sop up a flood of tears. *Cry fast! Get rid of the evidence!* I could not let him see me like this, not while we were working—certainly not if I wanted to keep him in my life. Damn, why had I pressed on when I knew I shouldn't!

I poured water from a jug into a metal bowl and splashed handfuls on my face, my fingers slapping away puffiness and tearstains. I ran damp fingers through my hair and got dressed.

If Robert thought clinking tin cups of boiled black coffee together that morning signaled that we'd settled our differences and could get on with our work, I resolved to go along with it. I was determined not to let emotions get in the way of doing my job. He and I worked well together. I imagined that not changing.

Late on our last day together, with Nils arriving the following morning to fly us back to Nairobi, I stood on the grasslands of the Serengeti while Robert photographed Maasai herdsman against the backdrop of the far-reaching plains. With the sun low, I watched him pause between frames and lift his right foot to scratch his left calf. I quickly pressed the shutter, grabbing a shot of him silhouetted in the classic stance of the Maasai, tall and straight, gazing across the vast plains.

He heard the *click-thunk* of my camera and turned to me, his face shadowed. The Maasai he'd been photographing began grouping around him.

"Please, Robbie. Let me take a picture of all of you." I managed to catch the sun's gold-rich light full on their faces, all of them wearing broad smiles.

When I returned to New York, the group photo I'd taken was used in the editor's pub letter in the issue featuring East African safaris. The photograph of Robbie standing on one leg with the other crooked to his calf, I kept for myself.

Chapter 14

ROBBIE'S HEAD LAY HEAVY IN MY LAP. I let him sleep, managing to slide my digital camera back in my pocket without disturbing him. A wisp of sultry air ruffled my hair as I tilted my head back. The gloaming was upon us, nightfall minutes away. Fireflies were already flitting in the blue-gray light. I breathed deeply, content to be spending the night in Spaulding. Perhaps over a quiet dinner, Robbie would be open to the talk I hoped we were both ready to have. Where had things between us gone wrong? Did it begin in the restaurant in Nairobi? My rash words spoken on the cot? Or much later, when damaging consequences were irreparable? The diamond ring was in my bag, waiting for the right moment to find out.

As if responding to my thoughts, he murmured, "It's nice having you here."

"You're awake."

"Wasn't asleep. Just needed to close my eyes for a bit." He stretched his arms back, then ran his hand down the side of my leg. "Hungry?"

"I could go for something, but we should look into getting rooms first."

I stood up, then reached down to give him a hand. His legs were stiff and he gripped my arm as we walked toward the car in darkness. By the time we got around to finding rooms for the night, there were no vacancies. The bed-and-breakfast where Robbie usually stayed when he was in Spaulding was fully booked with a wedding party. The only other B&B in the Historical District was closed for renovation. We sat in the car considering our options.

Robbie looked genuinely mystified. "Huh, never happened to me before."

"C'mon, you always left it to chance! Remember the night we slept on the beach in Villefranche?"

"Well, a lot of people slept on the beach in those days. Anyway, don't worry. I usually come up with something."

"Okay, let's see if your room karma works with those motels near the interstate." I pressed the ignition and pulled away from the curb. "We can get a bite to eat afterward."

But even the economy motels near the fast-food chains had filled up. I pulled into the last motel before the interchange, a sleek new three-story building with an overflowing dumpster near the entrance. With remnants of scaffolding on one side, the building looked like it was still under construction. I spotted a car with an open trunk parked in the lot. A man was setting luggage on a trolley. I pulled up and parked, leaving Robbie in the car while I hurried inside.

A cherubic desk clerk wearing a tan polo shirt with the nametag *Greg* was piling brochures on the counter next to a bowl of green apples. "Howdy, ma'am. Sorry, for the mess. We're officially open, but sorta behind."

"Do you have two rooms available?"

He looked down at the screen. "Only one left that's set up. No Wi-Fi or TV installed yet. Room one fourteen, if ya want to take a look."

I hurried down the newly carpeted hallway and circled

around an ice machine awaiting installation. The door to room 114 was standing open, smelling of fresh paint, a service trolley stationed outside. I took a quick look around. A handyman was screwing light bulbs into a bathroom fixture. A dark-haired housekeeper was making up one of the two queen-size beds. The walls were bare. The window had a sliding security device, which allowed a three-inch opening for fresh air.

"Hold the room a minute," I told Greg as I breezed through the lobby and out to the parking lot.

Robert stuck his head out the window. "Any luck?"

"One room, two beds. Clean. Airy. We can take it or check out places down the interstate. Your call."

"Sure, why not stay here?" He cocked an eye at me. "No monkey business, though."

"I'll try to control myself."

I patted his arm and went around to the back of the SUV to pop the trunk, smiling to myself. Sharing a hotel room with Robert was hardly a novelty, but on this occasion we would *not* be sharing a bed. The alternative, driving around in search of two available rooms, wasn't at all appealing. We'd manage, although I was surprised either one of us had agreed to the arrangement.

Before Robert could climb out of the car, I'd slung the camera bag on my shoulder, attached his satchel to my wheelie and made my way back into the lobby. By the time he joined me at the front desk, we were registered. I handed him one of the key cards.

"The room is almost ready. You can settle in while I get some takeout. You want pizza or burgers? We passed both on the way."

"Pizza sounds good."

"Great, there's a place just down the road. Back in a few minutes."

There was a time when accommodating Robert was part of my job. I knew, as I scrambled to supply a meal at the end of a day's shoot, that he'd want pizza, and I didn't have to ask what kind of topping. But behind the wheel, racing to pick up food to eat in our motel room, reality sank in. What slip in my thinking had made me imagine it would be okay to sleep together in the same room? Staying as a guest in Robert's house was one thing—sharing a motel room quite another. This was a different time, and very different circumstances.

I ordered pizza and sat waiting on a bench outside, a pager in my lap. The night air was mild, the sky a blanket of stars. I recalled another time years ago when we'd had no place to stay.

While Robbie was still in East Africa wrapping up the safari story, I flew to Rome to make arrangements for him to shoot a color feature on the Vatican. It was a tough assignment fraught with tight scheduling and security issues that had taken a toll on both of us.

After we finished the shoot, Robbie suggested that we unwind with a spur-of-the-moment trip to the South of France. We arrived late in the day, rented a car at the airport, and drove along a coastline crowded with late-summer vacationers. It was soon apparent there were no rooms to be had anywhere. At first I was furious he hadn't permitted me to let our hotel concierge in Rome call ahead, but Robbie insisted he had a place in mind to spend the night.

Meanwhile, he took me to a shanty on the beach, a tumbledown shack with a sloping roof sheltering a few tables facing the sea. We sat barefoot eating loup de mer roasted in a sandpit and drinking a local rosé. To add to the romance of dining at the seaside restaurant, an aging troubadour strummed a guitar and sang French ballads in the tiny bar. When the place shuttered for the night, Robbie talked the owner into loaning us a couple of straw mats. With our luggage locked in the trunk of our rental, we curled up on the beach, lying side by side under the stars until the sun woke us at dawn.

We strolled up and down the beach, splashing in the rolling surf, before returning to the restaurant for coffee and croissants. Robert handed over our rolled-up mats, tipping the owner generously. It was a magical eighteen hours that reduced the lingering tensions following our East African trip. After we left Villefranche that morning, it occurred to me that Robert hadn't really tried all that hard to find a room. Was it his way of showing me the romance of life without ties and expectations?

If so, what was he trying to show me now after yet another night searching to find accommodation?

The plastic pager vibrated noisily in my lap, its green lights flashing on and off. With our dinner secured by a seat belt, I raced back to the motel, breaking the speed limit to ask the desk clerk if another room had opened up.

"Nope, sorry," Greg said, shrugging. "Why? Something wrong?"

I shook my head, stifling an impulse to scream—*Yes, damn it! Everything!*

I shouldn't have come. I shouldn't be here, certainly not sharing a room with a man who was—what? A lover from decades ago, someone who—*damn it!*—still got under my skin, igniting memories of long ago passion, raw hurt and—*stop!*

I stared at the bowl of green apples on the counter, registering the thin layer of plaster dust covering them. With the pizza box warm on my hand and a bag of cold soda cans pressed to my chest, I headed down the hallway to room 114.

Robert was in bed, sitting up with pillows piled behind him, looking through images on his digital camera. He was wearing a tee shirt, his hair still damp from a shower, when I walked in clutching our dinner.

"Whoa there, you need a hand? I coulda gone with, you know." He put the camera aside and sat up a little straighter.

"No need. I managed." I slid the pizza box onto his lap and looked around the gloomy interior for a place to set down the drinks. There was no furniture, and the room was lit with a single overhead bulb in the entryway. I popped the tab on a can of Coke and handed it to him. "Thanks for giving me the bed by the window."

"You bet." He took a swig of Coke and lifted the lid. "Thin crust. Perfect. You take the first slice."

"No, go ahead. Start in while it's hot." Suddenly overcome, the room closing in on me, I mumbled, "I should wash my hands."

I grabbed my toiletry bag and went into the bathroom, closing the door. My heart was pounding, my breath short. I couldn't tell him I was going out for a walk—not now, with pizza waiting to be eaten. I peeled plastic wrap off a paper cup, filled it with tap water and gulped it down.

I heard the door to the hallway open, the sound of voices, probably housekeeping delivering a lamp or something. Robbie could handle whatever it was.

I washed my face and brushed my teeth. How long could I stay in here? This would not be a night I could sleep. There was no wine, no TV, no distraction, just the unsettling presence of Robbie in his tee shirt lying in the next bed.

His toothbrush—a blue one—jutted out of a paper cup. His small leather toiletry bag was zipped tight, nothing sitting out on the countertop. On the other side of the sink, my red toothbrush was in its own paper cup, my bag zipped up. Was there anything in either bag worth concealing? Not in mine. I ran damp fingers through my hair and took another moment before opening the door.

"You okay? Get in here. You've got a lot of pizza to catch up on."

"Sorry, just wanted to wash up."

He lifted a slice of pizza and held it out to me. "Here you go. And pour yourself a glass of wine."

"If only," I muttered.

"Right here. Your guy Greg just delivered it." He held a bottle by its neck, waggling it back and forth. It was already open. "The glasses are on the floor. Pour me some, too."

"What the hell? How did you do that?"

"Phone's working. I told your guy at the desk to get the nearest liquor store to send over their best Bordeaux." He glanced at the label. "By God, they did!"

I held wine glasses while Robbie poured. We clinked and I took a sip, savoring the fine wine. "Delicious! Thank you!"

"I also asked Greg if he had another room available. No luck."

"I don't believe it!" I laughed, realizing Robbie was finding this arrangement as awkward as I was. "I asked him the same thing on my way in. Sorry, but we'll have to make the best of it." I ruffled his damp hair.

"Hey, hey, don't get silly on me. Eat your pizza."

"Aye, sir." I plopped down next to him and took a slice from the box. "You've left more than half. I can't eat all that."

"Eat what you like. Drink what you like. There are no dos or don'ts. Seriously, stop fussing and planning. I'm thinking you oughta slow down and take a break for a while."

"My book tour's a break."

"Most people wouldn't figure it that way."

"I do. It's planes, trains, hotels mixed with signings and media events. A breeze, frankly. I enjoy it. It's only when I stop and, you know—that's when things get hard."

"Maybe you need to stop altogether and let things sink in."

"Thanks, Dr. Phil. How about topping me up?"

"All yours. You know me, I keel over after one glass."

"You don't have far to fall, but it's up to you." I took a sip of wine, swirling it in my mouth. "Funny, but I was thinking of Villefranche earlier. Drinking rosé. Sleeping on the beach."

He sighed. "That's going way, way back."

"Rome, too. Maybe it's the pizza. Anyway, I was thinking about how well we used to work together. Even on that tight Vatican assignment."

"Way too rushed, but turned out to be a terrific cover story."

"Still, we managed to play afterward. Took some time to ourselves. Remember our night on the beach? We had some great times together."

"The best." Robert shifted in bed, his shoulders resting against the headboard. "Those were the golden years, at least for me. Photojournalism meant something back then. Magazines were riding high. The sky was the limit on travel and expense. You remember the time Norm Jurgens bought a house for a local stringer he was working with in India and put it on his expense account? The company actually paid for it!" He laughed. "Those were crazy, good times . . . the stories we did, the places we went where no one else could go—"

"Too bad it all came crashing down."

"I was there for the crash."

"You survived, moved on. Guys like Norm, who lived high on the hog—the company's hog!—couldn't adjust. I can't say I felt sorry for him."

"Maybe he went overboard . . ."

"Maybe? C'mon, he'd swagger into the office with Leicas strung around his neck like battle trophies, everything heaped on the company's tab. You guys were kings."

"It was a time of excess. We all indulged."

"Couldn't last." I sipped wine, feeling a heady buzz. "At least we had a generous taste of the good times." I laughed. "And not just fresh caviar and iced vodka on Pan Am flights!"

"Not to be dismissed. Somewhere there's a TWA Heaven."

"*À la vôtre!*" I raised my glass.

"*Salute!* Take a swallow for me." He set his glass on the floor, stretched his legs out and pulled the sheet taut to his shoulders. "Good memories, babe. Those are the ones you want to remember. Forget the others. They'll just drag you down." His face was solemn, a warning note in his voice. "Seriously, just remember the good stuff."

Aware of his knee against my hip, I shifted away and reached for the bottle, filling my glass. "Thanks for this. It's hard to beat a good Bordeaux."

"You deserve it." Robert pushed the pizza box between us. "C'mon, eat up."

"That's it for me, the rest is yours. I'm going to have a bath." I stood and raised my glass in a salute. "Thanks again."

"Thanks for the pizza. I'm sacking out. I'm whipped. See you in the morning."

"Goodnight." I gripped his foot through the bedcover, jostling it. "Get some sleep."

I closed the bathroom door and sagged against the countertop, feeling shaky. Why did I shy away from confronting Robert when he warned me not to dredge up the past? Why make light of good ol' Norm Jurgens and ignore the role he played in what happened back then? My shoulder bag had been on the bed between us, yet I hadn't reached inside for the ring. What stopped me?

I turned on the taps, undressed and slipped slowly into hot bath water. With my feet planted against the far end of the shallow tub, I rested my head against the wall, closing my eyes.

Robbie had sounded wistful talking about the magazine and I understood. We'd traveled back decades, to a time that no longer existed. I'd moved on, leaving the magazine for personal reasons. For Robert, it had been a hard reckoning, but he'd also managed to adjust, mixing in corporate work while still doing reportage and editorial assignments.

For others like him, tethered to a magnanimous company

that provided seemingly bottomless expense accounts, refrigerators full of film, support staff and dream assignments to faraway places, the fall was precipitous. Most never saw it coming. Certainly not Norm, who had indeed charged a house for a stringer to the magazine and gotten away with it. The harshest rebuke he'd faced was being recalled from Paris to spend a week holed up in a New York hotel room with a company bookkeeper to bring his expense accounts up to date. He'd had to make do with room service and a well-stocked minibar while trying to recall how he'd spent the magazine's money. When the bottom dropped out of those high-flying times, some like Norm felt bitterly betrayed.

I reached for my wine glass and took a last swallow, recollections of those bygone days flitting through my mind. The Vatican assignment had come up fast on the heels of the East African safari story, leaving little time to regain our easygoing footing after hitting that rocky patch. I'd wanted to prove we could work together professionally and still be lovers, but every word and gesture seemed weighted with unintended significance. In retrospect, there was nothing I could have done; our course seemingly set.

The water chilled, and I shivered stepping out of the tub. Wrapped in a bath towel, I considered what I might wear to bed. Panties and a teddy would have to do. By now Robert would be sound asleep, but did it matter? I decided it didn't and tiptoed back into the bedroom, hearing the gentle flutter of Robert's breath.

As soon as my head sank into my pillow, I knew I wouldn't sleep. My body had been numbed by the bath, but my mind was alert. If I'd been on my own, I would have sat up, flipped open my laptop and set to work writing.

Instead, I closed my eyes and envisioned Jake as he always appeared to me on sleepless nights, his face slick with sweat, looking at me in surprise. It was an unnatural expression, fixed in astonishment. I'd sensed instantly that he wasn't really seeing me. He'd already departed even as his face registered disbelief. Why couldn't I replace that hateful last image of him with one more familiar, more as I'd like to remember him, instead of this insomniac's vision I wanted to forget?

For long minutes my mind patched pieces of his image together, rearranging his expression, wiping the surprise from his face. I wanted to see him as he was in life, not on the brink of death. Slowly the collage came together, with his close-cropped salt-and-pepper hair. Warm, liquid brown eyes in a handsome, always-tanned face. Rolling laughter welling up and bursting out of him in great, rumbling waves. I smiled, swallowing back tears. No one could hear that deep, happy laugh without laughing along with him.

Jake was a man who'd hugged, held and touched with an openness that was all-consuming. He was a year younger than me, an editor, who'd set me free to write the novels I wanted to write. He became my refuge, a safety net, my tether to the world when I thought I was going crazy. I was lucky to find him when I did. We'd made a future together at a time when I didn't think I had one.

I rolled onto my side, peering down at the floor. Where was the bottle of Bordeaux? At what point did a nightcap turn into a drink before breakfast? I'd weighed that question a good number of times over the years, never quite pinpointing the specific hour. How much wine was left? I calculated, picturing the bottle as I'd poured my dollop before bath time. There should be at least a glass left, maybe a touch more.

I shifted closer to the edge of the bed and stretched out my hand. I touched flesh and jumped.

Robert's fingertips caught mine. "You all right?"

"You're awake?"

"You only know that because you are. Can't sleep?"

"Not yet."

"Pour yourself some wine. It's okay."

"You know, that's probably a good idea. Maybe I will."

I fumbled on the floor for my glass and reached for the bottle, limned in a sliver of light at the side of Robert's bed. I pulled the cork and poured. There wasn't as much left as I'd thought. I sat back, plumping a pillow behind me.

"Still feeling pretty raw?"

I nodded, swallowing hard. "It's been over six months. I don't cry every two minutes anymore. I've stopped having to mention Jake's name every chance I get."

"You've barely mentioned him."

"People tire of it, so I try not to. Besides, it invites unsolicited advice. I'm told it's time to move on. Where to, I don't know. Where am I supposed to go? Wish I knew."

"People want to say something comforting, but don't know how."

"So they ask questions and sound impatient when I don't have answers. They ask why? How? Maybe it's the suddenness of his death that throws them off. I think they ask because they want to know what to avoid."

Robert chuckled softly. "So it doesn't happen to them—"

"I'm asked if there were warning signs. There weren't. We'd just finished playing tennis. I threw him a towel. He reached for it, then looked at me. I thought he was going to say something, but he just looked surprised. Then collapsed. I called nine-one-one. I did CPR, but I knew. Maybe I should just tell people 'beware of surprise'—it's a sure sign. A killer. A widow-maker."

"I'm so sorry, Livvie. Are you okay?"

"I miss him. Badly. I feel empty. A big, damn gaping hole I can't fill. I wish we'd had more time—even a day of knowing ahead, to plan, to say things. I'd take even a minute, instead of that damn look of surprise."

I heard the rustle of sheets, then felt the weight and warmth of Robbie settling next to me on the bed. He touched my arm. "You should take a break. Give yourself time."

Tears slopped down my cheeks. "Can't, not yet. More places I have to go. There are ads in the papers. Signs in the bookstores. My publisher..." I gulped again and caught my breath. "But it's hard without Jake. He was always there for me when I needed bolstering."

"I've been there. I know it's hard." He took the wine glass from my hand and set it on the floor.

My cry was a deep gasp, an unearthly sound I fought to muffle. I wanted Jake back, that terrible look erased from his face, his broad smile letting me know he was alive and well.

"Just let it go, Livvie. Don't hold it in."

Robbie pulled me toward him, holding me close and stroking my hair, letting me sob. I gulped, breathing in his soap-sweet warmth, my hands tangling in the thin sheet bunched between us. My chest convulsed in a hiccup, then another.

"Hold your breath, count to fifty."

I sucked in air, looking at Robbie through a glaze of tears. He held my gaze, touching my cheek where it bulged, his hand cool and dry on my damp face. With breath suspended, my thoughts raced, ricocheting with images of Robbie lying next to me in the sand, his moonlit face close to mine. I looked into his eyes for the full count, unblinking, lungs bursting, not wanting to break contact. With a whisper of a smile, he tapped my cheek and I slowly exhaled.

In a movement I didn't sense coming, he brushed my lips with a kiss. I blinked, my breath a startled intake before I hiccupped again.

He pulled back, his eyes crinkling with humor. "Too bad. That usually works."

"A kiss? Now who's getting silly?" Flushed, his nearness unsettling, I took a deep breath to thwart another oncoming hiccup. "You should've said 'boo' if you're trying to scare me."

"Sorry, Livvie. I wish I could help."

"Maybe I came here because I thought you could." The words came in a rush, tumbling over another hiccup. "I need to understand what happened."

He shook his head slowly, his face moving in and out of shadow. "I can't even stop your hiccups, much less ease your loss. I know the sorrow, Livvie. It'll get easier."

"But I keep going back, Robbie—way, way back to Norm, your aunt—trying to make sense of what happened, the choices made. Why you let me down when I needed you on my side!"

"You have to let it go." He reached for my hand, grasping my fingertips, squeezing gently. "Some things don't need to be dredged up. Keep Jake in your thoughts and let the rest go. Don't dwell on the past."

"You're telling me to move on, too?"

"With Jake, you did move on. Take that with you, Livvie. It's for the best." He released my hand and stood up. "Get some sleep now."

I lay back, my head sinking into the pillow, listening to the rustle of sheets as Robbie settled into bed. Still rocked by the sensation of his lips touching mine, I envisioned him again in the glimmering moonlight curled toward me on the straw mat, our toes in the sand.

As always, he was urging me to live in the present, but I couldn't with such an important part of my past still a mystery. The years with Jake had been a respite I hadn't wanted to spoil with ugly secrets. Without him in my life, I'd become consumed with finding out the truth.

Chapter 15

MORNING CAME EARLY. A loud cranking sound, followed by a thunderous roar and the smell of diesel, rousted me from deep sleep. A resounding *thunk* shook the room as the dumpster outside my window was trucked away.

Robert was gone, his bed made. The lingering smell of soap and dampness meant he'd showered and dressed not long ago. I glanced at the floor. The bottle and wine glasses were gone, but a faint whiff of last night's pizza hung in the air. I heard the click of the room card in the slot and pulled myself up in bed.

Robert shouldered the door open, two coffee containers balanced atop one another in one hand, a muffin on a paper plate in the other. "Hey, there, sunshine. I got the last of anything edible out there. The workmen decimated the rest. How're you doing?"

"Great. Your timing's perfect."

"I figure we better get a move on. The place is swarming with a crew laying flagstone around the pool." He grimaced, concentrating on the balanced cups as he made his way across the room.

I reached for the top container. "Thanks, got it." I took a sip, then handed the cup to Robert while I broke the bran muffin into quarters on a napkin. He sat down beside me and we both picked at the muffin, drinking coffee, sharing breakfast in bed. He licked his fingers, watching me dab up the remaining crumbs.

"We'll stop on the road for something later. Maybe get you some grits and gravy biscuits."

"You must've read my mind." I laughed. "Hey, I know where I'd like to go. How about a day in Weymouth?"

He blew out his cheeks and gave me a look. "Told you, it's not a good idea."

"I'd just like to see what the town looks like, that's all."

"That's all?" He stood up, drained his cup and reached for mine. "See you outside. My bag is by the front desk, ready to go."

I touched his hand. "Hey, thanks for last night. It made a difference."

He looked at me for a moment, then raised my hand to his lips, kissing my fingertips. "Hope so." He slid my empty cup inside his, and left.

I watched the door click shut, not moving. We'd crossed a threshold with two brief kisses in a span of hours. He'd embraced me, comforted me and dried my tears, but was he willing to share what I wanted most? Just the truth, that's all.

I threw off the coverlet and stood up, shaking crumbs off my teddy. If there was a chance of visiting Weymouth and the house on Orchard Street, I didn't want to leave Robert with too much time to come up with a counterplan. I quickly showered and dressed, zipped up my wheelie and hurried to the front desk. Robert was hovering near the entrance, his satchel at his feet, waiting for me with two green apples in one hand, fresh containers of coffee balanced in the other. I took the top cup.

"I already checked us out." He stuffed the apples in his jacket pocket and picked up his satchel. "We're getting the bum's rush because a tractor-trailer can't pull into the parking lot until we're out."

We crossed the noisy courtyard, past a driver scowling at us from a truck idling where the dumpster had been. I slid my wheelie and Robbie's satchel into the back of the car and climbed in. "Hang on, I'm going to try to burn rubber peeling out."

Before Robert had parked his coffee in the drinks holder and hitched his seat belt, I'd crossed the service road and turned south on the interstate, back toward Weymouth. He didn't object.

He slid his seat back, crossed his long legs and looked out the window. "I hope you don't mind me bringing up Jake again. I awoke this morning thinking about him. He helped me through a shaky time when I got assigned to cover Ulster in the early seventies. I wasn't sure I could handle Northern Ireland after Angola. But he had my back, saw me through it."

I nodded. "That was Jake."

"It's a good while since our paths crossed, but his death still came as a shock. A reckoning, I guess. I have a lot more miles on me, you know. Hardly seems fair."

"Fair?" I shook my head. "Since when does this world run on fairness? If you're looking for a reason, he was a guy who embraced life, ate what he liked and had the cholesterol count to show for it. Jake was not a moderate man. He had big appetites. He indulged. Martinis. Beefsteak. He worked around the clock when he had to, then played hard. It's the price he paid for being who he was. You know how he lived, always in the thick of everything. Why am I telling you?"

"I guess I'm just someone else asking why him, not me?"

Indeed, why Jake and not Robert? The question hung between us. Who could say?

But I knew what Robert was thinking. Aside from gobbling life with that great appetite of his, Jake was essentially a deskman, an editor who did his share of traveling but not on the scale Robert did. Jake didn't court danger in war zones, jeopardizing his life in the world's trouble spots as Robert always had. While covering the war in Angola, first from the government side, then going back to the same territory at the behest of a rebel leader to tell their side of the conflict, Robert came as close as he ever had to losing his life. He had scars on his arms and legs to show for it. But his life hadn't ended abruptly, in sudden surprise. He was still alive. Jake was dead.

"Anyway, the obit mentioned your place in Connecticut. You're keeping the house up there?"

"No reason to sell. Jake loved Willow Creek. It's where he wanted to retire. He probably had it in mind to die there, too, just not so soon."

"You were smart to keep it while you were living overseas."

"I guess. The rental money made a lot of things possible. It's how we could afford nice digs in London all those years when he was running the bureau there. But then, you never sold the Orchard Street house, either. You could have done that years ago."

"It's where I live."

"You told me you couldn't wait to get back to New York."

"It's a little late now."

"I know." I stole a glance at him. Our eyes caught. "I never figured you'd retire in Weymouth. How'd you let that happen?"

He shrugged, looking ahead. Robert had grown up in the house his aunt bequeathed him. I'm sure he never intended to end his days there, but that now seemed almost inevitable. There was no reason for him to pull up stakes and move on at this stage of life, which would have pleased Aunt Dorah.

Clearly not wanting to talk about his own living arrangements, Robert shifted the conversation back to me. "Living in a small New York apartment, don't you miss the house?"

"Not really. I can always move back someday. A young professor and his wife are leasing it now. They have a kid. The university is spitting distance. Jake taught there whenever we were back for a while."

"I know. He invited me to come up as a guest lecturer a few years ago to share some old war stories. Sorry it didn't work out."

"I remember. You would have stayed with us, of course." I glanced at Robert. "Anyone who came up to lecture was always welcome to the guest room over the garage."

He nodded and began polishing one of the green apples on his shirtsleeve. Jake told me about the invitation after he'd already extended it, which wasn't unusual when he booked guest speakers. It wouldn't surprise me to know Robert declined the engagement because it would have meant being our houseguest. When he'd cited a scheduling conflict, I was relieved. Our relationship was over long before I met Jake, but that didn't mean I was eager to sit at the breakfast table with my husband and a former lover, a scenario packed with potential awkwardness considering my history with Robert. I'm not sure I could have handled it without blurting out our sorry backstory over bagels.

"Want some?" Robbie held up the well-polished apple, turning it in his fingers. I shook my head. He took a bite, the snap spraying a mist. "Hmmmm, good." He smacked his lips.

"Okay, changed my mind!" I laughed and turned my head just enough to bite into the apple. Sour pulp puckered my mouth, a splash of juice trickling down my chin.

"Anyway, you were always more of a New York gal."

"Nothing like a convert."

He laughed. I shrugged. His comment, while true, fell short. I'm also a London, Paris and Tokyo gal, all the cities where Jake was stationed. A part of me resides everywhere I've ever traveled and written about for various newspapers and magazines. I'm a "places" gal, but New York works for me, the place where I have to keep coming back.

I was single and had already left the magazine when I moved into my rent-stabilized garden apartment in the West Village, which eventually became a co-op, the first property I ever owned. It's also the home that's been part of my life the longest; a bolt hole, refuge and repository for keepsakes, college texts, my old yellow polo coat and letters I hope to burn while there's still time, but can't yet bear to destroy. Those are the items that never made it to the Connecticut house, which we leased out shortly after we bought it and moved to London, later Tokyo, then Paris.

Jake spent little time in what he called my "gold-plated pied-á-terre," a reference to my willingness to pay for maintenance and repairs while staying there infrequently. I didn't want to sublet it, but would occasionally invite friends to make use of the place when they passed through New York. I would never have offered it to Robert, who was no longer living in New York by the time I moved in. I wouldn't have wanted him to have a key, nor the privilege of hanging anything in my closet.

"It's too bad you gave up your studio."

"I don't think I meant to. It just happened. Norm didn't have a place, so I let him stay. Eventually, you know—" Robert dropped the apple core into his empty coffee container.

"I remember."

"I didn't know when I'd ever be back in New York—"

"I remember."

"By the time . . . anyway, Norm took it over."

"Yes, I remember." I gripped the steering wheel, hoping he'd tell me more than what I already knew.

He bent the cup in his hand, twisting it. "You know, we won't be able to stay in my house tonight. I get the feeling that's what you have in mind. But we can't. The power is off."

"So you said. But there'll be enough daylight to see it."

"I'm not sure it's safe. There was a lot of damage."

"When do you think you'll be able to move back in?"

"Not sure. Anyway, we'll just drive by it on our way through town. You can see the outside."

"Sure. Maybe stop nearby and have some lunch. Or just sit on the veranda."

"Or head straight on up to Lakeville. There's a good barbecue place you'd like."

"Hey, no need to make plans. Let's just see what we feel like doing."

Those were words usually spoken by Robert. I sensed his discomfort hearing them spoken by me. He shifted and recrossed his legs. If plans were *not* to be made, he would be the one to not make them. I let him stew, knowing he was regretting his momentary lapse in allowing me to turn south on the interstate.

After a moment, he switched on the radio and raised the volume, a not-so-subtle signal he was tuning out for a while. I glanced at the dashboard. The gas tank was still half full. There'd be no need to pull off, giving Robbie an opening to change our course. It would be a rare instance if I got the upper hand.

If it made Robert uncomfortable talking about his West Village studio, I understood. I'm sure he hadn't meant to give it up, but then he seldom thought ahead or considered consequences. Unlike Jake, he acted on impulse, not plans. He just wanted to get out of New York and put distance between himself and new management at the magazine—and, as a consequence, me.

Change had been in the wind for a while, beginning with the departure of our managing editor after he suffered a massive heart attack. Horace Greenwalt, an import poached from a rival, less-regarded newsmagazine, was not widely appreciated by a staff expecting a successor to emerge from its ranks, certainly not from a publication they considered inferior. He was not Ivy League, didn't drink and, as Brígh observed, "doesn't come from distinguished lineage."

The drinks trolley was the first institution to go. The first innovation to arrive was a female writer stashed in the health and education department.

Brígh lamented the first instance—"Without the drinks trolley, is there any reason to observe Friday anymore?"

She exalted in the second—"In my lifetime, a woman writer on the twenty-seventh floor—imagine!"

We watched the new hire step off the elevator, trim in a skirt above her knees, her hair in a bouncy flip. She carried a briefcase and a potted philodendron, its vines trailing over her elbow, as she walked to her newly designated office with a window.

Brígh, her arms and legs spindled tightly around each other as though trying to contain her exuberance, murmured, "Bringing with her a bit of green that shall have daylight! Wonder of wonders, they've given a woman a window!"

"She doesn't look all that young," I said, eyeing her sensible shoes and battered shoulder bag.

"Nor old," Brígh said, reaching for her white coffee mug. "The world has skittered past me, but damn, I'll still have a hand in it!"

"What?"

"We're taking her to lunch. Today. Book a table."

Mona Larsen was pleased to join us at O'Reilly's, but a bit startled to see Brígh knock back three martinis, two of them before her chicken curry arrived. I struck a neutral balance, ordering a single Campari and soda, the aperitif I'd adopted since covering the Vatican story with Robert. Mona had iced tea, but her tongue was loose enough to satisfy the questions on everybody's minds. Aged thirty-two and newly married to an NYU professor. Childless (but how long would that last?). Connected (Horace's cousin by marriage). Courtesy of a mole in personnel, Brígh learned Mona would be earning a third of the salary paid any male writer.

"Still, she's established a beachhead, may her philodendron thrive!" Brígh crowed.

It was evident Horace Greenwalt had a clean sweep in mind, wielding his broom to wipe out excess and profligacy in every department. "Let's cut the fat, folks. We need to get more bang for the buck!"

He was organized, expedient and cheap, spending the company's money as though it came from his own wallet. There would be no more Norm-size gestures tacked on to expense accounts. No more four-star restaurant meals served in the conference room, nor limo rides home for the staff. Everyone kept their heads down, but a few still rolled as Horace replaced editorial staff members with cronies from his own circle.

"Why let excellence flourish when mediocrity is within reach," Brígh commented after the first rash of pink slips eliminated one of the ranking senior editors. But I noticed she kept her feet off her desk and cut her normal two-hour lunches back to one.

My boss, the lovable suspender-snapping, pipe-smoking picture editor, who had graduated from Yale with the recently departed managing editor, was also let go. Moses Ward was his fired-up replacement, a short, wiry guy with a nasal voice and an all-consuming desire to make the department his own. He was curt, his comments withering and hurtful. I loathed him.

Robert chafed under his overweening manner. His story ideas were met with scorn, and he was subjected to pointed barbs about the costly cover projects that were Robert's trademark. His photographs were critiqued in front of staff. His expense accounts were scrutinized. Robert reacted by spending even less time in the office, avoiding the editorial department by going directly to the photo lab on the floor above to drop off film and pick up supplies.

The upshot was that Moses Ward became aware of a rarely used office space that could be put to better use. Robbie lost his hole-in-the-wall office and all but disappeared from the twenty-seventh floor. Newly hired photographers, several formerly with various wire services, were assigned major stories that would otherwise have been covered by Robert.

The strain of dealing with Moses and the loss of camaraderie all of us in the picture department had enjoyed took its toll on our relationship. I was increasingly snappish and irritable. Robert became even more remote. When we spent an evening together, too often we fell into rehashing problems from the office. Robert was furious at losing out on plum assignments that were going to other photographers.

"Look, you're only hurting yourself by not showing up. You had an office of your own up there, for God's sake!" I flung an arm in the direction of boxes stacked in a corner of his studio that I'd been in charge of packing and clearing out. "You were crazy to give that up!"

"Excuse me, what? You're saying I've given up prime real estate by not exercising squatter's rights? You want me to fight my eviction?"

"You know what I'm saying. I go to work every day. I deal with him. Everyone adjusts because he's the boss. You just have to find a way to work with him."

"He's an idiot! He has no eye. He's worthless, an incompetent ass. He should be selling film to tourists on a boardwalk, not be charged with editing pictures for a major news magazine! What's wrong with you?"

"Oh, gosh, I don't know. Maybe it's rent that I have to pay. Bus fare, now that there are no more limos. Groceries, now that we don't get fed on the job."

"Thanks for the sarcasm—"

"It's not fun for any of us. We'll be supplying our own grease pencils next."

"Listen to you! That's what this work means to you?"

"It's my job. It's what I do to support myself so I can keep writing, keep eating. Do you know what it takes for someone like me to carve out a career in this city? I know how damn lucky I am to have a job like this. I'm grateful. Do you understand that?"

"No."

"No?"

"It's not the job, it's the work I do. That's what matters."

We looked at each other, both of us radiating incredulity. I was still wearing my suit jacket and pumps, fresh from the office, my handbag dangling on my arm. He was barefoot, wearing jeans and a shirt, his uniform in the studio. I'd arrived as he was hauling boxes containing the detritus from his former office in from the doorway where the company courier had dropped them off.

We stared at each other, disbelief shifting to stances a shade more intractable. Unfortunately it was a Friday night and we had a weekend to spend together. If we were to get along, adjustments had to be made. He smiled first.

"Glass of wine?"

"Yes, please, since there's no longer a drinks trolley at the office!" We both laughed.

Robert padded to the kitchen. "Now that austerity has set in, I suspect the magazine goes to press a little earlier? I didn't expect to see you for at least another couple hours."

"We're damn near nine-to-five these days, but O'Reilly's appreciates the business when we close early."

I took the glass of Sancerre that Robert handed me, pleased to see he was pouring himself one, too. "Sorry, I jumped on you, but it's not the same up there without you."

"The culture's changed. It's not for me."

"But he's just one guy. Maybe together we can turn him around." I peeled off my jacket, kicked off my shoes, striving to reduce stridency from my voice. "We had a good thing going. We can't let him spoil it."

"You're nurturing a lost cause. Won't work."

"I'm trying to put things right."

He tapped his glass to mine. "As it is. Let it be."

He took a sip of wine and put his glass down. I knew he'd be having no more to drink. He kissed me and we settled down on the couch. There was no Coltrane playing on the hi-fi. The candles weren't lit. I'd arrived far sooner than expected.

I nestled closer, making sounds of contentment, but replaying the words we'd just spoken. *Nurturing? Putting things right?* Were we talking about the office or ourselves? *Won't work?* A shiver of uncertainty rippled up my spine.

It was becoming far less easy to separate work from our relationship. I was no longer the outsider he'd found refreshing. I was enmeshed in the day-to-day operation of the department. I stood up to Robert when it was my job to do so. We no longer had the freewheeling budgets he took for granted, and that had become my job to rein in. Deadlines had to be met. Film could no longer be couriered on chartered flights. Attempts I made to ease tensions between Moses Ward and Robert only infuriated him and further distanced us.

I took a sip of wine and glanced at Robbie, whose gaze shifted from the middle distance and focused on me, his eyes lighting with warmth. He tilted my face toward his and kissed the tip of my nose, then my lips.

"You know, I was thinking that it might do us good to get away for a while. How would you like to go camping on St. John?"

"The Virgin Islands? Never been there. I'd love it!"

"Good. It's been a while since I was back bumming it on those beaches. You've got vacation time to use. Pack a swimsuit. It's all you need. I'll take care of the rest."

Villefranche had given me a taste for sleeping on the beach. I looked forward to a week under the splendor of the night sky with Robert all to myself.

Chapter 16

ROBERT TUNED THE RADIO, flashing through bursts of news, noisy commentary and raucous music before settling on a local station playing twangy bluegrass. He settled back in his seat, looking out the window.

"I read your new book, did I tell you?"

"Really? I didn't want to ask."

"So?" he teased. "Figured I had to with you coming to visit."

"Shucks, I was going to leave you a copy as a house gift."

"Signed, I hope. I can always use an extra. Add it to the collection."

"You've read my other books?"

"A couple." He turned up the volume and drummed his fingers on his knee in time to banjo music, humming along with the lyrics. "Always a tug at the soul," he murmured.

"Thanks. I was on tenterhooks wondering."

"Talkin' about the music. That high lonesome sound always pulls me in."

I bit my lip and glanced at him. He gave me a gotcha look and laughed, hamboning his chest, thighs and the dashboard in time to the music.

"And your book, too, girl. Pulled me in. Tugged at the soul."

"Damn it, Robert! Did you honestly like it?"

"Yup."

"That's all you have to say?"

"Good story and I can hear you talking on every page. You expecting a book report?" He hummed, energetically slapping the dashboard and his knees.

"You're not fixing to yodel, are you?"

He let loose a bloodcurdling yodel. I laughed and joined in, making my own joyful noise.

"There, now, nothin' like bluegrass to build up an appetite for some good barbecue. How 'bout it, girl? Finger lickin' good! Why not bypass Weymouth and head on up to Lakeville?"

"You sure have the twang down." I tightened my grip on the steering wheel, sending a clear signal I wasn't going to change course.

"The junction's coming up. Take the turnoff and go straight cross-country. Food is sure good."

"Tell me more about what you thought of my book."

"You write funny, tell a good story. Your characters come off real, so I reckon you've gotta be drawing on people you know. Maybe Jake?"

"Of course. Now I'm glad I did and that he got to read it."

"Figured that."

"He didn't mind. Jake understood it's the downside of knowing a writer."

"Just so you don't write about me."

"Really? You think I haven't already? Or wouldn't?"

He darted a look at me. "Anything I should know about?"

"Why? Is there anything you wouldn't want me to write about?"

"Depends on how you go about getting your licks in. We kinda take different views on some things."

"Maybe so, but I write what I see in the same way you take photographs that capture what you see."

"Except a camera tells the truth. It doesn't make up a story."

"Of course it does! The lens creates its own story the moment you click the shutter. It's how you frame it. Remember your shot of Richard Nixon in a flop sweat during the debate with Jack Kennedy?"

"Unaltered. It's just what happened. Jack had been in the studio since four o'clock, preparing. Nixon raced in just before airtime. Didn't shave, didn't want makeup—"

"So you caught him mopping his face, his eyes shifting to your lens, looking malevolent. Your picture said he wasn't to be trusted—not that he needed a shave. Were you getting your licks in?"

"Maybe." Robert smiled. "And he didn't let it happen the next time."

"I remember." When Robert photographed Nixon years later, he greeted him waving an electric razor and said, "You don't get me twice."

"So, I should be worried?"

"Beware. I'm going to start another book, so you never know—"

"Two can play that game." Robbie picked up his camera and snapped a picture of me, then another. "Beware yourself, girl!"

I laughed and raised my hand to block his shot. "C'mon,

even if I did write about you, you might not realize it. People don't, you know. If they do think I've written about them, they usually get it wrong."

"Well, that sure puts my mind at ease," he mumbled.

"Does it?" I relaxed my grip on the wheel. "You know, I was thinking about St. John earlier. I never went back there after our trip together."

"Neither did I. I'm sure it's built up and choked with tourists by now." Robert shifted in his seat and pulled the sun visor down. "I can't imagine you'd want to write about that. Don't even know what made you think of it."

"You mentioned Norm Jurgens and giving up your studio. It all came back."

He leaned against the window, turning his head. "I'm listening. Just have to close my eyes a bit."

"Go ahead, take a nap."

"Anyway, don't remember much about that trip."

Liar! "I do. It was an idyllic place. Sand and crystal blue water. No one but us and a whole lot of jungle."

"Forest, actually. Deep underbrush."

"We spent most of the time in the water, face down. Snorkeling. "

"You made friends with a big, old grouper, I recall. Followed you around in the water like a hound dog."

"Huge thing! Scared the hell out of me when I first saw it. I thought it was going to eat me alive."

"He just wanted to be your buddy, but you damned near sprinted on water getting back to the beach. Never saw anyone explode out of the water like that."

"With you laughing, of course, because I lost my bikini top. See? You do remember."

"It was damn funny." He pushed the seat back, reclining further. "Don't remember much else."

"Really?"

There was no response. I thought about the matchbook in my shoulder bag, and the diamond tucked behind match heads. If he recalled nothing about St. John, would seeing the ring jolt his memory? If I wanted him captive when I showed it to him, now would be the time. But his eyes were closed, his head turned away. I reached over and turned down the radio, letting him rest.

If he didn't remember the trip, I recalled our six days camping on the island in vivid detail. I'd taken him at his word, letting him plan everything because he was so familiar with the island. He'd made his first visit to St. John when he was still in college and had returned several times on solitary camping trips, generally to the same strip of remote beach. He claimed I would be the first person he'd invited to stay there with him. It would also be one of the few trips we'd taken together that didn't involve a photo shoot. I tried not to get too carried away with a fantasy that I hoped would include a marriage proposal.

"It'll be primitive," he warned. "No discos. No trips into town. Don't expect a mint on your pillow."

I packed a duffel bag with swimsuits and the basic gear I'd need to camp on a tropical beach, not forgetting insect repellant, sunscreen and moisturizer. When I arrived at his apartment the night before our departure, I found him sorting through a mound of camping gear, including a tent, an inflatable kayak, sleeping bags, packets of dehydrated food and cooking utensils. It was my first inkling of just how primitive our encampment would be. I looked over his checklist and made a quick trip to the deli on the corner. He laughed when he saw me return with chocolate bars, instant coffee and rolls of toilet tissue.

"Don't worry, we'll pick up anything else we need once we're down there."

As promised, after our early morning flight to St. Thomas, we went straight to a local market to pick up supplies. Not trusting the dehydrated packets, I filled a string bag with cans of tinned tuna and salmon, peanut butter, crackers, chocolate, marshmallows, papaya and bananas before we caught the Red Hook ferry.

Robert had arranged for Osgood, a driver he'd met on his first trip to St. John, to meet us when we pulled into St. Cruz. While we were still on board the ferry, Robert pointed out a tall, courtly-looking hipster standing on the dock wearing a too-small seersucker jacket, tattered gray flannel dress pants cut off at mid-calf and a porkpie hat.

"That's Osgood, and damn if he isn't wearing the same old jacket!"

Once we'd docked, he and Robert greeted each other like long-lost brothers, a quick handshake fusing into a rocking, backslapping embrace.

"Too, too long, man," Osgood said in the island's lilting cadence. He cast a sidelong glance my way, his smoky gray eyes with dark-blue rings appraising me. "This time you don't come alone, my friend."

Robert introduced us, and Osgood reached for my weighty bag. "A feast!" He laughed, surveying the cans bulging against the woven string, "For a cat!"

"It's that or Robert's C rations. Thank God, I remembered to pack a can opener."

He laughed and slapped his thighs. "She's a good, good one, man! You keep!"

I looked to Robbie, grateful for Osgood's endorsement, and hoped I'd make the grade. The closest I'd come to camping was a cookout with my Brownie troop. At least I'd stashed away all the ingredients for s'mores and a bottle of rum bought in the duty-free shop for late nights around the campfire. Dinners of dehydrated pork chops and a star-filled sky would carry us just so far alone on a beach for a week.

We loaded the open Jeep and I sat in the back, my arms gripping duffel bags that threatened to bounce out of the hold with each jarring pothole. On the far side of the island, we drove down a dusty rutted road to a stunning expanse of white sandy beach in a pristine, uninhabited cove. I pitched in unloading the Jeep and Osgood stayed on to help Robbie set up our encampment.

By late afternoon, our food cache was secured, a latrine had been dug near the brush and the tent was pitched above the high-water mark. I plopped on the beach, digging my toes into cool wetness under the hot sand, wondering what I'd gotten myself into. Aside from Robert's transistor radio with its intermittent signal, we were essentially cut off from civilization. Only Osgood and the coast guard knew where we were. While this was the paradise pictured in travel brochures, I would not have wanted to be stranded there with anyone but Robert.

We'd signed in with the coast guard patrol before leaving the harbor, which was required if we were to camp in that remote location. We'd agreed to stand on the beach twenty feet apart and wave our arms at eleven o'clock every morning as a coast guard cutter passed by the cove. After being logged in for the day, if we were swept to sea or catastrophic illness befell us only minutes later, no one was likely to come to our aid until the following morning. Once he left, we wouldn't see Osgood again until ten o'clock Sunday morning when he'd drive us back to catch the ferry.

With everything unloaded and set up, Osgood and Robert swam far out into deep waters, their bobbing heads barely visible. I paddled out a safe distance and floated, buoyant in the clear, azure water, drifting with the sun warm on my face and my hair streaming like seaweed around my head. I swam back to shore and sat on the beach, my elbows planted in the white sand, and looked around at the unbroken horizon. Listening to the surf lapping along the shoreline, I was blissfully at peace, ready for adventure.

As soon as Osgood waved goodbye and drove away, Robert went off to gather kindling and firewood. I was instructed to unpack our provisions and assemble a cook stove kit.

"Very basic," he'd said, before heading up the beach in search of driftwood. "The pieces all fit together. Simple, just needs unfolding. We'll have stew for dinner."

The cook stove, a relic of many previous camping trips, was an unwieldy, soot-stained contraption. The pot, sticky to the touch, looked none too appetizing. I scoured it with sand and rinsed it in the ocean, giving the plates and utensils the same treatment. By then, Robert had returned with an armload of firewood. He worked his magic with the dehydrated food packets, which largely meant adding water and stirring.

Sitting in the dusky gold of early evening, metal plates heaped with stew balanced on our knees, we ate watching the sun dip to the horizon. As long as one didn't think too much about the ingredients, the stew was tasty and filling, but I was glad I had tuna fish on hand as backup to pots of reconstituted mush.

As night fell and a full moon rose in a star-filled sky, Robert broke out the rum and we roasted marshmallows to press between squares of melting chocolate and graham crackers. Snug in our tent on the beach, we made love to the sounds of breaking surf, conscious of the enormity of the world outside and our own isolation from civilization. I was already thinking six days together in this glorious setting would not be long enough.

We awoke just after dawn and sat huddled on the beach, wrapped in our sleeping bags, watching the sun splay glitter on the rippling ocean. Even without making plans, our days took on a pattern. After waving to the coast guard patrol boat, we'd hike deep into the forest. Often we'd picnic at an abandoned sugar plantation, sitting on a rough wall of stone covered in lichen, eating papaya and sharing a can of tuna fish.

Afterward we'd explore one of the trails that led into the hills, spotting through the trees the crumbling remains of an old estate house or the ruins of a sugarcane mill. Wildlife chittered in the brush and birds twittered high in the branches overhead as we made our way through thick forest. In the afternoons, we'd swim and snorkel, then nap on mats under a shady overhang of rock and fern.

Late in the afternoon of our second day, Robert led the way up a steep path off the beach to the ruins of a sugar mill. We followed a winding path until we came to a stone cistern thick with vines on a mossy ledge looking out over the ocean. Robert plunged a length of hose into the cool rainwater to hook up a makeshift shower. We stripped off our bathing suits and stood on the ledge in the hot sun spraying each other with cascades of icy water. That night we feasted on sea perch he'd caught.

By midweek we were lean from swimming and already deeply sun bronzed. I hadn't used a comb in days and my dark hair was a tangled mass of sun-bleached curl. We snorkeled for hours on end, built sandcastles and splashed in the surf half-naked like castaways on our own desert island while freighters and fishing boats passed by far out in the ocean. While Robert caught fish for our supper, I strolled our strip of beach from one end to the other, filling my string bag with heart-shaped stones.

In the late afternoon on our final day, still dripping from the ocean, our feet sandy from the beach, Robert and I mounted the mossy stone steps to the cistern. The climb up the slippery path had become a ritual, every lichen-covered rock and spray of fern familiar. With a pang I realized this would be our last alfresco shower, our last night together on St. John. I looked back down at our small encampment on the beach, the tent and campfire pit, and felt a pang. I didn't want to leave.

More than that, I wanted to be with Robert. Forever. A calm had settled over me in the time we'd been together on the island. I'd savored our long, languid days, the unhurried treks deep into the silent brush, exploring ruins and photographing wildlife. Cut off from the rest of the world, I'd absorbed his rhythms as my own, living the moment without agenda, as he did. I couldn't imagine life without Robert.

I recalled the night we'd made love on a narrow cot in a tent in Africa, and I'd whispered, "I love you." More than a year had passed, but the painful memory remained fresh. We still made love, laughed and spent much of our time together, but our relationship remained "as it was" and no more. The words "I love you" had never slipped out again, nor had we talked about a future together. Had Robert had a change of heart? Was that why he'd brought me to St. John?

Night after night, lying in his arms in the stillness of the tent, I'd look up at the wedges of sky visible through the flaps, my thoughts drifting to the sleeping loft in the studio and the skylight that bathed our bed in pale moon glow. When we got back to the West Village, I pictured myself emptying the contents of the shoebox into a drawer and unpacking my suitcase to stay. I'd have a closet of my own and a shelf in the medicine cabinet. I'd proved I could adapt myself to his lifestyle, living in the moment, content with everything as it was.

I saw the week on St. John as a test run, the glide path to permanence that I was confident Robert had in mind. He wasn't a train leaving the station that I had to scramble to catch. We'd found each other. After this trip, I was sure we'd be together forever. I counted on it.

A balmy breeze ruffled my damp hair and dried salt water in tight, sticky patches on my shoulders as I climbed the steep trail to our last outdoor shower on the island. Ahead of me, Robert's long bronzed legs moved up the pathway, my footfall landing on each step he vacated, our strides matching. Slung over his arm was a canvas bag stuffed with our jeans, shoes and tee shirts. Nearing the top, he swung himself up onto the landing, grabbed a weathered post and reached back to give me a hand. We locked fingers and I hoisted myself onto the parapet in one easy movement.

Shirtless, his tanned skin smelling of sun and salt, he

pulled me into an embrace. I kissed him, licking his lower lip, tasting the salty sweetness. I slipped my fingers inside the loose band of the cutoffs that hung low on his hips. He kneeled in the mossy earth, pulling me close.

The sun was a rich golden glow by the time I sat up, bracing myself on an elbow. I stroked his stubbly beard, hoping he wouldn't shave it off when we got back to New York. I shook my hair back on my shoulders.

"Any chance we can tell Osgood we're staying another week?"

He smiled lazily, his eyes still closed. "I'd do it every time I was here if there was a way. I always hope he won't show up."

"But he always does?"

"Like clockwork." Robert opened his eyes and sat up. "But we're here now. That's all that matters."

He kissed me lightly on the lips and stood up. I watched him uncoil the length of hose and rig the cistern as he had every evening, unselfconsciously naked, his movements spare and unhurried. I lay back, looking at him framed against streams of light breaking through a bank of low clouds, willing myself to imprint that image of him forever in my brain.

"Hey, there. Don't get too comfortable. We've got some bad weather coming in."

He was right. The gold-and-crimson sky was a fiery copper behind a roiling bank of dark clouds. I jumped to my feet and grabbed the bar soap from the satchel. Robert held the hose high and we stood close as he released his thumb on a cascade of sun-warmed water that quickly grew frigid.

We showered, soaping each other down, the icy water washing away sticky sweat. Afterward, barefoot and naked, we stood shivering on the parapet, arms spread wide, air-

drying in the last of the warm sunlight. The black clouds re-
ceded farther out on the water. We dressed in jeans and tee
shirts. Lulled by the sounds of slapping water and a faint
blowing mist, we sat for a long time, saying nothing.

Then Robert began speaking. I don't recall what he said
at first. His voice was soft, the tone casual, but the words
jarred. Alarm swelled in my throat as I tried to make sense of
them. I turned to see him scanning the horizon as though
tracking the flight of a bird.

"No, wait. What are you saying?" My chest was tight, my
heart hammering. "You said you're leaving the New York bureau? Is that what you said?"

"Hey, easy. No need to get upset."

"But when are you going?"

"Don't know yet. Maybe a week or two."

"No! Why? When did you decide?"

"You're getting upset."

"Damn right I'm getting upset!"

"I don't know why. I figured you could see it coming. It's
all we've talked about for weeks." He glanced at me, then
looked away. "I told you, the guy grates on me. Hates my guts.
I'm not getting assignments I want. What's the point of hanging around?"

"So you've told Moses Ward this? He knows you're leaving?"

"As of last Friday."

"You mean, this happened right before we left? And you
didn't say anything to me?"

"I didn't want to spoil the trip. I figured you might take it
like this."

"Of course I would. I can't believe you didn't tell me until now." I looked across the pockmarked ocean, shocked he'd kept this to himself. "Then it's definite? You're really leaving?"

"Not the magazine. I'll just be working out of the Rome bureau."

"But what's the point? He'll still be your boss."

"At a distance."

"Why didn't you talk it over with me? We should've discussed this."

He looked at me, his eyes as opaque as the graying sky. "Why?"

"Because I can't just up and leave like you can!"

"There's no need for you to go. You can handle the man, I can't."

"It's not about him, damn it!"

"You're upset again."

"What do you expect? I don't want you to leave—I mean, not without me! If we'd planned this together, maybe I could've arranged a transfer to the Rome bureau. It's not as easy for me. For you, it's different—"

"Yes—"

"But I love Rome. I'd love to be there with you. Maybe—"

"But I won't be there. I'll be working out of their bureau, but I'll be in Africa."

"Where? What's the story? No one's said anything to me about doing another piece on Africa. What's it about?"

"I can't say yet."

"It's my job to know! Is it a big color project? Why haven't I been told?" A new horror dawned. "Wait, is there more to this that I don't know? Am I losing my job? Is everyone in the picture department fired and no one's told me yet? Tell me, for God's sake! What's going on?"

"No, nothing like that. It's just that I'm not permitted to say anything about the story yet. It's being set up on the QT. I need State Department approval. I think Moses gave his blessing just to see my back."

"Seriously, all this happened before we left on Friday and you kept it a secret?"

"Nothing was going to change while we were here. I've got another week, maybe—"

"You said two weeks. Damn it, Robert! You should've told me!"

"You'd get upset."

"Stop saying that! I *am* upset."

"See what I mean? You'd brood the whole time. The trip would be spoiled."

"It *is* spoiled!"

I hit him. Hard. It was a strike with the back of my hand that caught him on the shoulder. I didn't feel it coming, nor did he. Registering his stunned look, I gasped, horrified, my hand still throbbing from the blow.

"Robert, I'm so sorry! Really sorry!" I reached for his hand. It was gripping the stone ledge, the knuckles white. I gently folded my fingers over his. "I shouldn't have lashed out. Forgive me."

"It's okay. I shouldn't have brought it up."

The tautness in his hand did not ease with my touch. I pulled away and hugged my knees, wishing I could reel back to the laughter we'd shared minutes earlier, both of us naked, rushing to pull clothing on our damp, chilled bodies. I shivered, looking down the crumbling sea wall at the water battering the rocky shore, my heart racing.

Anger swelled with the temptation to hit him again. Hit

harder! *Shouldn't have brought it up?* Why had I been the one to apologize?

Fat drops splat the stone ledge. The storm clouds had returned. We scrambled to our feet, and I hurried down the path, Robert in my wake, as icy rain slashed across the parapet. By the time we reached the beach, sheets of rain ripped across the sand. We took cover under an overhang of dense brush, cocooned inside a dry, silent arc of shadow.

I rubbed my wet, chilled arms. Robert moved closer, standing behind me, wrapping his arms around my shoulders, pulling me toward him. Why had I lashed out? I shouldn't have hit him, but how could he not know how I'd feel?

Wind swirled sand around the tent, the thundering rain almost flattening it. Robert nudged my cheek, his breath warm in my ear.

"It'll be all right, you know."

"Will it? Because I don't see how it could get worse."

He squeezed my shoulders. "It's battened down, everything rolled up inside."

He'd meant the tent, not us. It struck me as funny, yet tears sprang to my eyes.

"We'll be spending a soggy last night here. Sorry, Livvie, but I didn't see this coming."

"Me, neither," I muttered, my head pressed to his shoulder. "Anyway, if you're leaving, I'll look after your studio while you're gone. I can forward your mail. I could even move in and pay rent. I'd like living downtown."

"Thanks, but I told Norm he could stay."

"Norm Jurgens?"

"His wife gave him the boot. He's out of work."

"You gave your studio to Norm?" If there was a light at

the end of this tunnel, I couldn't see it. "I wish you'd said something to me first."

"Sorry, it didn't cross my mind that you'd want to stay there. It's a studio—"

"I know what it is. I love it. I hate where I am uptown. Is there any way you can change things?"

"Sorry, but he called just before we left and asked to sleep on the couch—"

"Wait, he'll be there when we get back?"

"I expect so."

Another wave of bad news sank in. Norm—a man I despised!—was going to take over Robert's place while I made do with a bed by a window looking out on an airshaft.

I gazed at the flattened tent, imagining Norm going through my shoebox under the bed.

Chapter 17

ROBERT WAS STILL NAPPING, or pretending to be, as I crested a hill and looked out on the snug little town of Weymouth. His picturesque hometown, with its church steeples and neat two-story brick and timber buildings, was nestled in a valley with a river running through it fed by streams from a ridge of pine-covered mountains.

As Robert might say, Weymouth was "as it was," a thriving small town, its prosperity having much to do with its namesake, Woodrow L. Weymouth, a pharmacist known to everyone as Woody. He'd established Weymouth's drugstore on Main Street in the early years of the last century and began dabbling in his own line of herbal-based salves and ointments. He eventually built up a mail-order business and branched out into herbal skin-care products, then food supplements. Many mergers and acquisitions later, the Weymouth brand of products had lost its original name and become the cornerstone of a vast international health-food conglomerate.

However, Woody's modest drugstore still remained on Main Street dispensing medications and the company's various herbal products. According to Aunt Dorah, who'd provided me with a complete rundown on Weymouth before I ever

set foot there, many of its residents owed their family for-
tunes to early investments in Woody's enterprise, including
Lloyd Ellerbe.

"Lloyd and Woody were good friends," Aunt Dorah told
me. "He invested with him and even set up his clinic next door
to Woody's pharmacy." Then, with a sharp note of regret,
she'd added, "It's just a shame Lloyd didn't invest more."

Diagonal parking remained in effect on Main Street.
Black wrought-iron baskets overflowing with flowering
plants hung from old street lanterns. I recognized several of
the shops, including Woody's pharmacy, but Lloyd Ellerbe's
medical clinic had been razed, a brick office building taking
its place. I pulled up at a traffic light, my signal blinking to
turn into Orchard Street, which flanked Weymouth Park,
when Robbie cleared his throat.

"You know, this isn't a good idea," he said, his eyes still
closed.

"We'll just drive by, maybe stop and have a chat on the
veranda."

"We won't be able to sit on the veranda."

"Something's wrong with it?"

"Not safe. I had to take the rocking chairs in."

"So we'll stand. Or perch on the railings. Honestly, does it
matter? I'd like to see the place again." I made the turn and
pulled into a space next to Weymouth Park. "C'mon, we can
walk along the bridle path to your house."

I unbuckled my seat belt. Robert opened his eyes but
didn't move. He was pale, his expression stony.

"You can't leave things be, can you?" His voice was barely
audible. "I thought after all this time you'd be over it."

"That I'd moved on? I did. Now I'm back." I shifted in my

seat to face him. "Did you think we'd just flirt and pick up where we left off? Like nothing else happened?"

"Of course not!" He threw me a sharp look, then turned away. "Sorry to be harsh, Livvie, but it's pretty clear you came with an agenda. You want to rake up the past and blame me. All that talk about St. John—I know where it's leading."

"I thought that's why you invited me here, so we could finally deal with what happened. You owe me that."

"I do?" He eyed me coldly. "You invited yourself. I went along with it because I was sorry about Jake. I understand. I know it's hard losing someone you love, but grief takes its own time."

"This has nothing to do with Jake. I thought you might be open to seeing me because you wanted to make amends while you still had a chance. Maybe you lost your nerve and changed your mind, but we still need to talk."

"What do you want from me? Life happens. You take it as it comes." He turned away, looking out on the park. "Neither of us handled things very well. It was a difficult time, but it all worked out for the best."

"Maybe for you, but not for me."

"Did you ever tell Jake what happened?"

"No, why would I? By the time I met him, there was no reason to mention us. But now that he's gone—" I gulped and caught my breath. "Sorry, this isn't about Jake. I came here because the past came flooding back. I need answers, Robbie."

"So you can write about it? Is that it? Damn it, don't do this!" He exhaled in a rush, his face anguished. "Drop it. You don't know what you're asking. It's not going to do you any good. Or anyone else."

"C'mon, Robbie. I need to know—"

"Reminiscing is one thing. But I'm not going to rehash." He reached for the door handle. "I have to get to the post office. The box section closes early on weekends."

"Wait, I want to show you something." I dug deep into the side pocket of my shoulder bag and pulled out the matchbook. "Mulligan's, remember?"

"Yeah, so?" But as I lifted the flap on the matchbook, his hand fell away from the door handle.

"Look familiar?"

He sank back in the seat, his eyes fixed on the diamond ring I slid from the matchbook. I turned the slim gold band in my fingers, the diamonds glittering in the sunlight.

"Where'd you get it?" His voice was barely audible.

"I found it at Norm's mixed in with travel receipts from St. John. Did you bring it with you on our trip?"

"I'm sorry, Livvie," He shook his head, his gaze still fixed on the ring. "The time wasn't right for us. I was leaving, maybe not coming back. It wouldn't have worked."

"But why not later? After what happened?"

"I couldn't be what you wanted, that's all. Leave it at that."

"Please! Tell me. If you meant the ring for me, I need to know what changed your mind. Why did you betray me when I needed your help?"

"That's your view, not mine." He fumbled for the door handle. "I have to get to the post office."

"Wait, I'll drive you over. We can talk later." I pressed the ignition, glancing at him as I turned on the blinker. His breath was ragged, his eyes clouding. "You okay?"

"Just pull into the loading zone."

I swung back onto Main Street, heading toward the old

brick post office, now twice its former size, with a parking ramp adjoining it.

"Will you be long? Maybe I should I park."

"Just pull to the curb." The car had barely come to a stop before Robert released his seat belt and opened the door. "When I get back, we'll drive you to the airport. Whatever the fare difference is, I'll cover it. No point in having you hanging around here."

"Then take this." I held out my hand, the ring in my palm. "It's not mine."

"It was my mother's. You found it. That makes it yours." He climbed out, closing the door. "Keep it."

I sat motionless. He'd spoken so softly I barely heard him, yet the words thundered in my brain. *My mother's!* I hadn't expected that. I couldn't have known or guessed. I watched him slowly mount the steps to the post office, favoring his left leg. With the ring heavy in my hand, I turned off the ignition and let his words sink in. *What had happened?*

It was the question roiling my mind as I stood under dripping branches waiting for the storm to pass that last night on St. John. *What had happened?*

The squall blew out to sea, leaving a thin, cool mist hanging in the night air. I shivered. Robert wrapped his arms around me, squeezing my shoulders. "C'mon, before it gets too dark."

He loped across the wet sand and shook the tent flap to drain off pooling rainwater. After securing loose stakes, he tied the tent flaps open. Before going inside, he glanced back at me under the canopy of dripping leaves, but said nothing.

I stayed where I was. How had I so misread signals? Norm, a master at trumping, had trumped me. But Robert had not led me on. He'd made no promises and we hadn't discussed a future together. It had all been wishful thinking on my part. If he loved me, it wasn't of a variety that led to a ring on my finger. That's what I wanted, but it was the dream Brígh had told me not to nurture. Her warning echoed in my mind: *He's single, very single. Beware, and tiptoe softly, my girl.*

I looked up at the darkening sky and felt the shadows of the forest closing in behind me. I had no choice but to move on. I walked around the sandy area under the thick overhang, picking up pieces of driftwood and twigs that were slick with surface moisture but not soaked through. I carried my haul back to the campsite. The cooking pot was lying on its side, half-filled with rainwater. I set it upright in the sand and looked around for the folded camp stove.

"Ready for cocktails?" Robert emerged from the tent, two tin cups in his hands. "Sun's well over the yardarm."

"Thanks, matey." Not feeling in the least jocular, I played along, taking one of the cups and touching it to his. "What's this? A fancy rum drink without an umbrella?"

"Get yourself in here, lass. I've got a smorgasbord set up. Take a look."

I peered inside the tent, startled to see an elaborate display of food artfully laid out on a driftwood plank decorated with bits of lichen and mossy twigs. He'd assembled a feast of all our leftovers, including the last of the dry salami, hardtack and tinned salmon. Even the jar of peanut butter looked decorative set on a bed of seaweed.

He'd also lit the last stub of candle and plumped up rolled sleeping bags as cushions. With the flickering candlelight and the flaps open to the sounds of rolling surf, the tent was cozy and inviting. In spite of everything, my spirits lifted.

"Well done! You have to photograph this!"

"I already did." He lifted his camera and took a picture of me raising my cup in a toast. "I don't think it's a night for sitting around the campfire."

I sat down next to Robbie and took a sip of rum. "Fine with me. I don't think I could have faced cooking up another one of those desiccated food packets."

"Me, neither." He handed me a piece of hardtack slathered with salmon. "How about a steak dinner when we get back?"

"Tomorrow night?"

"Why not? We'll be getting in early enough. I was thinking Mulligan's."

"You're on."

"Good. I'll tell Norm to crash somewhere else for the night."

"Really?"

"Yeah, really." His voice caught and he cleared his throat. "Look, I'm sorry, Livvie. I was rushing around, not thinking. Norm sounded so forlorn on the phone that I said okay. It never occurred to me you'd want to stay in the studio on your own. Anyway, now that he's been holed up there for a week I can't vouch for what the place will look like when we get back, but—"

"We'll find a sink full of dishes, but I don't care." I clinked my cup to his. "Let's hope we don't walk in and see him sitting in his Fruit of the Looms watching *Gunsmoke*."

Robert laughed, looking relieved. "Don't worry. We'll drop everything off and go have steak and a bottle of decent red."

"It'll feel odd not eating barefoot."

Robert handed me another piece of hardtack laden with tinned salmon. I was drawn back into life as he lived it, but the fact that he was making plans twenty-four hours ahead felt like a milestone, reason enough to take hope. If something could be salvaged, I didn't want to burn bridges. I couldn't imagine not having him in my life, whatever the terms.

The driftwood was dry enough to burn. Once we'd polished off the smorgasbord, Robert lit a campfire and we toasted the last of the marshmallows. The sky had cleared, the stars out in abundance. I wasn't fool enough to think I'd be tagging along to Rome, but neither did I want to think our relationship would end with dinner at Mulligan's Grill.

Perhaps Robert was thinking along the same lines. He slipped his arm across my shoulders and pulled me close. "We're good together, Livvie. I've known that from the beginning. It makes this all the harder. I'm sorry."

"It would have been easier if you'd let me in on it sooner."

"I should have. I know I've hurt you, but there was never a chance I could take you along where I'm going. That doesn't mean we won't see each other again."

"Maybe meet up in Rome?"

"Let's take it as it comes. Anything could happen."

A door that had seemed shut tight stood ajar, a bit of light glimmering through. All I needed was an opening, a bit of hope. *Anything could happen.*

We broke camp early the next morning, stowing everything back in canvas bags and cases. We'd barely finished by the time Osgood showed up. Despite our talk about wishing we could stay longer on the island, I was relieved to see the dusty Jeep bumping down the rutted road. I was sure Robert felt the same way.

While he and Osgood loaded the gear, I slipped back to the campsite with the string bag of heart-shaped pebbles I'd collected. Saving a blood-red stone for my pocket, I dropped the others in the sand where our tent had been set up.

With all our cases loaded, I climbed into the back of the Jeep. Osgood and I watched Robert sweep the sand with stiff palm leaves, leaving no sign that we'd ever been there. Aside from the stones I'd dropped back on the beach, our campsite was unmarked, as we'd found it, *as it was*.

Chapter 18

I ROLLED DOWN THE WINDOW to get a cross breeze and shifted in my seat. What was taking Robbie so long? Focusing on the doors of the post office, I blinked back tears, his mother's ring squeezed in my hand. It had to be precious to Robert. Had he intended to give it to me at Mulligan's as a promise of a future together? If so, what had stopped him?

The scream of a siren startled me. A red paramedic truck pulled out of the fire station a block away, lights flashing, and roared down the street toward me. *Robbie!* I knew at once something had happened to him. I looked back at the post office, willing him to walk out the doors. *What's taking you so long? Come out, please!*

A squad car pulled up alongside me. A freckle-faced female police officer motioned to me. "Gotta move it, ma'am! You're in a loading zone. We got an emergency vehicle pulling in here."

I pressed the ignition and jammed the SUV into gear, my eyes shifting from the red truck thundering down the street to the doors of the post office.

Please, Robbie, please, please come out!

The red truck pulled up behind me, sirens blasting. I pulled out in front of the squad car and turned the corner.

Tires squealing, I swung into the parking structure and found a space halfway down the ramp. Grabbing my shoulder bag, I jumped out, pressing Lock on the fob as I ran for the stairs. Reaching for the handrail, I raced up the steps two at a time, heart pounding.

A small crowd had gathered near the door, arcing around paramedics working on Robert, crumpled on the floor, blood pooling under his head. I rushed toward him, but was blocked by the ginger-haired police officer. "Sorry, ma'am. Please, stand back."

"But I was with him! What happened?"

She shook her head. "Can't say yet. Let the medics do their jobs."

"Poor man's had a stroke, I'm sure of it," a woman murmured, moving next to me. She was wearing tennis shorts, a sun visor clamped into graying blond hair. "He dropped his mail and looked at me funny-like, then keeled over just like that."

Trembling, I imagined that look of—surprise? *Not again!* His face was stone gray, his forehead and cheek smeared in blood.

"He just came in to check his mail," I mumbled, seeing envelopes on the floor, some stained in blood. His camera lay near his feet.

A thick-necked medic squatting next to him caught my hand as I reached for the camera. "Just leave it be, ma'am. You know him?"

"Robbie," I said, my voice choking. "His name's Robert Yardley. Will he be all right?"

He looked up at me, his voice brisk. "Don't you worry, ma'am. Just take it easy. I'll be with you in a minute."

"Such a sweet, dear man." The woman in tennis shorts turned to me. "So sad. Did you say you were with him?"

"Ma'am?" The medic looked up, addressing me. "If you know this gentleman, maybe you can provide some information?"

"Of course, he's—"

"We all know him around here," the woman interrupted, pressing closer. "Mr. Yardley lives just down the street from me. He's sort of famous, if you know what I mean."

"I figured it was him." The medic stood up, looking from the woman back to me. "What's your relationship to Mr. Yardley, ma'am, if I could ask?"

"I'm his wife."

"Really? My word!" The woman stared at me, startled, her eyes narrowing. "His wife? Well, that's something no one knew."

"We'll just move over here where it's quiet," the medic said, steering me toward an alcove near the door.

"I can't believe it," I mumbled, my mind spinning. "What do you need to know? His full name is Robert Lloyd Yardley. He grew up here, just down on Orchard Street, number four twenty-one. All his identification and medical cards will be in his wallet."

"We've got those, Mrs. Yardley. Medications? Do you know what he was taking?"

"Uh, not offhand. I mean, drops for glaucoma, but otherwise—" My eyes were on Robert, strapped to a gurney, his camera and the envelopes in a plastic bag next to his feet. "Please, let me go with him to the hospital—"

I hurried back to Robert, walking alongside the gurney as he was transported to the truck. His eyes were closed, an oxygen mask fitted over his face. "Robbie, I'm here. I'm with you. I'm not going to leave you."

The other paramedic, a slim black woman, stepped up. "Ma'am, it might be better for you to drive directly to the hospital. Just go straight into Emergency. That's the best thing." She climbed into the truck and turned to close the doors. "Don't you worry, now. My name's Gloria. I'll look out for you."

"Thanks so much, Gloria." I stepped back, bumping into Robert's neighbor standing directly behind me. "S'cuse me. So sorry."

"That's okay." She touched my elbow, her eyes radiating concern. "You know, I could take you to the hospital, if you'd like. Just drop you off there."

"Thanks, but I've got a car."

"You must be new here. You know the way?"

"Yes, of course, but thanks. I appreciate the offer." I turned toward the parking ramp.

"It's no trouble. My name's Marietta Satterthwaite. I check on his house when he's away. I already watered his plants today."

"Thanks so much. Very kind of you."

"Not at all. Sorry, but I didn't catch your first name, Mrs.—"

The siren wailed. I pretended not to hear the question. Yet I'd heard her say she was watering his plants. Where? Indoors? She had a key?

I raced to the car, but it took far longer to reach the hospital than I'd figured. The three-story brick structure I remembered had been replaced by a sleek steel-and-glass facility spread across two city blocks. By the time I found the entrance to the parking facility, I'd completely unraveled.

Banging my hands on the steering wheel in desperation, I wound my way up the ramp in search of a space. I parked and ran down the winding steps rather than wait for an elevator. I rushed into the glass-enclosed reception area and spotted Gloria coming out of the ER wheeling a gurney. Without a word, she pressed the entry button and gestured for me to go straight in.

Breathless, I nodded thanks and hurried through the parting pneumatic doors into the refrigerated air. I looked around, exhaling slowly to calm myself, and caught the eye of a stocky young nurse emerging from a cubicle.

"Robert Yardley? Do you know where he is?"

She gave me a quick glance. "Gloria said to look for you. He's in ICU."

"Was it a stroke? Is he all right?"

"They can tell you more. Go on over, ma'am. Around the corner, up the ramp and turn right."

"Thanks so much," I said, already hurrying down the hallway.

My lie held with the nurse at the reception desk, a terse middle-aged woman with cropped gray hair. "An attendant will take you in shortly, Mrs. Yardley."

I hovered near the windows, too anxious to sit. Turning my back on the clusters of visitors in the lounge, I looked across at the forested ridgeline of a state park some miles in the distance, dabbing the tears spilling on my cheeks. An attendant called my name and I followed him through doors and down a corridor to a draped cubicle.

A heavyset nurse with dark hair wound into a tortoise clasp was attending Robert, her bulk obscuring him. My stomach seized as she moved aside and I caught a glimpse of him. He was hooked up to monitors and a drip, a bulky gauze pad covering one side of his face. His eyes were closed, his face slack and gray.

The nurse looked up. "Give us another minute, please." She motioned me to step back so a young male attendant could wheel a small trolley out of the cramped quarters.

Next to me, a nurse with a thick blond braid, her back to me, slouched on one foot while tapping a keyboard. I glanced up at the monitor, trying to make out the blocks of text cascading down the screen. She turned, shifted her weight and regarded me without comment before turning back to the keyboard. I edged aside but looked over her shoulder, mesmerized by the fresh burst of text streaming onto the screen.

"You're Mrs.—?" she asked, without looking at me.

I glanced at Robert, wondering if he could hear us. "Please, just call me Olivia," I whispered. "I go by Olivia Hammond—not, you know . . ."

"Yes?" She glanced at me, her frank look unnerving. I was about to come clean when she said, "I'm Sara, the attending nurse. He's coming around. He'll be fine." She glanced at the other nurse leaving the cubicle. "Go ahead, Mrs.—sorry, Olivia."

Had Robert heard the exchange? I moved closer, emotion welling up. He looked shrunken under the coarse flannel blanket. "I'm so sorry, Robbie," I whispered. "Forgive me. I didn't mean for this to happen."

His eyelids flickered, but didn't open. "Oooooolivie," he breathed, his voice a quiet wheeze. "Sorry, too."

I brushed his cheek with my fingers. "Nothing for you to be sorry about."

The corner of his mouth twitched. "Always the way with us," he breathed. His face relaxed and he drifted off again.

"Doesn't have to be," I whispered, brushing the dampness from my cheeks.

I rested my hip against the railing and stroked his hand. Mottled skin, almost transparent, slid across tendons and veins, offering no resistance, not settling back.

Sara touched my elbow. "Let him rest now." I followed her out of the enclosure into the hallway. "If you want to stay in the waiting room, I'll call you when he's awake again."

"He's going to be okay, isn't he?"

"Oh, yes. So far, so good." She smiled and patted my arm. "We just need to stabilize him. He should be fine."

The sun had set by the time I returned to the waiting room. I poured coffee from a decanter on a service trolley and settled into a green vinyl armchair facing the window. The dusky gloaming cast the ridgeline in deep lavender shadow, a crescent moon already on the rise.

By this time tomorrow I'd be in another city, arriving at a bookstore to sign copies of *September Girl*. Should I cancel my appearance? I'd never done that before. Still, who would look after him while he recuperated? Where would he go if his house weren't habitable? He needed me—*stop!*

I stood up, tossing the container of tar-black, foul-smelling coffee into a rubbish bin. I'd spent less than forty-eight hours with Robert, our longest time together since camping out on a beach in St. John. Yet, I already saw myself stepping in as his caregiver. After all these years, was I still that young woman who was thrilled to oblige him, while content to keep a shoebox of toiletries under a bed?

Robert left New York less than a week after our return from the camping trip. There was no farewell party for him at the office because no one on the staff knew he was leaving for anything other than another overseas assignment. If Moses Ward was aware that I knew Robert had been reassigned to another bureau, he did not let on.

Robert shipped film for a story he covered in Morocco, but I had no inkling of his exact whereabouts. Other than sending him a telex through the Rome bureau, I had little means of reaching him. He did not get in touch with me.

It was more than a month after he left New York that Brígh mentioned Robert had secured a visa from the Portuguese Embassy enabling him to cover guerrilla warfare in the African provinces of Guinea-Bissau, Angola and Mozambique. There was still little media coverage of the growing conflict and Robert wanted to photograph it on his own terms, embedding himself with ground forces.

It wasn't until the office received a telex from Robert in Luanda that I learned he was on his way to join government troops in Guinea-Bissau. He kept sporadic contact with the Rome bureau, making brief forays out of the bush to ship film. Months later, we heard he would shortly be on his way to Lisbon. Brígh, who was still in charge of the World section, persuaded Horace Greenwalt that it was necessary I go to Lisbon to handle his trove of film. She knew it was imperative for me to see Robert in person.

She'd guessed that I was pregnant. She confronted me one morning when I was late to work and so nauseated I could barely navigate from the elevator to my desk.

"What're you going to do about this?" she asked bluntly. "Any thoughts?"

I burst into tears. "I need to see Robbie."

"So the bastard doesn't know yet?"

I shook my head, feeling another wave of nausea. "No chance to tell him," I managed to say, my stomach churning. "Couldn't reach him."

"This is one instance a shot of single malt won't help. We'll talk later," she said as I fled to the bathroom.

That evening, while I drank ginger ale and tried to retain some chicken soup in my stomach, Brígh consumed a half bottle of Pinch and poked a veal cutlet around her dinner plate. I tried not to look.

"You're creeping up on the now-or-never stage," she said, her voice unusually husky. "If it helps, I know someone, if that's how you want to take care of it."

I shook my head. "I thought about it, but—no."

"Then you've got a tough road ahead, but I understand. Maybe you're right. I still regret what I did and it was a long time ago." She acknowledged my quick look with a nod and reached for my hand. "You can't ever undo what you decide now, so you want to make sure."

"I know that. But then I try to figure out how I'll ever be able manage on my own with a baby." I swallowed hard, feeling sick. "If only I could see him—"

"It's still all up to you, not him. And he's a long way away." She squeezed my hand. "Let's see what we can work out."

Soon after I confided in Brígh, the opportunity came up to meet Robert in Portugal. I thought back on my flight to Paris, the romantic weekend that only Brígh had known about. This time Brígh, who had won approval from Horace, would be masterminding a rendezvous in Lisbon. She took charge of booking my flight and reserving rooms for us at the Hotel Metropole.

My bag was packed. I was prepared to catch an overnight flight when another cable arrived from Robert via the Rome bureau. An intermediary had put him in touch with Holden Roberto, leader of one of the rebel factions in Angola. He would be joining his ragtag forces in the northern section of the province instead of traveling to Lisbon. I unpacked my bag.

I had no idea when I might have another chance to see Robert, but the clock had already run out on making any choice other than having his baby. I tried not to consider the possibility that he'd chosen to trek through jungle in a hail of bullets rather than see me. Brígh, guessing my thoughts, insisted Robert had already signaled his change of plan before getting her cable that I would be joining him. She swore his decision had nothing to do with my arrival. I chose to believe her.

Wavering between sheer fright and a state of numbed resignation, I handled my situation as best I could. I had little control over my thoughts or emotions, and certainly none over my body. I was already showing, but fortunately tent dresses that swung wide and loose from the shoulders were the fashion. I invested in two that concealed my thickening figure, although my roommate became suspicious. I confided in Patty on condition she promise not to tell Stuart, who would spread word around the office.

Patty already knew that Robert had moved to Rome, and she wasn't that pleased that I was spending more time in the apartment. She and Stuart had come to regard our bedroom as their private love nest. While I'd expected some show of compassion from Patty, she considered me a Typhoid Mary.

"Oh, my God! Preggers?"she yelped, stepping back as though I were contagious. "You shoulda been more careful, kid. Can you get rid of it?"

"It's a little late for that, Patty. But I'm going to try to work as long as I can, so please don't say anything."

"My God, Stuart's the last person I'd tell. But he's going to see it. Guys aren't that dumb. And I've got to tell the other girls."

"Okay, I'll tell them myself."

"They won't like it. I mean, how will it look when guys come around? You're going to have to find another place, kid."

"When I can, I will, all right?"

Not long after the confrontation with Patty, Brígh warned me that my bump was becoming obvious. If I wanted to avoid rumors, it was time to turn in my notice. Since in my case there were no company provisions for medical benefits or pregnancy leave, I had to resign. Quitting a job I knew I was lucky to have, doing work I enjoyed, was wrenching, but I had no choice. I made ends meet working at home doing free-lance editing for a book publisher Brígh knew.

One afternoon, she called from the office to tell me she wanted to drop by after work. Brígh had never been to my apartment. I wasn't eager to have her see the chaotic hovel I called home. The chipped planter with a dead aspidistra still stood in the entryway. No one had vacuumed in weeks. I suggested meeting somewhere for drinks since I had no liquor on hand for her.

"I'll bring something, dearie. On my way."

The moment I opened the door and saw her face, I knew Brígh was too sober to be making a social call.

"This is about Robbie, isn't it?" Panic lapped at my throat. I could barely breathe. "Something's happened? What?"

"I'm so sorry, Livvie." She reached for my arm and pulled me toward the living room. "Please, sit down first."

"Tell me! What happened? Is he all right?"

"Sit, please. We don't really know yet." I sat down on the edge of the couch. She perched on the arm, her hand on my shoulder, her eyes dark in hollowed sockets. "I wanted to be the one to tell you. A telex came in this afternoon. It's not good news. Robert was caught in gunfire with rebel troops in Angola. He's missing, but—I'm so sorry, Livvie. It's presumed he didn't make it. That's all we know."

"No!" I groaned. "No, no, no!" My hands gripped my stomach, trying to quell a swelling tide. Searing pain seized my belly and I cried out, writhing against the back of the couch. "Stop! No!"

Brígh called an ambulance, then remained with me at the hospital, comforting me throughout a long and terrible night.

Chapter 19

VISITING HOURS WERE ALMOST OVER, my stomach soured on stale Cheez-Its washed down with tepid Dr. Pepper. I was about to leave when the nurse at the desk beckoned me. "Sara says you can go in for a minute."

I hovered in the hallway outside the draped enclosure, waiting. Eventually, Sara pulled the curtain aside and joined me in the corridor.

"I'm sorry the doctor wasn't available to see you."

"That's all right. How is he?"

"Resting comfortably. We'll keep Mr. Yardley over night because of the head injury, but he'll probably be released tomorrow."

"What?" I gasped. "But he had a stroke!"

"No, not a stroke." She shook her head. "And no broken bones. He neglected to take his blood-pressure medication, which, in his case, is serious enough. He could have had a stroke." She lowered her voice. "Look, I don't know what your situation is—none of my business—but please make sure he takes his medication, okay?"

"Sure." I nodded. "So, it wasn't—"

"He said he forgot his medication at home when he went away for a couple days. All he had to do was call in. I mean, any pharmacy would have filled a prescription."

I nodded dumbly, taking it in. So why the hell hadn't we gone to his house to get his pills instead of rushing off to the damn post office? Given the circumstances—the urgency! Why didn't he tell me?

"Mrs.—I mean, Olivia . . . are you all right? I can get you some coffee. A juice?"

"No, I'm fine. Relieved, of course. May I see him?"

"Sure. We're keeping him in here, rather than moving him, but he's doing fine." She patted my arm and left me alone with Robert.

His face was gauze white in the light cast by a beeping monitor. A drip was connected to a port in his wrist. His eyes were closed, a faint wheeze of breath escaping his lips.

I gently touched his arm. "Robbie, it's me. You're going to be fine. You'll be out of the hospital tomorrow, so. . ." My voice, a bare whisper, trailed off.

I had no idea what I was going to say next. Had I been about to tell him I would leave, head to the airport? How could I do that? Who else but his "wife" could pick him up from the hospital and take him—where? Someone had to take charge. Who, if not me? Would Marietta Satterthwaite attend to him, as well as his plants?

He was asleep. I sank into a chair next to his bed, overwhelmed, trying to sort out what to do. Tomorrow, he'd hear about the "wife" he didn't have. My cheeks burned thinking about his reaction.

When I was released from the hospital, Brígh insisted I stay in her spare room rather than return to my own apartment. I spent my days in bed with the shades pulled, my nights lying awake grieving for Robert. I felt dead, my world empty, except that I still carried a life inside me. I hadn't miscarried, which would have provided an expedient solution.

Dwelling entirely on my own situation, I did not consider the extent of my imposition on Brígh, who was hardly the sort to house a roommate with a noisy newborn. But once I'd moved out of my Upper East Side apartment, I could not go back. Patty had quickly replaced me with another roommate, making it clear I wasn't welcome to remain with a baby.

"Guys get squeamish," she said, shuddering at having a nursing mother sitting on the couch when gentlemen callers arrived.

In frigid late February, I was in no condition to search for an apartment. Meanwhile, I managed to crawl out of bed a few hours each day to cook and clean, trying to earn my keep, which wasn't necessarily appreciated.

"Lumpy gruel?" Brígh asked one morning, attempting to identify the alien substance in a bowl I offered her.

"Yogurt with muesli and raisins, something to line your stomach," I said helpfully. "It's good for you."

"No need to gum up the works, but I'll try it." Knowing she'd get a rise out of me, she tipped a jigger of gin into the bowl before taking a bite. "Yummy, but it's the mixers that'll get you. I'll take my breakfast neat." Her eyes narrowed. "Besides, you're making me fat."

"What?"

"No more of the noodles and cheese, okay? That stuff can kill you. If you keep force-feeding me, I'm going to turn into a blimp like you."

"Sorry, I thought you liked macaroni and cheese."

"I do. Especially the crumbled bacon on top, so stop making it." She reached for her cigarette, took a deep drag and blew out a stream of smoke that momentarily obscured her from view. "They may eat like that in Minnesota. Here, we order in Chinese."

"Okay, Chinese." I smiled. "Sweet-and-sour pork. Plain rice."

"Good girl," she cooed. "See? You're learning."

I even offered to pay room and board. Brígh refused to accept any money. Despite reassurances, I realized she might be regretting her rash invitation when she saw me stockpiling supplies for the birth that was fast approaching. Under the circumstances, there'd be no baby shower for me at the office. I was grateful when one of Brígh's neighbors, a mother with two young children, offered me a bassinet, baby clothes and a good many other used items she was discarding.

Brígh looked askance as the woman's husband delivered everything to her door, dumping cartons and overflowing bags in the small entryway.

"You'd think a cradle and a blanket would do it. You really need all that stuff?" she asked, lighting a fresh cigarette.

"I'm afraid so." I sighed. "Sorry, I'll stash it all in my room." I picked up the wicker bassinet, then stopped. "Seriously, if you're having second thoughts now—"

"No, no, not at all." She exhaled in a rush, her eyes bleary behind a haze of smoke. "Besides, where would you go? I mean—"

"Now?" I repeated, the wicker bassinet cradled in my arms.

"Of course not *now*." Her voice trailed off in a throaty wheeze. "Something will work out."

We regarded each other across a frayed strip of Turkish

carpet, the basinet in my arms, a cigarette cocked between her fingers. I was tired. She was drunk. I didn't want to cry and feared I might if I spoke. What could I say, anyway? She was well aware that I was short on options.

She took another drag on her cigarette, regarding me through a dense fog of smoke. "I like having you here." She waggled her cigarette at me, her voice husky.

"Thank you, Brígh. I don't want to be a nuisance."

"Nuisance? Not at all." She tottered back to her desk, spilling ash I would vacuum up in the morning. "All I was questioning is how a creature so small and God-given requires such a lot of equipment not available when mankind was created, but then, I guess it's not the only thing the nuns couldn't answer."

I watched her weave into the hallway, letting her comments sink in. She'd covered her ungracious lapse in admirable Brígh form, but her wit wasn't meant to conceal her true feelings, and it hadn't.

I carried the bassinet to my room and made several more trips with bags and cartons. When I was finished, I checked on her. She was still at her desk, folded over, snoring softly with her head cradled in her arms. Her lipstick-smudged cigarette had joined a multitude of others in the heavy glass ashtray. Her wine glass was empty.

I didn't lead her to bed or cover her with a blanket. She would hate to have me do that. Given time, she'd eventually awaken, require a top-up of red wine and drift off to the couch, where she slept most nights. I only emptied the ashtray and cleared the path from desk to makeshift bed, removing books and papers that would end up shoved to the floor. I turned the light low and went to bed.

I understood that however much Brígh valued our

friendship, she didn't want me to see her passed out at her desk, sleeping on a couch, or retching in the early morning before she could medicate herself with straight Bombay gin to face a new day.

In the meantime, I was only weeks away from giving birth, but had no job, no medical coverage and no means of supporting myself with a child. Brígh, anxious about how I would cope on my own with a newborn, confided in Dorah Ellerbe, who had traveled to New York to meet with Robert's attorney and representatives from the magazine. He was still missing, presumed killed in an ambush by Portuguese government troops, possibly the same forces he'd been traveling with several weeks earlier. His body had not been recovered, but there was little hope he had survived the attack and escaped.

After a private meeting with the managing editor, Dorah stopped by to see Brígh. She asked about me, surprised to learn I was no longer working for the magazine. Brígh explained my circumstances, telling her about my pregnancy.

"She asked how you'd taken the news about Robert. I had to tell her," Brígh said in her hurried phone call. "I mentioned you were staying with me and she insisted on seeing you right away. I couldn't say no. You'll understand when you see her. She's devastated. He's all she had left in the world. She spends every waking minute praying for a miracle, hoping he's alive."

"Has she heard anything?"

"Sorry, nothing to report. If we had any news about Robert I'd let you know. But she hasn't given up hope that he'll be found, one way or another. Like you, she's suffering terribly. I think seeing you can give her some comfort."

"You told her everything? That I'm carrying his child?"

"Yes, I did." Brígh sighed. "Listen, it won't hurt to have someone like her in your corner. Do you understand?"

"Sorry, I'm not up to it." My face flushed, imagining the conversation they'd had about me. I was mortified that Dorah would see me in my condition. "I know what she'll think. Careless. Knocked up. Serves me right!"

"Stop that. It's Robert's child, that's what she'll be thinking." Brígh turned brisk, her voice commanding. "Be a good girl now. Comb your hair and put on some lipstick. She'll be there any minute."

"Yes, sir!"

"I mean it." Brígh's voice softened. "And remember, you're both suffering. Be kind to each other."

She hung up, cutting me off from saying another word. I put on one of the knit tent dresses that hiked up in front and stretched tightly across my belly. I barely had time to run a comb through my hair before the doorbell rang. I took my time navigating down the hall. The bell rang a second time before I could open the door.

Dorah looked wan and shrunken inside her mink coat, her shoulders hunched with the effort of holding her handbag and a bouquet of small pink roses. Her eyes glistened wetly when she saw me.

"My darling, beautiful child. I wish you had let me know, my dear."

I melted into her arms, breathing the smell of roses and the fragrance of Worth perfume clinging to her fur. We wept together, my bulk pressed against her tiny frame.

"Come in, please. Come in." I took the bouquet, my fingers interlocking with hers. "Thank you so much. It's good to see you, Mrs. Ellerbe."

"Please, you must call me Dorah, remember? We know each other better than that." She squeezed my fingers. "And we're going to know each other even better. You've become very special to me. I'm sure you understand what I mean, my dear. You mustn't be alone in a time like this." She hesitated. "Your family is supportive, of course?"

"Actually, I haven't told them anything about—this, yet." My face flushed as I looked down at my swollen belly, knowing I couldn't make that call home. "Not that they wouldn't understand and help me out, but . . . you know." Heat burned my cheeks.

"Poor thing, of course I know!" Dorah exclaimed. "Your family would embrace you and see you through, but . . . I suspect you are of a more independent spirit, am I right? You want to forge your own way, as so many young women today want to assert themselves, yes?" She smiled and patted my arm. "You're a girl after my own heart. How much you remind me of myself at your age. That means such a lot!"

Her warmth lifted my spirits. Isolation had weighed heavily. Other than Brígh, I saw no one. I hadn't confided in family and couldn't face doing so. Alone for great stretches of time, I'd fought off thinking ahead, which only brought on waves of shaky anxiety and fears that I wouldn't be able to cope. If Robert's aunt was reaching out to me, I sensed a glimmer of hope in my future.

I hung up Dorah's coat and showed her around Brígh's cluttered apartment, where tables and chairs alike were piled with books, magazines and jumbled stacks of paper. When we reached the kitchen, I put the kettle on for tea. I rummaged through Brígh's cupboards for a vase, which helped cover awkward moments when I felt Dorah's eyes on me, taking in my awkward bulk.

"You're due soon, I see."

"A month to go." I slowly arranged roses in a crystal vase, avoiding her gaze.

"Brígh made arrangements for me through her doctor. Afterward, I'll stay here with the baby until I get a job and a place of my own."

"Well, that's not quite my understanding, dear. Please don't think me too forward, but I had a little heart-to-heart with Brígh about your situation. I think we can do better. Will you trust me?"

The word *we* caught my ear. I held my breath while filling the teapot. Brígh had been as wary of Dorah Ellerbe as I'd been. If Brígh now endorsed a plan proposed by Robert's aunt, I was open to it.

"You may remember I'm in hospital administration. I'm in a position to give you some assistance I think you need."

"But that wouldn't be here in New York, though—"

"No, of course not. You're coming home to Weymouth with me. It's what Robbie would want and I insist. I'm leaving Sunday afternoon. I'll book a ticket for you on the same flight." She smiled, her eyes dropping to my bump. "The sooner we get you settled, the better, I should think."

"Wait, are you sure you want this? What will your friends in Weymouth think?"

"Whatever do you mean?" She stared at me, her eyes the steely blue I remembered from her photograph. "They'll think whatever I want them to think." She rearranged the cups I'd set on a tray and reached for the teapot. "Shall we go into the other room? It'll be cozier there and we have quite a lot to talk about."

By the time Brígh arrived home, I was already packing. I realized that the two women had discussed everything and settled on a plan together. It didn't come as a surprise that Brígh would collude with Dorah, who provided a perfect guilt-free solution. She had a spacious house, access to good medical care and the means to provide assistance until I could get back on my feet. Besides, Dorah was "family." She'd made all those advantages clear to me during our chat over tea. The arrangement also eliminated any need to get in touch with my own family. I readily agreed to fly back home with her.

I took only a suitcase and my typewriter, leaving everything else in Brígh's spare room, assuring her it would only be temporary storage. With a newfound sense of adventure, I was excited at the prospect of returning to New York with my baby, finding an apartment of my own and securing freelance editing work I could do at home.

As I lay in bed the night before leaving for Weymouth, I even dared play out dream-like scenarios in which Robert was alive and on his way home to me. I pictured him arriving at my door, envisioned embracing him, feeling his lips on mine. I replayed the loop again and again, embellishing it more each time until I drifted off to sleep. Anything was possible, even dreams coming true.

Chapter 20

ROBBIE WAS STILL SLEEPING. I brushed his cheek, whispering, "See you tomorrow," before slipping quietly out of the room. Regular visiting hours were long over. The SUV was one of the few vehicles remaining in the parking structure. I tossed my shoulder bag into the passenger seat and climbed in, my eye catching the gleam of his mother's ring I'd dropped in the drinks holder when I raced to park.

If I'd been Robert's wife—even his fiancée—how very different everything would have turned out for me. I tucked the ring back in the matchbook and slid it into my shoulder bag before heading toward Orchard Street. If Robert were released tomorrow, this would probably be my only opportunity to visit the Ellerbe home, where Dorah had invited me to stay.

Chatting with Dorah over tea in Brígh's apartment that afternoon, I was more hopeful than I'd been in a long time. Before she left, I took her to my room and showed her the baby supplies, including an array of infant sleepers, tee shirts and booties the neighbor had given me.

"I'm going to need quite a lot of these things. What do you think I should take with me?"

Dorah gave the items a cursory look and patted my arm. "You won't need any of it, my dear. We can arrange everything later. Just bring yourself and I'll take care of the rest. I don't want you to tire yourself packing."

In a wave of relief and gratitude, I embraced her at the door. "Thank you, Dorah! You've no idea what all this means to me."

I took her at her word, packing my well-worn knit dresses and a few personal items, but nothing for a newborn.

I was exhausted after our flight from New York, but felt a rush of exhilaration when the taxi drove down Orchard Street and pulled into the driveway of the Ellerbe house. I stepped onto the sidewalk and looked up at the imposing two-story home, with its ironwork and white pillars shrouded in twilight's ghostly lavender shadows. I remembered a snapshot Robert had shown me of himself, a gangly teenager at the time, standing near the wrought-iron railings on a sunlit afternoon, his bike leaning against a pillar.

For a moment, time stopped. I stood on the sidewalk transfixed, imagining Robert emerging from the deepening shadows, taking his place where he'd once stood as a boy, a sunny grin on his youthful face. I could almost see him in the fading light, his eyes looking into mine, welcoming me home.

"Home again, home again," Dorah trilled, stepping onto the veranda. "Come along, my dear. You can look around in the morning."

The paunchy, gap-toothed taxi driver had already set our luggage near the door. "Easy does it, ma'am," he said, taking my elbow as I climbed the three steps to the veranda.

"Thank you," I panted, breathless from exertion. I paused on the top step and gripped the railing, my eyes lingering on the shadows, hoping to catch another spectral glimpse of young Robert.

Dorah had already unlocked the front door and was flicking on lights. I picked up my suitcase and stepped inside. I stopped short, staring at a massive mahogany coat rack on the far wall of the entryway. Hanging on one of the pegs was a safari jacket, torn at one elbow.

"What is it, child?" Dorah turned and saw me looking at the jacket. "Oh, Robbie left that behind," she said briskly. "He'll be back for it."

She spoke without irony or wistfulness. I took heart in her conviction that, against all odds, he was alive. I followed her down the hall to the guest room, passing family photographs framed on the walls and displayed on a side table, all featuring Robert. It was comforting to know that while awaiting the birth of our baby, I would be staying in the house where he grew up, his presence everywhere.

Dorah showed me to my room and set out fresh towels in the adjoining bathroom. "I can see you're tired," she said, stopping to switch on a lamp, "but you need to eat something before going to bed."

While I washed up and pulled a nightgown out of my suitcase, Dorah set out supper in the small breakfast nook off the kitchen. We sat on bentwood café chairs at a round table that reminded me of the one in Robert's studio, and ate buttered brown bread with delicious homemade vegetable soup.

"It's Lilah's specialty, a little different each time," Dorah said. "She's my housekeeper. You'll see her in the morning. Now, I'll be off to work at seven-thirty. I'm home again a little after four o'clock in time for tea, but she'll take good care of you. Whatever you need, just ask her."

"Thank you. Maybe I'll go out for a walk and look around the neighborhood."

"Good idea. Fresh air and exercise is precisely what you need. You'll find Weymouth Park just up the street, but wear a sweater. The weather is still fairly raw." She ladled more soup in my bowl. "By the way, should you run into anyone in the neighborhood, just tell them you're the daughter of my old college friend back in . . . where did you say you're from?"

"Minnesota?"

"Excellent. Minnesota. I'll make a note of that." She put another slice of buttered bread on my plate. "No need to get too specific. I don't think it's necessary to mention Robbie, either, with everything so uncertain. You probably won't feel up to a lot of socializing. You'll find the house quite comfortable and there's a lovely garden in the back. Plenty of fresh air, good food and rest, that's what you need. Don't you agree?"

Her manner was warm and confiding, but it was clear I wouldn't be meeting her friends, nor would my connection to Robert be mentioned. If anyone inquired about me, I would be passed off as the daughter of an old friend, a "girl in trouble," who needed refuge. As Dorah had said, her friends in Weymouth would think what she wanted them to think.

I looked down at my brimming bowl of soup, no longer hungry. "Whatever you think is best."

"Good." She patted my hand. "No sense in raising a lot of questions we don't want to answer."

"So, I'm not supposed to know Robbie at all? Not even from the magazine?"

"Not really. People are so quick to put two and two together," she murmured. "You'll need to see a doctor, of course.

I'll arrange an appointment before the end of the week. How are you feeling?"

"I'm fine, but really tired."

"Of course you are, my dear. Go off to bed now. I'll do the clearing up."

"Thank you. It was delicious. I just can't eat any more."

"That's understandable. Just get a good night's rest." She made a move to get up. I hoped it wasn't to hug me.

"No, no, please finish eating." I turned toward the hallway. "Thank you for everything. I really appreciate it."

I hurried to my room and went into the bathroom, turning the key in the lock. I lifted the lid on the toilet and threw up, then flushed away swirling bits of squash, carrots and green beans. I looked in the mirror as I brushed my teeth, seeing hollowed eyes in a moon face that had grown swollen along with the rest of me.

So that's the way it's going to be.

But who could blame her? Dorah was right in that everything was uncertain. Why open ourselves to speculation and rumor? Worse yet, pity and disapproval. Why be forced to answer a lot of unwelcome questions about the father of my baby? Everyone could see there was no ring on my finger. It was best to remain anonymous and leave quietly after the delivery.

I owed it to Dorah, who would otherwise have to live in Weymouth facing the consequences if it became known I was giving birth to Robert's illegitimate child.

Chapter 21

I PARKED THE SUV IN THE DRIVEWAY at 421 Orchard Street and turned off the ignition. Quickly, before I could mull the consequences of entering someone's dark, locked house late at night, uninvited, I grabbed my shoulder bag and climbed out of the car. Shrouded in darkness but for the pale light of a corner street lamp, the house appeared to be intact, with no obvious signs of storm damage. If the power was still on and the house habitable, I would spend the night. I grabbed my wheelie from the trunk and set it on the veranda.

I ran my fingers across the top of the window frame, the second one on the left to the side of the front door. The key was still there, as I'd hoped it would be, gritty with dust and flecks of white trim paint. In the many years since I'd stayed in the Ellerbe house, how often had the exterior been repainted without the key being disturbed? I brushed it clean and opened the scrollwork screen door. If my luck held, the lock wouldn't have been changed.

The key turned with a soft click. I grasped the knob and gave a swift glance over my shoulder. Was I being watched? There were no ominous shadows in the spill of light on the wide veranda. The street was quiet. No cars passed by, but that didn't mean someone in the neighborhood wasn't observing me entering the house. If anyone reported me, my excuse was ready. I was there to pick up items for Robert, who was in the hospital.

I took a breath and shoved the heavy oak door open and flicked the switch to the right of the door. A low-wattage light glimmered in a ceiling fixture. Why had Robert told me the power was off?

The entryway seemed emptier than I remembered, then realized what was missing. My face did not peer back at me from the beveled mirror of a coat rack. The massive, elaborately carved mahogany piece, once thick with hats, umbrellas and Robert's torn safari jacket, was gone. In its place was a wall of bare brick, oozing petrified mortar.

I took a few steps into the room that Aunt Dorah called her parlor, my sandals slapping noisily on a bare, wide-planked floor. I stopped, unnerved by the hollow, eerie silence. I flicked another wall switch and gasped, stunned to see Dorah's parlor barren and empty. The room that once looked like a color spread in *Better Homes and Gardens* had been stripped of its elegant décor.

Where were her prized Aubusson rugs? Or the floral chintz settees and the cherrywood cabinets filled with Dresden figurines? Instead of hand-painted Chinese-motif wallpaper, there were smooth stretches of white plaster. Delicate porcelain wall sconces were missing, replaced with low-wattage light bulbs shaded by pierced-tin cylinders. The chandelier that once sparkled with teardrop crystals burnt nakedly with pricks of light in bare candle bases. In place of Dorah's costly furnishings and bric-a-brac, what remained were two armchairs covered in plain muslin flanking a square wooden table.

I pictured everything as it was long ago, recalling a pretty majolica vase that was no longer standing on the mantel, the carved mahogany stripped bare. Oil portraits, matching in size, of Aunt Dorah in pearls and Uncle Lloyd holding a pipe no longer hung on either side of the glazed-plaster fireplace that was now exposed bare brick.

I stood for long minutes, slowly to take it all in. The transformation was deliberate, a painstaking deconstruction, not caused by storm damage. This was Robert's work, similar to what he'd done in New York converting the old butcher shop into his studio. Is this what he hadn't wanted me to see?

"Why not!" I cried out, bursting into laughter. "Damn her, Robert! This is glorious! Wonderful!"

I stamped my foot, floorboards trembling, daring Aunt Dorah's hateful, ghostly presence to seep from the walls she'd spent her waking hours adorning with the best she could buy. Was she lurking here in spirit, house-proud and beside herself with grief at its systematic destruction? I imagined the horror at seeing her precious wallpaper stripped away, plaster crumbling and moldings pried loose.

I glared at the empty space on the wall where her painting used to hang, the original of the framed photograph Robert had in his studio.

"Damn you! Serves you right!"

My voice sliced through the silence in the stripped down room, harsh and echoing. Why would Robert not want me to see this? If only I could have stood next to him swinging a sledgehammer!

I walked through the dining room and saw that the mahogany table and chairs had been replaced with an industrial workbench and stools. How had Robert disposed of the furnishings? Had he put it all in storage or scrapped it? My hope was that he had donated everything to a local Goodwill shop or church bazaar where Aunt Dorah's covetous friends could pick over her prize acquisitions and buy them at bargain prices. A dining table and chairs, cabinets brimming with good china and drawers stuffed with fine embroidered linens would have been welcome in any consignment shop. Or sold at a rural flea market. Cruel irony for Dorah, who had scoured such places for many of her own finds.

Less had been stripped away in the kitchen, although the walls were bare aside from an old Bakelite clock hanging above the stove. The breadbox was also familiar, as were a pair of black-and-white salt-and-pepper shakers and a crock containing wooden spoons and a potato masher. The toaster was vintage. The deep ceramic sink and faucets were original. The black-and-white checkerboard floor tiles hadn't been replaced, nor the old refrigerator. I smiled. Would I find boxes of Kodachrome in the vegetable crisper?

I opened the fridge to find it stocked with lunchmeat of questionable vintage, a package of sliced American cheese, a puckered tomato and two eggs, but no boxes of film. Robert, who seldom drank, had an unopened bottle of good rosé stashed next to a milk carton. I opened the drawer next to the sink, gratified to find a corkscrew.

I poured wine into a water glass, not surprised Dorah's crystal had vanished, too. The cupboard yielded an unopened can of vacuum-packed mixed nuts. Things were looking up. There was also a can of tomato soup and a box of saltines if I got hungry later. With a tumbler of rosé in hand and the can of nuts tucked under my arm, I continued my exploration.

While awaiting my delivery, I'd stayed in the front guest room, with its canopy bed, flowered wallpaper and pale-yellow chintz curtains. That room, too, had been stripped down, the bed removed, the walls painted white. The sash window was covered with white muslin curtains and a plain roller shade. The floor was bare, the walls unadorned. A trestle table supported by two low filing cabinets was similar to the worktable Robert had had in his New York studio. I opened the closet door and saw that plain wood shelves had been installed to hold camera equipment and office supplies.

A large bathroom, with doors on opposite walls, interconnected the guest room at the front of the house with Robert's childhood bedroom. The tassels had been removed from the keys in the locks, but otherwise the bathroom, with its etched glass and vintage wood wainscoting, remained much the same as I remembered it.

Robert had told me that when he was growing up, he'd locked the bathroom door to the guest room and stashed the key away. Aunt Dorah had thrown a fit, but Uncle Lloyd backed him up, saying, "A boy needs his privacy, the same as a man." He forbade Aunt Dorah from looking for the key. Robbie said he gave the key back to her the day he left the Ellerbe home and caught a train for New York.

Robert's childhood bedroom, paneled in dark knotty pine, was in the rear of the house, with casement windows looking out on the garden. His single bed remained, as did the old rolltop desk tucked between two built-in bookcases. I opened the closet door and found several tan safari jackets, faded and well worn. There were also khaki pants and blue work shirts, pretty much the extent of Robert's timeless wardrobe. He was a creature of habit and simple tastes. It didn't surprise me that he would be sleeping in his old room, despite having a big master bedroom upstairs.

I sat on his bed and opened the can of nuts. Looking out on the garden, I recalled the pecan tree I'd watched topple during a fierce electrical storm. The sound of a thunderous crack had rocked the house, rattling the casement windows. I'd stood riveted, watching the dark mass rush toward me. Dust rose amid fluttering leaves as the tree crashed to the ground, its branches landing with a heavy thud just a few feet from the back porch. It was a near miss, but the house was spared—and so was I.

My eyes fell on a pipe rack, a memento of his uncle that Robbie kept on the rolltop desk. If Uncle Lloyd had still been alive when I met Robbie, would things have turned out differently? Could he have influenced Dorah in my favor? *What if?*

I passed through the kitchen to top up my wine. I walked back through the living room, looking again at the deconstruction of Aunt Dorah's once well-bred parlor, now relieved of its fussiness and pretense. Robert's stripped-down redo had an elegance and integrity of its own. Why wouldn't he tell me the house was under construction instead of making up an excuse about storm damage?

I went back into the darkened guest room Robert had converted into an office. Pale light from the street lamp seeped through the window shade. Even if neighbors didn't see me, they would notice lights turned on. I didn't want visitors.

Avoiding people and awkward personal questions had preoccupied me the entire time I'd stayed with Dorah. I set my glass of wine and the can of nuts on the worktable and pulled up a chair, once again hiding out in the Ellerbe house.

I threw up my first night in Weymouth. Afterward, while brushing my teeth, I talked myself into accepting that Dorah was right about keeping things secret. Everyone in town knew Robbie as the kid with the camera, who had gone on to a storied career as a globetrotting photojournalist. He'd been a local hero, a favorite son missing in action in some distant place no one had ever heard of while covering someone's war, a consequence of living an adventurous life. Dorah had risked a lot bringing me to Weymouth. I understood why she'd asked me to pretend I was her college friend's daughter, a young woman in trouble that she was helping out.

After waking up in Dorah's guest room that first morning, I sat in the big canopy bed, plumped with pillows, and looked around the airy room with high ceilings and flower-sprigged wallpaper. I pictured a bassinet and changing table in the corner. All that had felt so wrong the night before had suddenly seemed right. I resolved that if Dorah was doing the right thing by seeing me through the delivery for Robert's sake, I would keep up the pretense.

I was ready to get out of bed when there was a timid knock on the door.

"Come in."

G'morning, miss."

A short, stout housekeeper edged the door open, carrying tea and toast on a white wicker tray. She barely glanced at me as she set the tray across my lap.

"Good morning! Thank you, this looks wonderful." I glanced at the clock on the bedside table. "Oh, dear, I've really slept late."

"Mrs. Ellerbe told me you need your rest. You take your time, miss."

She spoke in a pleasing drawl more pronounced than Do-rah Ellerbe's. She wore a plain blue cotton dress, snug over her hips and ample bosom, with a white bib apron. Her dark skin, a burnished walnut, was smooth, her eyes a lustrous deep brown.

"You're Lilah, aren't you? Please, call me Livvie. Everyone does."

"Of course, Miss Livvie. Mrs. Ellerbe said to look after you." She tied back the pale-yellow drapes and sunlight streamed into the room.

Through the sash windows I saw two white rocking chairs on the wide veranda and imagined myself sitting out-side in the shade of the overhang, cradling my napping baby. Beyond the front garden and driveway I glimpsed Orchard Street, sun-dappled by giant sycamore trees. I breathed deep-ly, smelling lavender-scented linens instead of Brígh's stale cigarette fumes. For the first time in months I knew how it felt to wake up after a restful sleep.

"Anything you need, miss?" Lilah shifted her weight, looking uncomfortable.

"Thank you, Lilah. Everything's fine. I think I'll just take a bath."

"You do that. I'll have some lunch for you later when you want it." She stooped to pick up the bed cover that had slipped to the floor.

"Your soup was wonderful. If there's any more of it left, I'd love some."

She darted a glance at me, then looked away again. "Sure thing, miss. I'll heat it up when you're ready."

"Thank you." I hesitated a moment, aware of Lilah's dis-comfort. "Excuse me, but I was wondering . . . did Mrs. Ellerbe tell you anything about me?"

"Only that she knows your mother and—" Lilah turned away, straightening a lace runner on the bureau that didn't need straightening. "I'm sorry about your trouble, Miss Livvie. I'm sure everything'll work out just fine, the good Lord willing. I should get back to work now. I'll take your tray out later."

So that was the way it was going to be.

She left and I put my tray aside, my toast half-eaten. I unpacked and took a bath, but decided not to go for a walk in the park. Why chance meeting a neighbor until I had my story down? I pulled a sweater on over my knit dress and sat in the back garden under the pecan tree. I breathed deeply, filling my lungs with sweet, earthy smells. Pale fingers of crocus and hyacinth poked out of the mulched beds under the casement windows. Clusters of daffodils were beginning to bloom in the sunlit ground surrounding a birdbath. Under the dove-gray canopy over the kitchen windows, I spotted a bird's nest and the flicker of a bobbing head.

I sighed, grateful to be in the Ellerbe backyard rather than walking around the chill, windswept streets of New York. By the time I returned with my baby, the last blasts of winter would be over. A bubble of anticipation swelled inside me at the thought of starting fresh, with a new life to care for and nurture.

I settled back and closed my eyes, thinking over items I'd need for the baby, whittling the list down to bare essentials necessary for the short time I would be here. My mind turned, as it often did, to baby names. Robert was the obvious choice topping my list, but it could also be a middle name, since I was also partial to Andrew. If I had a girl, I'd give her my grandmother's name, Emma. I dozed off, my hands on my belly, dreaming again of Robert, seeing him on my doorstep.

I awoke to a chill breeze, with low clouds darkening the skies. I went back inside and found Lilah in the kitchen, the radio tuned to a soul station. She was folding towels while crooning backup to Aretha Franklin's "Say a Little Prayer," her voice rising on "forever, forever." She stopped singing as soon as she saw me and reached over the ironing board to turn off the music.

"No, leave it on. I like it." I hummed along even as she turned the volume down.

"That's okay, Miss Livvie. What can I do for you?"

"I was just wondering if there was a phone book handy. I'd like to take a look at the yellow pages."

"Sure, there's one on the shelf under the telephone table. I'll get it. Mrs. Ellerbe won't mind if you want to call someone."

"I just wanted to look up some local stores, places that sell baby clothes and basinets. Things like that."

"There's a good-sized department store in town has baby things." Lilah moved the clothes basket aside and went into the hallway. "But there's some fancy shops, too. Depends on what you want." She returned with a phone book and handed it to me.

"Thank you." I opened the book on the counter and scanned the listings. "Have you worked for Mrs. Ellerbe long?"

"Not more'n a year. My aunt did for her before that, but took sick."

"But you've known the family pretty well over the years, I imagine." When she didn't answer, I sensed her wariness. "I mean, through your aunt, of course."

"We're all local folk, miss." She took a moment, choosing her words while she unwound the cord on the iron and plugged it in. "I can't really say, if you know what I mean. Some folk don't like being talked about. I have to abide by that."

I nodded. "Yes, of course. I was just making conversation. None of us much like being talked about."

I went back to checking the listings, silence growing between us. The radio was still turned low, but I hummed along to Diana Ross on "I'm Gonna Make You Love Me." Lilah remained silent. I could feel her eyes on me now and then as she looked up from her ironing.

She struck me as someone naturally outgoing. I sensed she'd been warned to mind her tongue around me. Dorah probably anticipated I'd take the opportunity alone with Lilah to pump her for information, which is precisely what I'd had in mind.

I held up a notepad I'd taken from a tray on the counter. "Would it be okay for me to use this?"

"Sure, that's what it's for." She snapped a pillowcase straight, smoothed it out on the ironing board and sprayed it with water. "You want me to warm up soup pretty soon?"

"Yes, thank you. I'm getting hungry."

While Lilah heated soup and continued ironing, I jotted down the items I needed and the addresses of a few shops. By the time I finished, Lilah was carrying a tray with my lunch to the breakfast nook. I followed her.

"Smells delicious!"

"Good. Now take your time and leave everything. I'll clear later."

"By the way, are any of these stores within walking distance?" I handed her my lists. "I only need a few things. I thought I might take a look in some of the shops tomorrow."

She looked down the list, then shook her head. "These are all a fair distance, more'n you could walk. A taxi'd get you there, but I'm sure Mrs. Ellerbe will take you herself."

"Of course, but I didn't want to bother her."

She nodded and handed back the list. "It hasn't been a good time for her, but she's holding up. Maybe having you here will do her some good."

"I hope so. She's being very kind to me." I folded the list and tucked it into my pocket. "I was very sorry to hear about her nephew. Maybe she'll have some good news soon."

"We're all hoping for that, but nothing yet. It's such a shame, a good man like that. Everyone liked him."

"You must have known him, of course, working for Mrs. Ellerbe."

"Practically all my life. My aunt raised me, so she'd bring me with her sometimes."

"Really? You knew Robert well, then?"

"Rob. That's what kids called him back then." She smiled and nodded again. "He's only a year older than me."

"I knew him, too," I said quietly. "In New York."

"I figured that, but wasn't sure I should say anything. I'm really sorry for what's happened."

"Me, too." Tears came. I let them stream. "Me, too."

"We just have to keep praying." Lilah's cheeks were wet. "I'm going to pray for you, miss. I'm so very sorry for your pain."

Tears boiled up, spilling down my face. "He just . . . has to come back."

"He will. I'm sure of it." She pressed my head against her ample belly, stroking my hair. "You let it out now. I could see it coming on you, girl. I know it hurts." She mopped my face gently with her apron. "There, there. You don't want to hold that in. Can't do you or your baby any good."

My tears subsided. Lilah handed me a tissue from her pocket. I blew my nose. She patted my shoulder and picked up the bowl.

"You settle yourself, now. I'm gonna heat this up for you."

I slumped back in the chair, drained. How long since I'd let myself give in to the terrible loneliness that had become such a part of my life?

I hadn't really been able to confide my feelings to Brígh, who masked her own in boozy wit and bravado. Not in Patty, either. She had learned Stuart was married and had her own share of misery. Nor had I reached out to my family, who would have urged me to return home, a prospect I couldn't bear to consider. Certainly not Mrs. Ellerbe, for every reason I could think of. Lilah knew I needed to let go and it was comfort enough.

Within minutes she was back with hot soup and buttered bread. "You eat this now and let me know when you're finished. I've got something I want to show you before it gets too late in the day."

Chapter 22

I DRAINED THE LAST OF THE WINE from the water glass and walked back into the kitchen. I wasn't hungry, but other than salted nuts and Cheez-Its, I hadn't eaten anything since breakfast. I opened the cupboard and looked at the can of tomato soup on the shelf, reminded of Lilah's homemade vegetable soups and her slightly sweet brown bread flavored with cardamom and molasses. I could almost taste it. Where was she now?

I wondered what Lilah would have made of all the changes in the Ellerbe house. Had she stopped working here when Dorah passed away? She was probably retired, but I'd ask Robbie if he kept in touch with her. If there was a single person in Weymouth that I'd like to see, it would be Lilah. I owed her such a lot.

I had no appetite for canned soup and closed the cabinet door. It was getting late, but I wasn't tired, either. I slid my cell phone out of my pocket and flipped it open to check messages. The nursing staff had promised to get in touch if there was anything to report. I opened the fridge to refill my glass, then took the bottle with me back into the living room. I sipped wine, looking around at the sparsely furnished room. Dorah had made it clear she didn't want me to set foot in her house again. Was Robbie, pleading storm damage, honoring a long-ago promise made to his aunt?

I went into the hallway, my mind roiling with sour memories. Accepting Dorah's invitation all those years ago was a mistake that still haunted me. I hoped being back in the Ellerbe house as Robert's guest would help me come to terms with what happened. But skulking around, an intruder with no right to be here, only reinforced bad memories. I stood at the foot of the wide staircase that curved to the second floor, steeling myself to face the past.

With an elbow on the mahogany bannister to steady myself, I clutched the glass in one hand, the half-empty bottle in the other, and slowly began climbing the stairs. Stripped of the pale celery-green carpet I remembered, each footfall on the bare treads landed with a loud, hollow thud.

Two of the upstairs bedrooms had long ago been converted into a master suite with separate dressing rooms and baths. Uncle Lloyd's quarters had a library and a daybed. When he became an invalid, he spent most of his time there. Upon his death, that suite had become Dorah's day room, with a writing desk and a chaise where she napped in the afternoons following her tea.

The door to the day room was just off the landing at the top of the stairs. I turned the knob, surprised to find the door locked. I jiggled it, then stepped back, a shiver running up my neck.

Had my noisy climb up the stairs and my hand rattling the doorknob awakened anyone? Was someone else staying here, someone Robert didn't want me to know about? I shrank back toward the stairs, listening closely, my hand tightening around my glass of wine. Aside from my own rapid breaths, I heard only silence.

I waited a moment longer, looking down the darkened hallway toward Dorah's bedroom. The door was closed. Locked, too? I dared myself to find out. With a stride that belied my dread, I walked the length of the hall and turned the knob. The door swung open. I entered, boldly flicking a light switch that turned on a bedside lamp.

There was no need to imagine Aunt Dorah's boudoir as it was. The décor had been left essentially untouched, including cabbage-rose wallpaper and a Victorian hand-painted bamboo fire screen in the narrow fireplace. Botanical prints hung on the walls. The familiar white chenille bedspread she referred to as a "counterpane" covered her mahogany bedstead. The small step stool she used to climb into bed was positioned on the right side, as always. The etched crystal water glass, in which she deposited her dentures at night, was still on the bedside table. Empty, one hoped, although I lacked the will to see for myself.

Everything was in its place, but a good deal more had been crammed into every available space. Her bedroom had become a repository for all that had been stripped from the rooms below, including furniture, rugs, mirrors, pictures and knickknacks. The bed was heaped with mounds of silk and taffeta drapes, gauzy curtains and chintz slipcovers. In one corner, dust sheets covered the dining table and mahogany cabinets that were wedged together, the narrow spaces between stuffed with cushions and pillows. Chairs were piled one atop another. Packing boxes stacked tightly against the walls likely contained china, silver, porcelain and crystal.

I laughed, gaping at the disorderly clutter all around me

that Dorah would never have tolerated. I was at once reminded of the neat storeroom Lilah had shown me decades earlier
on my first day in the house.

After clearing away my lunch that first day, she'd said,
"There's some things I can show you back behind the kitchen,
if you'd like. But you can't tell Mrs. Ellerbe, okay? You promise?"

"Of course. I won't say a word."

I followed Lilah through the kitchen and pantry to the
laundry room. She slid open a pocket door next to the washing machine and switched on a light. "It's where Mrs. Ellerbe
stores the Christmas decorations and all the extra plates and
glasses she uses for bridge parties."

Lilah stepped aside and I looked around. It was a large
room, with metal shelving along one wall, everything tightly
packed and orderly. Cartons and plastic bins, all neatly labeled, were stacked against another wall. Two sturdy hanging
racks held garment bags. In the far corner, Lilah pulled a cloth
sheet off a disassembled baby crib. Its mattress, wrapped in
plastic, leaned against the railings, which were tied together
with twine.

"Mrs. Ellerbe probably has in mind for you to use this,
but you can't tell on me. You let her bring it up. Promise?"

"I'll act surprised, I promise." I ran my hand along the
lacquered vanilla railings. "It's lovely! I'm so glad she kept it."

"Nothing gets thrown away around here, I can tell you.
She had me go through everything last Christmas to make
sure nothing was getting mildewed. Look at this."

Lilah tugged a sheet off a white wicker bassinet on a

stand with wheels. She ran a corner of her apron along the rim and handles. "See that? Not even dusty. I could have this set up in your room as soon as Mrs. Ellerbe gives the word."

I gaped at the trove she'd uncovered. Packed inside the bassinet was an assortment of folded blankets, rattles and small stuffed toys, including a scruffy brown teddy bear missing a black button eye. I picked up the stuffed bear and danced it along the railings of the crib. Little Robbie's teddy bear, with the nap worn off its ears and belly, was a treasure I wanted for our own child.

"And this, too." Lilah pried the lid off a plastic bin filled with baby clothes neatly folded with packets of sachet. "Everything you could need is in there, all Rob's baby things." She handed me an embroidered bib and a tiny woolen sweater with matching cap.

I pressed the soft sweater to my cheek, smelling the fresh scent of lavender. "No wonder Dorah told me not to bring anything with me. She said I should leave it all to her."

"See that?" Lilah beamed. "As soon as I looked at that list you made, I thought of everything stored in here. It wouldn't make any kind of sense to go buying new. Mrs. Ellerbe wouldn't go for that. So don't you go off on your own and hurt her feelings."

"No, of course not. Besides, she'd want Robbie's baby to ... I mean, she'd ..." I stammered to a stop, my hand covering my mouth. I looked at Lilah, her eyes wide. "Sorry, I didn't mean to say that."

"Don't you fret none, you hear?" she whispered. "I figured that was the case, so no harm done."

"Even so, Mrs. Ellerbe would not be happy if she knew I'd let on about Robbie. She wants it kept secret."

"Then we leave it like that. It wouldn't do me any good for her to know, either." She leaned toward me, still speaking in a whisper. "It's best you know, Mrs. Ellerbe has her ways. You don't ever want to cross her."

"No, of course not. We won't say a word about this." I looked around at the open containers. "Maybe I shouldn't be in here."

"It's fine, Miss Livvie. You take a look around and make sure everything's back in place when you finish. I'll check it myself when you're done. Tea's at four fifteen, then supper's at seven o'clock. That's the way she likes it. I set everything out before I leave for the day."

"Thank you, Lilah. I'll put the covers back on everything."

"You feeling better now?"

I nodded. "Much better."

"Then you take heart, girl, and holler if you need me." She turned back toward the kitchen. "It's all going to be just fine."

Minutes later I heard the volume turned up on Motown sounds. But without Lilah in the room with me, I felt uneasy. I tucked the bib and sweater in the plastic container and put the teddy bear back in the bassinet, positioning it carefully. After re-covering the furniture with dust sheets, I left.

Lilah looked up from her ironing as I passed through the kitchen. "Already through in there?"

"All done. Thanks again, Lilah. I'm just going to lie down for a while."

"I'll let you know when it's time for tea. You get a good rest now."

I was napping when Dorah arrived home. I awoke to hear her talking with Lilah in the hallway, then someone coming up the stairs. Moments later, I heard a soft rap on my door.

"Miss Livvie? You awake?"

"Yes, come in."

Lilah opened the door a crack and looked in. "Just to let you know that Mrs. Ellerbe wants you to join her upstairs for tea."

"Thank you. I'll be up in a few minutes."

"That'd be good, Miss Livvie. I wouldn't keep her waiting," she whispered, closing the door with a soft click.

I rubbed my eyes and stretched, groggy from my long nap. I'd almost drifted off again when there was another knock on my door and I heard Lilah's muffled voice.

"Miss Livvie, you'd best come with me. I'm bringing the tray up now."

"Go on ahead. Please tell her I'm coming."

I hurriedly shook out my dress, brushed my teeth and ran a comb through my hair. With my awkward gait it took time to make my way up the stairs to Dorah's room. Through the open door, I could see her sitting, head down, sorting through mail in her lap. I knocked before entering.

"There you are," Dorah said, looking up, her voice cool. "Come in. I was afraid I'd have to ask Lilah to make a fresh pot of tea. If you're going to join me, do be on time."

"Yes, of course." I glanced at Lilah, who was at the open closet door, her back to me. She was hanging Dorah's suit jacket on a padded hanger.

"I'm so sorry. Lilah kindly woke me, but it took me a while to get ready."

"Well, you're here now. Do sit down."

While Dorah went back to sorting her mail, I eased myself carefully into the matching pink velvet-upholstered chair across from hers. She was wearing a loose floral-print cotton duster, buttoned up the front, the edge of her latex foundation garment peeking out below the hem. Her sheer hose, released from garters, had been rolled down into tight donuts around her primly crossed ankles. Little mounds of plump flesh rose like dough above black leather pumps. She was still wearing her earrings and double strand of pearls.

I shifted awkwardly in the low, antique chair, trying to stretch my knit dress to cover my knees. Lilah turned toward me. I caught her eye with a questioning look. She shook her head slightly and quickly looked away.

I glanced back at the silver service on the small round table. The tea was growing colder. Delicate crème-colored china cups and saucers with silver rims were set on the silver tray with a bowl of sugar cubes, a milk pitcher, strainer and tongs. Next to it was a dish with lemon slices and a small plate of brown bread rounds, spread with pimento paste and a slice of green olive. I was hungry and saw that the bread was already curling at the edges.

"I hope you had a nice rest," Dorah said, setting aside her mail.

"Oh, yes. Thank you."

She leaned toward the silver service, placing spoons on the saucers. "Sugar?"

"No, thank you. Just plain, no milk."

"Lemon?"

"Yes, thank you.

She poured tea, dropped a lemon slice into my cup and handed it to me. "If it's too strong, there's hot water. And do try a savory, if you like pimento."

"Thank you. The tea is lovely."

"Earl Grey, of course." She turned to Lilah. "I see there's

no shortbread on the tray. If we're out, put it on my shopping list, please. Are we having the baked pork chops for dinner?"

"Yes, ma'am. It's all in the oven. I'll have applesauce and string beans on the stove, ready to heat up."

"Good. You can leave us now, if you're finished there."

"Thank you, ma'am." Lilah shut the closet door and hurried out of the room without looking at me.

Dorah waited until Lilah had closed the door behind her. "Honestly, that woman manages to put more syllables in the word 'beans' than one would think possible." She smiled. "But she's a good soul. You know that she and Robbie played here together as children, don't you?"

"Really?"

She laughed. "Don't look so surprised. I'm sure Lilah told you, although I don't think the two ever became close friends. You got along all right with her?"

"Yes, fine. She heated up the soup for my lunch. It was delicious."

"Excellent. What did you do with yourself all day? I hope you got enough rest."

"Yes, I spent most of my time in the back garden. It's beautiful out there."

"Thank you, my dear. It's featured on the Garden Club tour each spring. We raise a good amount of money to keep Weymouth Park up."

I nodded, unaccountably tongue-tied. What could I talk about? The bird's nest? Daffodils sprouting around the fountain? *What?* She smiled and lifted the teapot, gesturing to my cup. I nodded again, my teacup clattering in the saucer. I held it steady with two hands as she poured, nervous I'd spill tea on the velvet chair.

"Did you find anything to read? The new Book-of-the-Month Club selections are on the side table in the foyer."

"Really? I'll have a look tomorrow."

She set the teapot back on the tray and reached into the pocket of her duster. "I happened to find this on the floor in the breakfast nook when I came in."

With her gaze fixed on me, she held the notepaper with my list of baby things pinched between her thumb and forefinger. "Lilah says it's yours."

"I must've dropped it." Tea sloshed from my cup into the saucer as I set it down. "I was looking in the yellow pages for baby stores that I thought I'd go to later this week."

"Very enterprising," she said quietly, looking over the list. "All very good, my dear, but I believe I told you I'd take care of everything." She folded the notepaper and laid it on the table.

"I know, but I didn't want to leave it to the last minute."

"Are you feeling anxious?" She smiled and patted my knee. "Not that it would surprise me. It must be very hard being alone at a time like this. That's why I invited you here."

"I know. I appreciate it. But I don't want to be a burden. I have some money saved up. I can buy things, unless . . . unless you already have things I can use. I mean—" The words were already out of my mouth. I couldn't take them back. *Why did I say that?*

"Have *things*?" Dorah looked puzzled, but her tone was sharp. "What things would I have?"

"I don't know, things." I folded my hands to stop them trembling. "You know, sometimes people just keep . . . things."

"You mean, baby things? Oh, my goodness, no. Why would I have that?"

I shrugged, laughing nervously. "I don't know, except my mother kept stuff—"

"Understandable. But in my case, no." She took a sip of tea and set down her cup. "Let's leave that for a moment. I spoke with Dr. Brennan today and set up an appointment for you at his clinic tomorrow afternoon. Two o'clock. Is that good with you?"

"Of course, thank you."

"He's a dear man. Retiring soon, but we all think the world of him."

"That's great. I hope you don't mind my asking, but..." I hesitated, trying to find the right words to ask if she'd mentioned Robert to him.

"Are you concerned about medical expenses? I've made all the necessary arrangements with the hospital and Dr. Brennan. I'll be taking care of it all."

"What?" My mouth fell open. "You don't have to do that."

"Of course I do. Brígh said you had no medical insurance. Weren't you going to ask me about the doctor's fees?"

"Actually, I was wondering... have you told him everything about me?"

"Dr. Brennan knows what he needs to know. He's discreet, as one would expect him to be. He's going to deliver the baby. There's no need to go into anything else with him. The less said, the better. Do you understand?"

"Yes, fine. I understand."

"Good. I've arranged for a taxi service to pick you up at one thirty and take you back here again afterward. Did you remember to pack your medical records?"

"Yes, everything."

"Don't forget to bring them with you tomorrow." She

smiled and folded her napkin, laying it on the table. "I'm going to rest for a while. Dinner is at seven o'clock in the dining room. I always have a glass of sherry beforehand. I'll remind Lilah to set out tomato juice for you."

Chapter 23

I PERCHED ON THE ARM of Dorah's Victorian lady's parlor chair. Its fraternal twin, a slightly larger gentleman's parlor chair, was also upholstered in rose-pink velvet. The two pieces of furniture were arranged as I remembered decades ago, a round mahogany table positioned between them, where afternoon tea was served.

All that was missing was Aunt Dorah herself, but I felt her presence sitting across from me wearing her cotton duster, her hose rolled to her ankles, pouring tea. I remembered the curling rounds of brown bread spread with pink pimento paste and the smell of tepid, overly steeped Earl Grey. The strong tea, soured with lemon, had turned my stomach. My fingers shook, the cup jittering in the saucer when she showed me the list of baby things. I wondered if hearing the clatter of bone china, knowing she'd rattled me, had given Dorah satisfaction.

She was solicitous, sometimes even affectionate with me, but I was always on edge around her. I flustered easily, never feeling quick enough. Her bright small talk and cultured drawl were disarming, but her sudden turns of frostiness unnerved me.

Had I compromised Lilah, who must have been interrogated about me? What did it matter if I knew that she and Rob had played together as children? Or that I'd shown Lilah the list of baby supplies and asked about shops? Dorah knew how to throw me off guard, her canniness nearly telepathic and very unsettling.

I filled the tumbler with rosé and set the bottle where there'd once been a tea tray. Lifting my glass, I toasted Dorah's spectral being, certain she was somehow present.

"Skoal! Prost! Cheers, you old bag."

I lost my balance and slid off the arm of the chair into the seat, sloshing wine on the pink velvet. I was borderline drunk and needed something to eat. I stared dizzily at the table, wishing I'd see a plate of curling brown bread with pimento paste appear. I refocused my eyes, wishing instead that I'd brought the rest of the can of nuts upstairs. The gnaw in my stomach told me I required food, not more wine. Heating tomato soup was not appealing.

I took a sip of wine, swirling it in my mouth, feeling a chill creep across my shoulders. If Dorah did haunt the Ellerbe house, I thought woozily, what form would she take? She would not be a benign ghost. There was no predicting how she might choose to terrorize, but it would probably begin with an act of kindness.

In my case, she'd begun by treating me to a fancy lunch, but making me promise not to tell Robert we'd met—then undermining me by telling him herself. Brígh had alluded to his previous romances and warned me that he was "single, *very* single." It occurred to me Dorah's meddling could be a reason. Did she vet all of Robert's girlfriends and intimidate them with honey-laced scrutiny? Or had she sensed I posed a particular threat? If so, I'd managed to fulfill her fears.

She'd used my neediness to her advantage, but had I really been taken in by her show of concern? I'd jumped at her generous invitation because it was expedient, an easy, cheap way out of the mess I was in. All that was relevant to me at the time was food, shelter and a good night's sleep. I was in survival mode, focused single-mindedly on giving birth—with Dorah picking up the tab.

If I'd given thought to anything when I left her boudoir after tea that first afternoon, it was the glass of tomato juice Lilah would set out for me instead of a glass of wine I suddenly craved. I'd given up alcohol for the duration. Pushing baby clothes and Dr. Brennan out of my mind, I concentrated on the next big event in my life—dinner alone with Dorah. I was too shaken to think about anything beyond pork chops and string beans.

With one hand across my bulging belly, I gripped the banister and carefully made my way back down the stairs. I checked out the monthly reading selections on the side table. The books included *Nicholas and Alexandra*, *The Electric Kool-Aid Acid Test* and *Rosemary's Baby*, all in hardback, the covers pristine. The Tom Wolfe book, which I'd already read, hardly seemed like the sort of reading I'd find on Dorah's nightstand, but perhaps it came automatically with her monthly subscription. I'd also read *Rosemary's Baby*, thanks to Brígh's advance review copy. All things considered, the book struck me as a poor choice to read now.

I picked up *Nicholas and Alexandra*, felt its heft, and figured it would see me through my delivery. I put the book on my nightstand and climbed into bed for a nap until it was time to change into my other knit dress, freshly laundered by

Lilah. I didn't want to think about my list of baby things that Dorah had kept. Had I also accidentally dropped my list of baby names?

Not wanting to be tardy again, I arrived in the kitchen shortly before seven o'clock. Dorah was standing at the stove, an apron over her housecoat, poking a fork into a casserole dish containing pork chops smothered in onions. The smell alone made my mouth water.

"Anything I can do to help?"

I peered into a saucepan bubbling with string beans in a shade of green that told me they were more than well cooked.

Dorah turned to me, a smile lighting up her face. "Nothing at all, my dear. I'll add some brown sugar and bourbon to the beans and let them simmer a while till they're done."

She thrust a fork into a pork chop. "This is my favorite dish. I taught Lilah to make it. The secret is Campbell's mushroom soup and a can of French's French Fried Onions. Lloyd loved it." She opened the oven and slid the casserole onto the middle rack. "We'll just keep it warm while we have our aperitifs."

I followed her into the living room, carrying my small glass of tomato juice. We sat in front of the fireplace, sipping our drinks and nibbling mixed nuts from a bowl on the low coffee table. The tension I'd felt during tea slipped away. I listened to Dorah chat gaily about the town of Weymouth, meeting Lloyd and renovating the house she'd persuaded him to buy.

"It almost broke us during the Depression, but in time became our single best investment." She laughed, adding, "Just as I knew it would be." She winked. "If you should ever happen to lock yourself out when Lilah's not here, there's a key on the ledge above the second window on the veranda. I've done it myself more than once."

She didn't talk about Robert. I took her lead and didn't mention him, either. It occurred to me that dining in the Ellerbe house was not unlike dinner with Brígh in New York, except that Brígh's cocktail hour extended well into the evening, punctuated with a brief bite of whatever I'd cooked for our supper. Dorah enjoyed her claret and poured liberally from a decanter; she, like Brígh, enjoyed companionship with a meal.

"Without you here, I'd be stuck eating leftovers for two days," she confided, making a face. "It's so nice having someone to talk with. After all these years, I still miss Lloyd, especially at dinnertime."

She looked away, pensive for a moment. It struck me how lonely she must be living on her own in this big house. The conversation could so easily have turned to Robert. Missing him, wanting him back safely, was constantly on my mind and had to be in her thoughts, too. I went to bed that night feeling relief, hoping the convivial evening I'd spent with Dorah marked a turning point in our relationship. She was family, my baby's grandaunt, and deserved a place in our lives.

I slept late again. Dorah had left for the hospital long before I was out of bed. Lilah was warm and friendly, but neither of us mentioned the storeroom. The closest I came to referencing anything of the previous afternoon was to promise not to be late for tea again. She smiled and rolled her eyes.

The morning passed slowly. I was keyed up, strolling in circles around the garden, unable to concentrate on reading a book. I'd been to a doctor only once since my New York hospital stay, a referral Brígh had arranged through her GP. With a blithe wave of her hand, she'd tried to allay my anxiety by saying, "Relax, babies are born in rice paddies and the back of taxis without harm," which afforded little comfort.

Well before one o'clock, I stood in the foyer, clutching the folder containing my medical records, waiting for the taxi to arrive. I was anxious to meet the doctor who would deliver my baby and assure me all was well.

The clinic, a cozy single-story brick building, was located in downtown Weymouth. I arrived early for my appointment, which was the first one scheduled after lunch. Within minutes of completing a lengthy new-patient form, a middle-aged nurse named Wanda led me to an examining room.

I changed into a gown. Wanda took care of preliminaries, recording my weight, temperature and blood pressure on a chart. I waited only minutes before Dr. Brennan rapped on the door. He breezed in wearing a crisp white coat and a genial manner. Despite white hair and a slight stoop in his shoulders, he hardly looked like a man on the verge of retiring. He was short and compact, with crinkling eyes and a tan. I guessed golf was his sport.

"Well, well, good afternoon," he said, gently shutting the door. He leaned against it a moment, his warm brown eyes taking me in. "It's nice to meet you, Miss Hammond. Welcome to Weymouth. You're a long way from home, aren't you?"

I nodded, tugging the cotton wrapper closer around me, and blinked back unexpected tears. "New York," I whispered, my voice faltering.

"There, there," he said soothingly. He set the clipboard with my patient forms on a counter and folded his arms. "You're going to be fine, trust me. Now, why don't we start with you telling me a little about yourself."

"I'm, ah ... I'm ..." I gave it up and let the tears stream. "I'm going to have a baby," I managed, gulping breath.

He smiled. "I think by now we know that, don't we? Well, you've come to the right place." He handed me a tissue and patted my shoulder. "You're not the first young lady to tell me that, you know. Although, occasionally, I get to tell them first."

"I'm sure." I laughed in spite of the tears that just kept coming. "I'm sorry.

Feeling a bit nervous. I didn't mean to break down like this."

"You're not the first to do that, either. This is a stressful time under any circumstance." He handed me another tissue and pulled up a stool to sit down. "But on top of everything, I realize you have additional concerns. This has to be very hard on you."

I nodded. "It's just ... waiting. Not knowing what's in store." A fresh flood of tears splashed down my cheeks. "I mean, it's not just the baby."

"I understand," he said quietly, setting the box of tissues in my lap. "A young woman in your position, on her own, isn't going to have an easy time of it. We're going to do our best to make you comfortable, I assure you."

"Thank you," I whispered, hearing his words as though on time delay, trying to match the sounds with the kind eyes that held mine. "Then you know all about me? Mrs. Ellerbe told you everything?"

"I believe so, yes." He nodded, his gaze drifting off for a moment. "Mrs. Ellerbe's husband and I were colleagues, so she spoke freely to me. As I'm sure you're aware, this has been a very difficult time for her. But despite the strain she's under, she's very sensitive to your situation. She wants to help you all she can. I believe that's why she brought you to Weymouth, to spare you the discomfort of having your baby elsewhere."

"Did she happen to mention her friend in Minnesota?"

"Yes, as a matter of fact. Your mother is an old college friend of hers. Is that right?"

I took a deep breath. "Is that everything she told you?"

He hesitated and lowered his voice to a near whisper. "I believe she and your mother have close ties, so it was only natural she'd reach out to her. You've got nothing to worry about. I promise, nobody back home will ever have to know." He set aside the clipboard. "Now, let's take a look here, shall we?"

As I suspected, Dorah had told Dr. Brennan no more than she'd imparted to her housekeeper. After a physical exam, I dressed and a nurse showed me to his office. When I joined him, he was looking over the medical records I'd brought from the hospital in New York.

"You could so easily have miscarried," he said, setting the report aside. "But you're young and healthy. Everything looks fine now. You should have a good delivery. Nothing at all to worry about."

His reassurance was comforting and I listened attentively to what he told me to expect in the coming weeks. "My nurse will give you some printed materials to take home with you. Mrs. Ellerbe has made all the arrangements at the hospital, but please call our office with any questions you might have." He smiled. "And please don't hesitate to ask anything."

"Actually, I do have a question. I was wondering how long after the birth before I'll be able to go back to New York with my baby?"

"Really?" He looked at me questioningly, clearly taken aback. "Forgive me, but I understood that you would be putting the baby up for adoption. That's not the case?"

"Adoption? No, of course not. Why would you think that?"

"I'm sorry, my dear. Mrs. Ellerbe indicated it was your desire to place the baby."

"Well, she's mistaken. I never said any such thing, so I don't know why she told you that. I'm keeping my baby. I'll make that clear to Mrs. Ellerbe when I see her." Trying to control my anger, I pushed my chair back to leave. "Thank you, Dr. Brennan."

"Oh, dear, I'm very sorry about the misunderstanding. Won't you please sit down? I can see you're upset. I don't want you to leave here like that."

"For God's sake, why wouldn't I be upset?" I remained standing, my voice rising. "I don't know where she got the idea, but it's the last thing I would do."

"Please, Miss Hammond, sit down. I'm sure you've thought this through. It's your decision, of course, but let's just take some time to talk things over."

"There's nothing to discuss. And, for the record, Dorah Ellerbe has never even met my mother. It's just a story."

"I see." He sat back in his chair, his hands steepled under his chin. "I promise, it's not my intention to change your mind."

I sat down, breathing hard, my hands across my belly. "Then you should also know that this is Robert Yardley's baby. Did she tell you that?"

There was a flicker in his eyes, but his voice remained calm. "She did not, but I may have guessed. I've known the

Ellerbe family a very long time. I was a young doctor, new to this practice, when Dr. Ellerbe arranged for me to deliver Robert. I brought him into this world."

"You did?" I sank back, shaking my head. "If that's the case, I really don't understand why she wouldn't tell you I'm carrying his baby."

"I can't answer for Mrs. Ellerbe. I'm sure she has your best interests in mind. Perhaps she assumed that under the circumstances it would be better for you to place the baby."

"Because we weren't married? Because he might be— might never come back?"

"It's certainly a consideration. It won't be easy on your own. You're young. You have your whole life ahead of you, my dear. That's something to think about."

"I've thought about it. You won't change my mind, Dr. Brennan, whether you meant to or not." I stood up. "I'm keeping Robbie's baby."

I walked out of his office and past the receptionist, my mind reeling. *What was Dorah thinking? Why didn't she mention adoption to me?* The nurse intercepted me on my way out the door.

"We've called the taxi service," Wanda said, handing me a manila envelope. "Here are the materials Dr. Brennan wanted you to have. Wouldn't you prefer to sit in the waiting room? We'll let you know as soon as the taxi gets here."

"Thank you, but I'll wait outside."

"You're all right, aren't you? You look a bit flushed. Would you like some water?"

"I'm fine, thank you. I just need fresh air."

She pulled the door open and held it for me while I stepped out onto the sidewalk. Feeling shaky, I stood in the shade of the awning over Woody's pharmacy, hoping the taxi would show up soon. *Dorah can't just take my baby from me, can she?* I needed to talk with Brígh.

I arrived back at the Ellerbe house too late to chance a collect call to Brígh in her New York office. I did not want to be in the middle of a telephone conversation with her when Dorah arrived home.

Lilah greeted me at the door. "How'd it go, Miss Livvie?"

"Fine, I'm good. Just tired. I'm going to lie down for a while."

"You sure you're okay? Mrs. Ellerbe called to see if you were back yet. She's going to leave work early and hopes you'll be up for tea."

"Did she say anything else?"

Lilah shook her head. I suspected she was holding something back. "No, you go ahead and rest. I'll let you know when to go upstairs."

I sat up in the canopy bed, my swollen feet and ankles elevated on a pillow, my eyes on the sash window and the front driveway. I was wound up, my mind racing as I refined exchanges I imagined having with Dorah. I didn't need to speak with Brígh. I could stand up to Dorah without coaching.

I watched Dorah's Buick pull into the driveway. The car door opened. She swung her legs out, knees together, and tugged the skirt of her tweed suit. She looked grim, her mouth tight. She slammed the door closed and headed toward the back kitchen entrance. I tensed, hearing her footsteps in the hallway, wondering if she would knock on my door. I held my breath until I heard her climb the stairs.

I got up, washed my face and put on shoes. Then waited. A good fifteen minutes passed before Lilah tapped on my door. She opened it only a crack. "You go on up now. She's expecting you."

I mounted the stairs slowly, stopping on the landing to catch my breath and glance down the hallway. Dorah was sitting in her parlor chair looking at me, hands folded in her lap. She was wearing one of her flower-print dusters with her reading spectacles hanging on a chain around her neck. Her eyes didn't waver as she watched me move awkwardly down the hallway, my fingers sliding along the wall for balance. I reached the doorway and stopped, my heart racing.

"Come in, Olivia."

"Sorry if I kept you waiting again," I managed, my voice breathy.

"Not at all. Please, sit down."

I let go of the doorframe and concentrated on moving toward the other parlor chair without knocking into the table. I sank down and gripped the arms, feeling lightheaded.

"Are you all right?"

I nodded, not trusting myself to speak until I regained my breath.

"Some tea, perhaps?" She set the strainer in a cup and began to pour. "I'm sure you're not surprised to hear I had a rather disturbing call from Tom Brennan this afternoon. I'm disappointed in you, Olivia. This is very unsettling."

"I'm sorry you feel that way, but there's something I need to talk to you about."

"Not until I'm finished, please," she snapped, holding the teapot poised over the tray. Regaining her composure, she poured the second cup. "I thought we had an understanding. I've opened my home to you and shown you kindness and generosity. In return, I've asked nothing more of you than to show respect. I'm not sure why you deviated from that with Dr. Brennan, but it's put me in a humiliating position. I don't appreciate being made to look like a liar—"

"Then you shouldn't have expected me to lie to him!"

"Stop! I haven't finished."

"You don't know my mother. And my baby is not going to be adopted."

"Listen to me!" Tea splashed from the pot as she forcefully set it down. "Of course the baby will be adopted, Olivia. There's really no other option for you. Surely you wouldn't want the child to grow up with the stigma of having been born out of wedlock."

"But it's Robert's!" I sputtered, gaping at her.

She gave me a fierce look, tears springing to her eyes. "Do you think I've forgotten that? But you're not married and he's—I can't even bear to think what's happened to him." She brushed away tears, her face furious. "You've no right to pretend he wanted you to have a baby. If he did, he would have married you. You weren't even engaged."

"He didn't know I was pregnant. If he knew . . . if I'd had a chance to tell him, it would have been different."

She glared at me. "You think so? What a fool you are. He'd already moved on. Telling him you're pregnant wouldn't have changed a thing."

"You don't know that. You're not being fair to Robert . . . or me."

"You think you're the first woman to pull this stunt to get a man to marry her? Well, it doesn't work that way. Believe me, if you trap 'em, they'll just feel caged and fight like raccoons to get out. Robert didn't want any part of you. That's why he left you."

"That's not what happened!"

"Oh, but I think it is." She took a sip of tea, eyeing me cynically. "Did he stay in touch with you? Brígh Donnelly indicated he hadn't even written to you. What do you make of that?"

Her words stung, the barbed truth hitting home. I imagined the conversation between the two women, with Brígh acknowledging that I'd heard nothing from Robert since he'd left for Rome. My throat tightened in silence.

Dorah nodded. "You see? You can't contradict facts. Nor can you appeal to Robert now. But if he were here, even seeing you in this condition, he would hardly return to you. He'd do only what I'm doing on his behalf, making sure you have a safe delivery and paying the bills. Sorry to be so blunt, but you've left me no choice."

I stared at her as she bit into the piece of shortbread held delicately between thumb and index finger. Flicking a crumb from her housecoat, she said, "I hope that's settled matters, Olivia."

"No, it hasn't!" Enraged, I dug my fingers into the arms of the chair, shouting, "Robert's baby is mine to keep. You have nothing to say about it. There's nothing you can do!"

With cool disdain, she finished her shortbread and licked her thumb. "If you really cared about Robert, as you claim, you'd do what is best for his child—if indeed it's his. You think I want to rob you of your baby, but my concern is what's best for the child and you."

"Hardly. It's all about you and your reputation, not Robert's baby—and believe me, it's his!"

She sighed, shaking her head slowly. "I hoped I wouldn't have to do this." Dorah put her napkin on the table and stood. "Come with me. I have something to show you."

I got up and followed her down the hall to Uncle Lloyd's book-lined den at the top of the stairs. By the time I reached her, she was already sitting at her writing desk shuffling through envelopes.

"Robert kept in touch with me, as he always has. I saved his letters, including this one that he sent shortly before he left for Lisbon."

She opened one of the envelopes, took out a snapshot and handed it to me. It was a picture of Robert, his arm around a young woman with long, curly brown hair. She was leaning into him, her head pressed to his shoulder, her hand on his chest. Both of them were smiling.

I glanced at the picture and started to hand it back. "It means nothing. Is this what you wanted me to see?"

"Her name is Annalisa. Pretty, isn't she? I know he's my nephew and I love him dearly, but that's men for you. Always on to the next conquest."

I shook my head. "You're so mistaken if you think showing me this changes anything."

Dorah put the envelope back in a drawer and turned the key. "Keep that photo. I have no use for it. I don't know her, but he wrote fondly of her. I'm sure she's missing him, too. "

"Did you hear me? Whoever she is, it doesn't change a thing!"

"I'm going to rest for a while." She walked out of the room, her words trailing behind her. "Please wash up and be ready for dinner at seven o'clock."

Chapter 24

MY GLASS WAS DRAINED, the wine bottle empty on the table. I blinked and shook my head, my thoughts clouded by too much rosé on an empty stomach. I considered going downstairs to heat up tomato soup, but knew my legs would buckle. I got up from the parlor chair and moved unsteadily toward Dorah's bed, collapsing back on mounds of draperies and needlepoint pillows. Closing my eyes, I sank down into soft, puffy folds of silk and muslin, my head spinning.

I was drunk, lying on Dorah's bed, flat-out skunk drunk. I laughed, but it was a strangled sound that barely left my throat. The yellow silk draperies crinkled around my face as memories of that night spun dizzily in my mind.

I'd tried to erase the image imprinted in my memory of Robert and the girl with the curly, brown hair, her expression adoring. How much better off I would have been had I believed my own words back then: *Whoever she is, it doesn't change a thing!*

I passed out, tossing fitfully in a drugged sleep. My body entangled itself in the jumbled silk draperies heaped around me. I heard sounds but couldn't move. Light flashed, startling me, but I sank back into dark oblivion in an instant.

I awoke again, coughing as I struggled to move my head. My eyes felt gritty. I ran my tongue around the inside of my mouth, gagging on the metallic taste of soured wine. My head was stuffed, my lungs congested. I could barely breathe, yet I smelled the strong aroma of coffee.

Something bumped my arm. My eyes flew open. Terror-stricken, I cried out, my arms shooting up to fend off an attack.

A man hovering over me jumped back, his hand gripping his shoulder where I'd struck him. "I'm sorry, I didn't mean to startle you."

I jolted upright, the suddenness making me dizzy. Blacking out, I grabbed fistfuls of silk drapery to steady myself. The man's face was familiar. Not his voice. Who was he? *Am I hallucinating?*

"Please don't be frightened. I'm sorry. Are you okay?" He spoke gently.

I nodded, trying to focus. "I sat up too quickly."

"I thought you were awake." He stared at me in wonder, as though seeing an apparition. "I sure didn't mean to scare you. Rob shoulda told me you were here."

Rob?

I shifted, swaying as I reached for the bedpost. He caught my arm, steadying me, his touch electrifying.

"Easy, there. Easy. Need some help?"

"No, I'm fine." His face was inches from mine. His caramel-colored eyes were filled with concern.

He moved away, leaving behind a woodsy smell and the penetrating feel of his hand on my arm. "I came in earlier this morning and flicked the lights on. I was afraid I'd awakened you, but you were sound asleep. Coffee?"

I nodded, my heart racing. How long had I been sleeping? Was it morning? I glanced at the table between the two parlor chairs. A tray with a coffee pot and two mugs had replaced the empty bottle of rosé and my glass. How long had he been here watching me, passed out, entangled in silk draperies?

"Sugar? Milk?"

"Unadorned, as God intended. Thanks."

I watched him pour coffee into mugs, taking my first good look at him. He was tall and lean, wearing khakis and a gray cotton turtleneck that tucked up under a strong jaw. He handed me a steaming mug, his eyes meeting mine—those caramel-colored eyes. Eyes so like my own.

I thought I saw the glimmer of a warm smile on his clean-shaven face. I took him in all over again. He looked just like I should have expected. Only the thinning hair was a surprise.

"Thanks for the coffee," I said.

"Sounds like you've got a cold."

"Feathers." I pushed aside a needlepoint pillow and took a sip. "I'm allergic to them."

"Funny, so am I." He sat down on the edge of a parlor chair, his elbows on his knees, regarding me. "I guess we have that in common. I sneeze like crazy around feathers."

"What are you doing here?" I blurted. "I didn't expect this."

"I might say the same. You know who I am, right?"

"I think so. Robert took me to see his exhibit in Spaulding. I'm pretty sure you're the kid on the bike in one of the photos."

A boyish smile spread across his face. "Yup, that's me, just out of high school. His picture of you is terrific. I asked him for a print of it." His smile grew lopsided, uncertain. "I'm glad he took you there. It means he probably told you everything."

"He told me nothing. I'm only guessing."

I took another sip of coffee, hugging the mug in my hands to steady them. "I don't know what the other people decided to call you, but I would have named you Robert. Maybe Andrew."

"They named me Paul." He smiled. "Paul Westfeldt."

"Nice to meet you, Paul. Seems like you know who I am, too."

"Oh, yes." He drew in breath. "I've been wanting to meet you for a long time."

His voice was hoarse. I barely trusted mine. I nodded, unable to take my eyes off him.

"Yes. Me, too, but I would have planned things a bit differently. Maybe run a comb through my hair, or something." I smiled and saw his face relax. "Sorry, but I think I passed out. I don't usually do that, you know . . . well, you wouldn't know, but . . . anyway, too much wine on an empty stomach. Was that your bottle of rosé?"

He shook his head, his eyes locked on mine. "I think it was in the fridge a while."

"So, this is you after all these years. I've tried to picture what you'd look like. I have to say, I like what I see." I raised my hand, fluttering my fingers in front of my face. "No, stop. Please, hold the compliments. I'm not what you expected, I'm sure."

He laughed. "Close enough."

He blew out his cheeks, expelling breath in a loud whoosh. "I've seen you being interviewed and you're pretty funny. And I've read your books, of course. There's a stack of them in the day room."

"Wait, what?" A startling thought occurred to me. "I'm sorry, but do you live here? Is the Ellerbe house yours now?"

"No, I live up north of here. I drove down in my pickup when the hospital called. I was kinda surprised to see the SUV parked out front. I bought it a few weeks ago and Rob said I could leave it in his garage until I got back down here."

"It's yours? Sorry, but I've been driving it."

"That's okay. Better you than Rob." He shook his head. "It's killing him that he lost his license."

"It would," I agreed, the reason now clear why Robert was so amenable to letting me drive. "Seems you two have known each other quite a while. And pretty well, too."

"Pretty well, yeah." He nodded, his eyes still not leaving mine. "He's my father, you know."

"Yes." I smiled at the irony. "I seem to recall that was the case."

I hugged my arms across my chest. Random thoughts bumped into each other, struggling to sort themselves out while I looked at the man I'd given birth to and had never met. "Once again, please. You didn't know I was here? Robert didn't tell you?"

He shook his head. "No, I came down because the hospital called. I wasn't able to see Rob, but his doctor told me he was coming around. A bad scare, but he'll be fine." He took a sip of coffee and leaned back in the chair. "He's a little forgetful when it comes to medication. This isn't the first time this has happened, you know."

"No?" I replayed his words, as though hearing them from a distant planet, faint and garbled. "No, but then I wouldn't really know that, would I? There's a lot I don't know."

"That makes two of us. The nurse mentioned his wife was in yesterday." He looked down at his hands, examining his thumb as though he'd never seen it before. "It seems she was with him yesterday when he collapsed. I guess that might have been you?"

"Guess so."

I slid off the bed, feeling unwell. My feet touched the floor with a cascade of yellow silk drapery sliding down around me. "I should probably find a bathroom."

He stood quickly, reaching for my coffee mug. "Sure thing. It's right around the corner there. Want me to show you?"

"No, thanks. I remember where it is."

But he took my arm anyway, setting my mug on the table and guiding me around the bed. I prayed I wouldn't stumble. "Just through there. Light switch on your right."

"Thanks, I'm good." I was feeling lightheaded again, my heart racing. My blood pressure had to be stratospheric, but my pills were in my wheelie downstairs. The last thing I needed was to emulate Robbie and end up in the hospital. On the other hand, I could be hallucinating and I had no drugs for that.

"You okay?"

"Just a little stiff this morning."

"Well, take your time. I picked up groceries on the way, so I'll make us some breakfast."

I reached for the doorjamb and felt cool tile under my foot. I stepped inside and shut the door, locking it. Safe at last, I hung onto the towel rack and closed my eyes. When I opened them again, I would awaken from this crazy dream. The son I hadn't known would still be someone I didn't know. I would not have driven his SUV. He would not be cooking my breakfast.

I opened my eyes and looked into the mirror above the

sink knowing I was experiencing neither a dream nor a nightmare, but a reality more outlandish than anything I could have imagined. Still, what peculiar premonition spurred me to come back to Weymouth after all these years? Was it instinct, the sort mothers purportedly have—or a widow's conviction that my husband was pulling strings from the grave, manifesting wild phenomena far beyond strewing random pennies for me to find? *Jake, is this your doing? Have you set me up to find the boy I never told you about?*

The woman staring back at me in the mirror nodded agreement, certain I'd been spirited back to this house to fulfill a secret dream of one day reuniting with the child I'd lost. Had I somehow divined that Robert knew his son, while I did not? If ever there was a time when I needed to come to terms with what I must have somehow suspected, it would be now—albeit seriously hungover and in a sorry state to deal with it.

I looked derelict. Pale and puffy, my eyes bleary from too much wine and not enough sleep. I could rectify some of the damage with a hot shower, but what about everything else? Paul would have questions that were hard to answer.

Didn't he wonder why I'd given him up, only hours old, to strangers? Had anyone told him what really happened? Did he have any idea why I'd disappeared from his life? How could he not judge me, even knowing the truth?

My stomach erupted. I turned the faucets on in the sink, then the shower, before lurching sideways to lift the lid of the toilet seat.

I'd thrown up after my second tea with Dorah, too, heaving what little there was from my stomach before falling into bed, drained, my head bursting. After the harsh words we'd spoken, how could she expect I'd join her at the dinner table? Lilah offered to heat soup and bring it on a tray to my room.

I knew I couldn't keep food down. My stomach was in knots. *Annalisa?* She looked to be about my age, my height. Who was she? How did she know Robert? I should have dropped the picture on Dorah's desk and walked away instead of taking it with me to my room. *Annalisa? Who is she?*

I slept fitfully, unable to find a comfortable position for my unwieldy body or stop the terrible thoughts and images colliding in wakeful dreams. I dozed off as morning light glimmered through the pulled window shades.

I awoke hours later, hot and aching with a thundering headache. I managed to crawl out of bed and make my way slowly to the bathroom. Dizzy, my vision cloudy, I leaned over the toilet, retching.

Moments later, sinking to my knees, I felt Lilah's arms gripping my shoulders. Slowly she shifted me onto a throw rug, holding my head in her lap.

"You're feverish, Miss Livvie. We gotta call the doctor."

"Saw him only yesterday . . ." My breath was rapid, shallow, gasping for dry mouthfuls of air that parched my lips. "Thirsty."

"I'll get you some water. You just lie here."

Lilah eased my head onto a bathmat. I heard the tap run, then felt cool water squeezed from a cloth dribbling into my mouth. She brushed the damp cloth across my lips and folded it across my forehead.

"This isn't good, not at all." She sounded worried, her voice catching. "Don't move, now. I'm going to make a call."

She hurried out of the room, her footsteps jarring on the

tile. I dragged the cloth down my face and pressed it to my mouth, breathing in the moisture, trying to slow my breath. I rose up, steadying myself against the cold porcelain of the toilet, then convulsed and blacked out.

I have dim memories of being jostled on a stretcher and the sweet smell of Lilah's sweat, her breasts brushing across my arm with the sway of the rushing ambulance. Later, I heard voices, recognizing the clear, brisk sound of Dr. Brennan, but not comprehending his words. I heard Dorah, too, her voice mingling with Dr. Brennan's, both of them muffled and distant.

"Toxemia," I heard. "Get her into the operating room ..."

Moments later, Dr. Brennan spoke again, his voice firm. "She's had a seizure." Then, "No, we can't wait, Dorah. She's critical."

Dorah's face hovered above me, the scent of Worth heavy and close. Her voice was quiet, each word clear and insistent. "My dear child, Tom Brennan assures me he's doing his very best for you and the baby. You'll both be fine, but ... if anything goes wrong we have to be prepared. For your baby's sake, you need to sign this."

"What?" My body was leaden, my brain seizing in panic. "Why?"

"Listen to me. Just in case ... nothing more. Lilah's right here beside me. Lilah?"

"I'm here, Miss Livvie," she whispered, her voice weepy. "You're going to be fine, just fine."

"Lilah's here to help me with this. You understand, don't you? Just nod."

Alarmed, I turned my head, trying to find Lilah. "No, no, I don't understand what ... ?"

Dorah laid her hand on my cheek. "Just in case, that's all. Tell her that, Lilah."

"As she says, Miss Livvie. Just in case."

I looked up at Dorah, her face only inches from mine, feeling the pull of her fingers on my cheek.

"You see, Lilah? She nodded. She understands. Good girl. Now, you just relax. I'm going to hold your hand, help you sign this . . ."

Feeling woozy, my panic subsiding, I drifted off. Sometime later I awakened in a recovery room, with Lilah gently stroking my arm. I turned to her and she smoothed her hand across my forehead.

"You're coming around, Miss Livvie. You're going to be just fine now."

"The baby?" I whispered. "Tell me."

"Oh, real good. A baby boy, healthy as can be." She smiled and patted my arm. "You rest now. I'm going to stay right with you."

"But everything's all right? Mrs. Ellerbe . . ."

"Don't you worry now. You came through fine and so did your baby."

"So, nothing's happened? My baby's safe?"

"Safe as can be," Lilah said, her face solemn. "Mrs. Ellerbe can tell you. She's right down the hall."

A nurse came into the room, her face bright with a smile. "Hi, there. I'm Jeannie. How're you feeling? You had us a little worried, there."

"Thirsty—"

"Well, we can sure take care of that. Let me finish up here, won't take a minute."

"My baby?"

"A beautiful little punkin', ma'am, healthy as can be. Five pounds, ten ounces." She smiled broadly, then seemed to catch herself. "Even a mite early, he came through just fine. Nothing to worry about."

"I want to see him. He must be hungry."

"Oh, we're taking care of that. We just need you to rest. You've been through a lot, you know."

"Jeannie, I want my baby."

"Oh, dear, I'm not so sure about that." She glanced at Lilah, looking flustered. "I don't know what they told you, but..."

"Now!" I started to push myself up in bed. "I want to see my baby now."

"I'm going to get Dr. Brennan, ma'am. Right away." She hurried out of the room.

"My baby, that's all." I gripped the side table, woozy and nauseated, shakily screaming, "Now!"

"Miss Livvie, you gotta settle yourself. Miss Livvie!"

Sharp pain shot through my skull. My vision blurred and I convulsed again. I sank into darkness. That's all I remember, all I've ever been able to recall.

I stood under the shower in Dorah's bathroom, my face pressed against the water washing over my shoulders in soapy rivulets, trying not to think.

I reached for the plastic bottle of conditioner on the wire rack hanging below the showerhead. I missed it, my fingers closing around an empty space. I tried again, then once more before managing to clamp my fingers around the slippery bottle. Holding it in both hands, I concentrated on flipping the cap open with my thumb. I squeezed conditioner onto my palm, carefully setting the bottle back in the rack, relieved I hadn't dropped it.

All these years later, among the lingering complications of eclampsia is an occasional inability to judge spatial distance and chronic hypertension requiring medication. After giving birth, I remained in the hospital thirteen days, the more serious problems reversed with antiseizure medication. What could not be reversed, I was told, was the second document I signed three days after giving birth.

I was still recovering from multiple seizures, barely coherent. I opened my eyes to see the blurred faces of Dr. Brennan, Dorah and a portly man wearing a suit and rimless eyeglasses. I recall only flashes of what transpired that afternoon. Dr. Brennan spoke of "fostering care" and "the baby's needs." But I did not understand at the time the decision I was being asked to make. Nor do I remember signing a consent document. By the time I was discharged, my baby was living with strangers in another town.

"I know it's not what you wanted," Dr. Brennan said before releasing me from the hospital, "but your child will grow up in a very good home with parents who already love him as their own."

"I don't care. I'm well again and I want my baby. I'm not giving him up."

"Of course I understand your feelings, but that's not something I'm in a position to change. Besides, you still have a period of recovery ahead of you. I've told Mrs. Ellerbe she can pick you up later today. You can recuperate at home."

"So I've heard, but I won't stay in Weymouth any longer than I have to. How soon can I travel?"

"Whenever you feel up to it, but give yourself time to regain strength. I recommend regular checkups. You'll need to monitor your blood pressure and take medication." He also warned me that future pregnancies would be difficult, perhaps not advisable.

I used the pay phone at the hospital to make a collect call to Brígh in New York. "They've finally sprung me. I'm going to try to take the train back tomorrow. Can you put me up until I find a place?"

"Of course, can't wait to have you back. But hold off another couple days, if you can bear it. I'll book you a flight. I might even have a job lined up for you. How're you feeling?"

"All the better for hearing your voice." I sighed, not wanting to cry, which was all I'd been doing for days.

"Hang in there, gal. We'll get you home. I'll let you when I've got your flight booked."

"Thanks, Brígh. I just need to get out of here and back to civilization."

"Listen, I know what you're going through hurts like hell, but we'll have you back on your feet in no time. See you soon."

The tears came anyway. Would I never stop crying? An orderly wheeled me to the hospital entrance where Dorah would pick me up. I mopped my eyes, not wanting her to see a tear-stained face.

"We'll be home in time for tea," Dorah said brightly, as I settled myself in the passenger seat of the Buick. "I've had Lilah do up a nice banana bread as a special treat for your homecoming, how's that?"

"Nice." I gritted my teeth and looked out the window.

At an intersection, she reached over to pat my knee before making a left turn. "I know it's all hormonal, but there's no need for you to look so glum. You're a very lucky young woman to be alive today. Tom Brennan said the mortality rate in cases like yours is extremely high."

"So he said."

"There, so you should be thanking your lucky stars. Why can't you look on the upside?"

"Because I don't have my baby to take home with me."

"That again." She shook her head. "You can always have another baby when you're settled and it's time to start a family. You've got to be reasonable about this."

"Reasonable?" I stared at her. "Have you any idea how much I regret signing that consent form?"

She glanced at me quickly, frowning. "This is not a discussion I care to have while I'm driving. We'll talk later."

"Will it make a difference?"

We rode in silence.

Numbed, and feeling more uncertain than I would ever admit to Dorah or anyone else, I stared out the window at the small, neat bungalows we passed at twenty-five miles an hour. The wood-frame houses were set apart from each other with boxwood hedges or picket fences. Most had a border of flowers running along a walkway to the front steps. Was my baby somewhere in a house like this, with a backyard and a room of his own?

All that I could provide was cramped, temporary accommodation, his cradle next to my bed, and the constant worry that a squalling baby and nighttime feedings would awaken Brígh. There would also be lingering fear each time I picked him up that medication could fail. I'd have a seizure. What then? And what about a job? Daycare?

I gripped the armrest, frightened and overwhelmed. Even if I were up to the challenge of fighting the adoption, would it be fair to my child if I did get him back?

Chapter 25

AFTER DORAH DROVE ME HOME that afternoon, we had tea in the parlor so that I wouldn't have to climb the stairs to her boudoir. I'd hoped to avoid tea altogether. It wasn't an option. Dorah steered me into the sitting room, where Lilah had already arranged a tea tray on the low coffee table.

"Please, sit down," Dorah said, placing her handbag on the settee. She unbuttoned her suit jacket. For a change, she would be having afternoon tea without wearing a flowered duster and hose rolled down around her ankles.

"I told Lilah she should leave for the day as soon as we arrived back home. She's been privy to quite a lot already. It's my experience that the help never keep anything to themselves. Worse, they always get it wrong."

I held my tongue. Without waiting for Dorah to pour tea, I put a slice of banana bread on a plate. The sooner I could get to my room and close the door, the better.

"Good, I see you're hungry. That's a welcome sign." She set the strainer in a cup and began pouring.

"Perhaps because of my position at the hospital and all I've experienced there," she continued, "I take a broader view. To you, this may seem like the end of the world, but one day you'll appreciate the outcome. You'll be able to make something of your life, while bringing great happiness to a couple dearly wanting a child. You've done the right thing, Olivia."

"No, I have not. I didn't even know what I was signing."

"We waited a full three days after the birth, so everything was perfectly legal. Tom Brennan vouchsafed that you were cognizant, fit to sign. There was a notary on hand. Nobody rushed you."

"And nobody told me it was irrevocable. That can't be legal."

"Mind what you say. You don't want to make wild accusations."

"Tell me, why are you so damn anxious to rob me of my baby?"

"Language, please! I'll overlook this outburst, but you must temper yourself."

"I'm fine and I'm not leaving my baby with strangers. Who are they, anyway?"

"Never mind. They are entitled to privacy. That's the law. It's enough to know they're worthy people, who would otherwise not have a child."

"But they can't have mine!"

"You almost died, Olivia. Who was supposed to care for your baby while you lingered at death's door? Was I supposed to drop everything and do that, too? It's enough that I paid for all this, something you don't bother to acknowledge. Come to your senses, for the good of the child."

"I can't listen to this." I put down my plate, the banana bread untouched. "I should never have come here in the first place."

"No, far better you should saddle that poor drunk in New York with your bastard."

"Robert's child!"

"A pregnancy you engineered. Don't deny it!" Her face was livid, her voice trembling with anger. "I saw through you from the beginning. You could never have been a fit mother for his child. I've seen your type before. You want to trumpet the fact you've given birth to Robert Yardley's baby and try to collect. Forget your pipe dreams. You'll get nothing!"

"You think that's why I want to keep my baby?" I gripped the arms of the chair. My heart was racing, my vision growing cloudy. "I only want my baby, nothing more."

"Olivia, are you all right?" She picked up my teacup and held it out to me. "Here, sip this."

The cup, a fading mirage, hovered in a space beyond my reach. I shook my head and woozily sank back in the chair.

"You're not at all well, my dear. Don't move. I'm going to get you some water."

She hurried out of the parlor.

I took another breath and eased myself up from the chair, concentrating on moving across the carpet, a footstep at a time. I reached my room and shut the door behind me, turning the lock. A wave of nausea overcame me as I sat down and leaned my head against the back of the chair.

Dorah knocked on the door, calling out to let her in. I stared up at the ceiling, ignoring her pleas. I wasn't well enough to battle her. Weak and outflanked, the odds didn't favor regaining my son. Short of a miracle, strangers would keep him.

I pulled the ties tighter on a cotton robe I'd found hanging on the back of the bathroom door and looked around Dorah's pink-tiled bathroom. It was the first time I'd been in here, and I didn't want to leave anything behind. I threw the pants and shirt I'd slept in across my arm, went into the bedroom and slipped on the sandals I'd left there. My wheelie, containing toiletries, medication and the wraparound dress I'd wear, was downstairs in the entryway. I shivered in the morning chill and took another quick look around, grabbing a white cardigan hanging on the back of a chair.

Paul was in the hallway looking through mail as I came down the stairs. He turned, his eyes widening when he saw me.

"What?" I smiled. "Is something wrong, or are you just amazed I clean up so nicely?"

"No, just … thrown for a second." He shook his head. "Sorry, my mind was somewhere else. You ready for breakfast?"

"As soon as I get dressed." I pulled up the handle on my tangerine wheelie. "Give me ten minutes."

"Fine, I'll get started in the kitchen."

We stood awkwardly for a moment, taking each other in. He was taller than I'd first thought, perhaps with an inch or more height than Robert. The shape of his face and thinning hair were familiar, too, but weren't traits he shared with his father.

What was Paul seeing in me? He was looking at me intently.

"What?" I laughed. "I'm not a ghost. It's really me."

"Sorry. I didn't mean to stare."

"I know, me neither. This'll take some getting used to, won't it?"

He nodded, looking perplexed. "I guess so. It's just … very unexpected."

"For me, too." We continued to gaze at each other. It was

apparently left to me, the senior member, to break the stand-off. "Okay, then, get the eggs going. I'll dress and join you in the kitchen."

I swung down the hall to Robert's old room at the back of the house. I flipped my wheelie open on his bed. I shook out the print wrap dress, my usual traveling outfit, and set them aside with fresh undergarments and a pair of pumps. As I dressed, I glanced out the casement windows.

The sky was overcast and the weather seemed much cooler than the day before. The trees were shedding their autumn leaves, and the plants around the fountain were curling and turning brown. I sat down on Robert's bed to put on shoes, recalling the day I left to return to New York.

Chapter 26

THE MORNING HAD BEEN STORMY, with persistent rain, lightning and high winds that had rattled windows throughout the night. I'd already had breakfast and was packed, but still had more than an hour to wait before the taxi would arrive to take me to the airport.

Lilah came into the bedroom and stood with her arms tucked up under her heavy breasts. "Don't you worry none. The radio says this'll pass before your plane takes off." She winked. "Otherwise, you'll be spending another night with us."

I made a face. She laughed.

"You'd see me setting out on foot down the highway before I stayed here any longer."

"Oh, now, aren't you gonna miss me? I even packed you a whole loaf of banana bread to take with you."

"You're all I'm going to miss, Lilah. Thank you for everything. I mean it."

"I wish I could've done more." She grimaced and hugged herself tighter. "You know, there's something that needs saying. Mrs. Ellerbe made me witness that signing. I didn't want to, but she said I had no choice as you were gonna die. I hope you don't hold it against me."

"No, of course not. If it hadn't been you, it would've been one of the nurses."

"Oh, she tried that, too, but they backed off. You shoulda heard her! Now, I'm gonna tell you something because I just can't keep it in. The reason I agreed is because she held up your baby's birth until she got that paper signed. Dr. Brennan was beside himself, said we'd lose both you and the baby if he waited any longer, but she insisted." Lilah lifted a corner of her apron to blot tears flooding her eyes. "I couldn't let that happen."

A thunderous crack suddenly shook the house, rattling the casement windows. I looked up to see the massive pecan tree crashing down toward us, its topmost branches scraping the roof and back porch as it fell with a trembling thud. We both gasped as a cloud of dust and swirling leaves rose up outside, darkening the bedroom.

I shuddered and caught my breath. "My God, that was close."

"A judgment as sure as anything," Lilah said, her voice trembling.

"I'm not so sure," I whispered, my arm across her shoulder. "I think it just means the Ellerbe house won't be on the garden tour this year." Then we looked at each other and laughed.

The kitchen, usually the sunniest room in the house, was cast in twilight, the windows completely obscured by leafy branches. We sat at the table sharing a pot of tea and a plate of warm banana bread.

"No matter what, I had to own up," Lilah said. "I'm so sorry I had a hand in all this. I sure wish things could be different, but it just wasn't meant."

"But I'm not giving up. Somehow, I'll find a way to reverse the adoption. If it comes down to it, would you be willing to tell what you know?"

"I'll stand by you, Miss Livvie. You have my word, but that doesn't mean anyone's going to listen to me."

"But you'll state that Mrs. Ellerbe held up the delivery until she got that consent order signed, right?"

"I will indeed. It was awful, what was happening." She sighed and put down her cup. "But you've got a hard road ahead. You won't be the first giving up a baby and regretting it, but—"

"What?"

"Are you real sure you're up to it? You're still healing. I can see it." She nodded toward the teacup I had to hold steady in two hands. "I don't want you to lose heart, but think hard before you do anything. That's all I'm gonna say."

She reached into her pocket for a scrap of paper. "If you ever need to reach me, here's my address. I live with my sister and her family. You can find me there."

"Thank you for everything, Lilah." I leaned over, hugging her shoulders. "I'm going to stay in touch."

I smelled bacon and fresh coffee, reminding me that Paul was waiting for me. I stood up and pulled on the white cardigan. Wouldn't Lilah be surprised to know I'd soon be sitting in the Ellerbe kitchen having breakfast with my son? I took a minute to apply a bit of concealer under my eyes and a touch of blush and lip gloss. My face in the mirror looked expectant, confident.

Robbie would soon know that I'd spent the night in his house and had met Paul. Neither piece of information would please him, but both gave me immense satisfaction. I pushed up the sleeves of the cardigan and went to have breakfast with my son.

He was standing at the counter whipping eggs in a bowl,

his weight on one leg in a stance so familiar it made me smile. I was reminded of my first visit to Robbie's studio the morning after the blackout when he made scrambled eggs for breakfast. It also made me think of the stock of cello-wrapped toothbrushes I'd found in his medicine cabinet. I laughed at the memory.

"Hey, what's so funny?" Paul turned and smiled. "Okay, I gotta say it. You clean up very nicely."

"Thank you. By the way, when I was snooping around upstairs last night I noticed that the door to the day room was locked. Any reason?"

"Yeah, full of file cabinets stuffed with negatives and prints. Rob's donating his archive to the university and wanted to keep it safe from plaster dust." He grinned. "Sorry, just a lot of books and photographs, but no skeletons in there I know of."

"Just as well," I said, laughing. "While we're at it, the wife who showed up at the hospital yesterday? Full disclosure, I lied because I was afraid they wouldn't let me see Robert otherwise."

"I figured."

"But I felt justified because, to my knowledge, he was on his own. I didn't know about you. For that matter, I know nothing of the people who raised you."

"My parents?" He poured eggs into the skillet and set the bowl aside before looking at me. "They both died, my dad quite a while ago."

"I'm so sorry." I pulled up a stool and sat down. "Please, tell me about them."

"I'm afraid you're not going to like hearing some of this." He set two mugs on the counter and poured coffee, handing me one. "And it might take a while. You mind if we sit at the table first? I'll wreck the eggs otherwise."

"Of course." I dropped two slices of whole wheat bread in the toaster and watched Paul scramble eggs. His movements were quick, assured, just as Robert's were. They had the same build.

The only traits we seemed to share were caramel-colored eyes and an allergy to feathers. He seemed decent, kind and clearly knew his way around a kitchen, but I'd had no hand in his upbringing. I could take no credit for the sort of man he'd grown to be. Thinking about the lost years we'd never retrieve, I was engulfed in a wave of sadness. How could I begin to know him?

"Do you have a wife? Kids?"

"What?" He turned his head, giving me a quick glance over his shoulder. He looked pained, his eyes reddened. Had the same thoughts occurred to him?

"I was just wondering about your family. You're married?"

"Yes, Christine and I celebrated our tenth wedding anniversary last year. We met in high school. We've got a son named Bobby. He just turned nine." He cleared his throat and shifted his weight again, stirring the eggs in the pan. "Christine's dad is called Robert, too, so that's how he got the name. Anyway, the kid's a computer geek and a wiz at math. And we've got a six-year-old daughter, Beth. Loves ballet."

"That's great. I'm very happy for you."

"Yeah, a boy and a girl." His voice faltered. "It's really something to see 'em grow up."

He slid the skillet to a back burner and turned off the stove. His shoulders trembled. I knew he was weeping, but then I was, too. I touched his sleeve, then took his arm. In the next moment, I was holding him close, his face wet against my shoulder, my cheek pressed to his chest.

"Damn, I'm so sorry. So sorry," he said.

"Don't be. Just let it out. I'd have given anything to have those years with you, watching you grow up."

We held each other for long minutes, his cotton turtleneck soaking up my tears. He smelled of bacon and the outdoors, a mingling of pine, warmth and a freshly laundered shirt. My arms tightened around his waist, not wanting to let him go, but I could feel him releasing my shoulders.

"You'd like Christine. She'd love to meet you."

"I'd like that. And your children."

"Yeah, they're good kids. We have a lot of fun. Bobby is working on a project for a big regional science fair next month. We'll all be going up to Charleston for that. "

"Wonderful. And what about you?"

"Me?" He leaned back against the counter. "I'm a landscape architect. I've been working on a waterfront project most of the year." He tore off a couple sheets of paper towel and handed me one. "Christine teaches sixth grade. Sorry, it's a lot to throw at you all at once, but . . ." He wiped his eyes and blew his nose. "Have to start somewhere."

"I want to hear all of it. I think you know a whole lot more about me."

"I've kept track. Christine's a big fan of your books." He exhaled, looking at me sheepishly. "Chris and a couple of her friends went to one of your book signings in Charleston a few years back."

"What! And she didn't say anything to me? I don't believe it!"

"It . . . I didn't think it was the time to reach out. Chris wanted to, but we didn't know how you'd feel about everything."

I shook my head, not comprehending. "That doesn't make sense. I had no idea you even knew who I was. Or would care."

"Truth is, for a long time we didn't give much thought to getting in touch. We heard you were living in Europe. You were married and had your own life, so we didn't want to bother you."

"Don't say that! Didn't you ever wonder what happened back then? Why I gave you up? I didn't want to, you know."

"I know. Lilah Jackson finally told me. I came into Weymouth one day a few years ago and ran into her in a diner. She was working as a waitress by then and we got to talking. I think it bothered her that I didn't know that part of the story. She didn't hold back. I'm grateful for that."

"Lilah's still around?"

"Not anymore. She moved to Chicago some years ago to be near her sister." He picked up the skillet. "The eggs are hard. Sorry."

"But still warm, so let's eat. I want to sit at the table with you. There's too much we have to catch up on."

Chapter 27

ON MY FLIGHT BACK TO NEW YORK, I thought about Lilah, picturing her face after the pecan tree fell; the look of horror, and her words. *A judgment as sure as anything.*

What fresh horrors were awaiting me? I rang Brígh's doorbell with trepidation, not knowing she'd already taken care of the one thing I dreaded about returning to her apartment. I should have trusted she would.

"There you are. Welcome home!" she said, opening the door with a glass of red wine in hand. "This is for you. Mine is on my desk."

I laughed and took the glass. "Thank you. Just what I needed."

"I should think so. You'll find it's a very nice Saint-Émilion. Just shove your suitcase inside and give me a hug."

I embraced her warmly, then looked around the cluttered entryway. "Everything looks the same. It's good to be back."

"You've been gone less than a month. Come on in and get settled."

I picked up my suitcase and started down the hall, Brígh close behind. I took a deep breath, then opened the door to my room. I saw at once that the bassinet and all the other baby supplies had been removed. I looked at Brígh.

"You're starting fresh, my friend. I had the porter pack

everything up and haul it down to the storage room. Someone else will have use for all that stuff."

I put my suitcase down, unable to speak, imagining for a moment standing in that spot cradling a baby in my arms. Just as quickly, the image vanished, replaced by a surge of relief that I wouldn't have to spend the night in a roomful of reminders of what could have been.

"Thank you, Brígh," I managed.

"Not at all. Come along," Her voice was brisk. She was already moving down the hall to her desk and the glass of wine she couldn't be without. "Wash up, if you want, and then join me in here. I've got a lot to catch you up on."

I wouldn't have my old job back, nor would I be working in the picture department.

"You wouldn't want to, anyway," Brígh said. "The personnel have changed, but the ogre is still in charge. You'll be working at a safe distance at the clip desk. I know it's a demotion, but it's only temporary until something else opens up. I figured it was better you had a paycheck as soon as possible."

I agreed. On Monday morning we took the bus together to work. I was glad to be back and pleased to be working with Stan Daldry, the balding old-timer who'd supervised the "Morgue" for nearly thirty years.

It was a gentle reentry, with none of the pressure or long hours I'd had to work as a picture researcher. There were no overt reminders of Robert, either. I was also still recovering, dealing with occasional dizzy spells and monitoring my blood pressure. I could not have been more grateful to Brígh for my soft landing back in New York.

My way of thanking her was to look for a place of my own as quickly as possible. Now that I had income again, I pounded the pavements on weekends, real estate listings in hand. I was lucky. Walking down a quiet side street in the West Village early on a Saturday morning, I spotted an elderly man taping a For Rent sign on the front door of a small apartment building. I hurried up the steps and asked to see the apartment before he'd even managed to post the sign.

The moment I walked into the airy garden apartment and saw the beamed ceiling and working fireplace, I told the superintendent I'd take it. The rent was one hundred and ten dollars a month, slightly more than I'd budgeted, but I couldn't imagine living anywhere else. I had enough money in my bank account to write a check to cover the deposit and first month's rent. There was nothing left over to buy a bed. I spent the rest of the weekend cleaning the apartment and moved in on Sunday night with two suitcases, my typewriter, boxes of books and a sleeping bag. Brígh gave me a spare teakettle and a few other kitchen items that saw me through until my next paycheck.

I was blissfully happy. I was on my own. I could write late into the night without disturbing anyone. On sunny days, I could read in my garden. On a stroll through my new neighborhood, I walked past Robert's old studio, which was only a five-minute walk from my apartment. I assumed Norm Jurgens was still living there and I had no desire to see him. I also knew that I didn't want to stay with the magazine. I was already looking for a new job. It was time to move on with my life. I thought about getting a cat.

A telephone hadn't yet been installed in my apartment, or I would have received an early morning call from Brígh. She was among the first to hear that Robert had been found alive in a remote Angolan field hospital. It was left to Stuart to break the miraculous news to me as we rode up in the elevator together later that morning.

"Hey, you hear about Yardley? Someone told me he was rescued from some jungle hospital. He was shot up pretty bad. Might've lost a leg."

"What? Robert's alive?" Stunned, I stared at Stuart as though he were speaking in tongues. "You're sure? Where is he now?"

Stuart shrugged. "That's all I know, kiddo."

We stepped off the elevator. I stood, dazed, letting the news sink in. Brígh, hovering near my cubicle, hurried down the hall toward me.

"You heard, then? Robert's alive. He's been airlifted from Luanda to Lisbon for medical treatment. We're meeting with the managing editor in a few minutes for an update. I can tell you more after that."

"But what do I do? If he's in Lisbon, I want to see him. I have to go!"

She grabbed my hands, squeezing them tightly. "Just get hold of yourself. Right now, we know very little about his condition. There's nothing you can do. Hang tight, okay?"

"But, Brígh, if he's alive, if he's coming home . . . the baby."

"It changes nothing, you hear me? Trust me on that. We'll talk later."

Brígh hurried off to her meeting. I went to my desk and sat immobile, unable to shut down the turmoil raging in my head. Brígh was wrong—this changed everything. I had to see Robbie, to tell him what happened and try to undo the adoption.

I was sure Dorah Ellerbe had been the first to hear the news Robert was alive. As his next of kin, she'd be notified immediately. I picked up the phone to call her, then put it down. What would I say? "He's alive, thank God! Now give us back what is ours!"

Brígh took me for an early lunch, a liquid one for both of us. She was on her second martini when my soup arrived. I tasted it, then let the rest go cold. I hung on every word, asking her to repeat things so I wouldn't miss anything.

"What about his leg?"

"He hasn't lost any limbs, though his leg was badly injured. The gunshot wounds got infected from parasites in the swamp water. Apparently when they found him he was severely dehydrated and delirious. He'd been kept hidden, possibly as a source for ransom. Who knows? He's lucky to be alive."

"When is he coming back?"

"I told you, no word yet."

"I'm sure Dorah knows more than we do."

"You're not thinking of calling her, are you? If you're not on good terms, I'm not sure she'll appreciate hearing from you now."

"A card?"

"A card with your new address, of course. Don't go overboard. You know she's not going to want to put you in touch with Robert."

She reached across the table and took my hand. "Livvie, look at me. You are not going to get your baby back. Do you understand? The adoption was final. It's too late."

Yet, reclaiming my son was all I could think about. I was obsessed, spinning one scenario after another in which Robert and I fought to get our boy returned to us. If I'd been coerced into signing, was the document legally binding? Wasn't there a grace period in which a distraught birth mother could change her mind? Wouldn't Robert also have to agree for the adoption to go through?

I sneaked time at the clip desk to look up case law regarding adoption in Robert's home state. I needed answers and couldn't afford to hire an attorney. Lunch hours were spent in the Morgue combing through the Legal Affairs section.

One day I came across clippings culled from the *Weymouth Reporter*, and other newspapers across the country, about a custody battle that had raged between two warring sisters, Dorah Ellerbe and Blanche Yardley. My fingers trembled as I leafed through flaking, yellowed clippings in a thick file that revealed the long, drawn-out fight for custody of Robert.

I read as much as I could before my lunch hour was up. I flagged the files for access later, but did not log the materials out of the Morgue. I did not want to chance alerting Brígh to what I was pursuing. It was better to have the clippings remain private, a potential arsenal for use if Robert and I had to wage our own battle to regain custody of our son.

As soon as I finished work for the day, I raced back down to the Morgue and asked Stan if I could stay late. He obliged me with another hour while he finished up his own work. I gathered the files and retreated to a table some distance from his desk.

The custody story had become national news when Robert's mother, Blanche Yardley, was accused of abducting the five-year-old, defying the terms governing her visitation rights. She was characterized as emotionally unstable, having a history of "endangering the child through her erratic behavior."

A front-page story in the *Weymouth Reporter* read: *Following a tipoff from an alert desk clerk, Blanche Yardley and her son were found in a motel room just outside of town only a day after the child had been snatched from the backyard of the Ellerbe home, despite the watchful eye of the family housekeeper. The boy was returned unharmed to Dr. and Mrs. Lloyd Ellerbe, the legal guardians of the child.*

"But he's my boy! How can I be guilty of kidnapping my own son?" Blanche Yardley pleaded, in one of the few stories in which she was quoted. "My older sister has coveted my baby since the day he was born. She can't have one herself, so she wants mine. It's all trumped up, everything she says about me. I'm a full-time mother to my son. He's my life!"

Despite that heartbreaking plea, sentiment seemed to lie entirely with Lloyd and Dorah Ellerbe. They were described as "a childless couple, who could provide a visibly stable home life" for young Robert, who was only a few months old when they first petitioned for guardianship.

Blanche was depicted as a "good-time girl who lived a bohemian lifestyle" and had given birth out of wedlock. She had no known means of support or employment, although she claimed to receive regular cash assistance from the child's father, whom she refused to name.

Blanche, who had been granted limited visitation rights under supervision, had "fought tirelessly" to regain custody, according to her account, and was "thwarted at every turn" from seeing her son. Dorah Ellerbe countered that her sister "indulged in carousing with men of all types," and was not a fit mother for a young boy who needed the "steady influence of a proper father."

Following the kidnapping incident, the court granted full

custody to the Ellerbe family "for the good of the child." A court order was in effect, preventing repeated nuisance visits, the day Blanche Yardley wrapped her car around a telephone pole only blocks from the Ellerbe home.

The file box also contained pictures, both family photographs and black-and-white news photos. The two sisters, standing arm in arm in a youthful snapshot, were a study in opposites. Dorah, the taller of the two, wore a boxy chemise dress, her dark hair cut in a bob. Her handsome face, with its high cheekbones, caught sunlight as she looked straight into camera. Blanche, standing in her shadow, was girlish and slim, her full-breasted figure fetching in a low-cut summer dress. Her light hair, long and wavy, framed a pretty face with a sweet smile. One looked bold, the other shy. Even with their arms linked, they appeared to lean apart.

A news photo pictured Blanche, distraught, with wild hair and a tear-stained face, reaching for her sobbing toddler. Dorah, her eyes fierce, held Robert, dressed in short pants and a shirt with a Peter Pan collar, tightly to her bosom. The photograph was a vivid tableau of misery, a feud between battling sisters, with the boy caught in the crossfire.

I reread the clippings, wondering what sort of lasting effect this conflict could have had on Robert. It occurred to me that Yardley was Aunt Dorah's maiden name, but I came across a guardianship document allowing Robert's last name to be changed to Ellerbe. When and why had he changed it back?

Stan, who had finished his work and was itching to leave for the day, saw that I was still poring over the clippings. He offered to make copies the following morning and leave the packet on my desk. I suspected Stan was eager to put the newly installed Xerox machine to work, but it also meant I'd have my own permanent copies of the news articles. Still, I weighed whether I wanted Stan to see the clippings and question my interest in these stories about Robert Yardley.

I carefully tucked the last crinkling news clipping back in the file box and handed it to Stan. "Are you okay with keeping this just between us?"

"Don't you worry," he said quietly. "You wouldn't be the first one asking me to keep something under wraps. At least you didn't try to sneak anything out of here. That's been tried, too."

"Thanks, Stan. Maybe I'm being overly protective, but Robert Yardley's rescue from Angola is a major news story. You never know what some writer will want to dig up as background material on him."

"That's your interest?" He cocked an eyebrow and gave me a look that told me he wasn't buying it. "Whatever you say, sugar. The file's not getting into the wrong hands. They don't call this place the Morgue for nothing."

The following week, while Robbie was recuperating in a Lisbon hospital, the managing editor sent the entire staff copies of a dispatch Robert had dictated giving an account of his months-long ordeal on patrol with Angolan rebels:

It was early in the morning, but I'm not sure of the date. We'd been walking for days and I'd lost track by the time we reached a small settlement. I slept fitfully on the dirt floor of the mud-and-thatched-roof hut the rebel soldiers had provided me. It was either on the Congo side of the border, or not. Borders are not too important in the bush. This was the day we would move deep into

Angola and try to hook up with Holden Roberto's ragged posse of underfunded, underfed and underequipped rebels.

We were on the move by first light. I made sure my "water bearers" had the two canteens of boiled river water that would be my lifeline. These guys were used to all the local bugs and infestations, and would drop to their knees and drink from any puddle, stream or other water source without a second thought when they got thirsty. I didn't have that option.

I ate a quick breakfast of my meager leftover portion of chicken soup from dinner the night before. I think it was chicken. I hoped it was chicken. The rebel "camp follower," a young woman who had prepared my dinner and boiled the river water for my canteens, had given me a toothy grin and flapped her elbows, making a "cluck -cluck" chicken imitation when she handed me the tin plate.

We left the tiny settlement, about a dozen rebel soldiers and me, and started walking into the Congolese jungle—an awful lot of walking without a break. About 12:30 that afternoon we came to a wide, sluggish river the color and consistency of pea soup. One of the guys waded in and found it was shoulder deep, but out of deference to me and the cameras I had slung on my shoulders, we continued walking upstream where the river narrowed. We eventually found a dead tree that had fallen across the stream, making a natural footbridge. The rebel leader waved me back, indicating I should bring up the rear.

Two rebel soldiers hung back to cover me and were crossing the log bridge about three meters ahead. I was looking down to make sure of my footing when I noticed little droplets of water spurting up from the surface of the river. My immediate reaction was, "How nice, a little rain will cool things off."

It's funny how long it takes for sound to catch up to sight. It *was a good second before my mind raced from thoughts of cooling rain to hearing the gut-wrenching staccato echoes of AK-47s chattering from somewhere upstream. Government troops, perhaps the very ones I'd traveled with weeks earlier, had spotted us and set up an ambush.*

My compatriots up ahead had instinctively rolled off the log, tipping me into the gooey, foul-smelling, evil-tasting river. Under fire, they fished me out of the slime and hustled me to the middle of the ranks for protection and doubled-timed us out of the vicinity. Our leader indicated the government forces probably would not try to follow us, but we should "bugger out" anyway. Two of the rebels hoisted me up and we were out of there fast.

Once in the clear, we stopped to regroup and survey the damage. None of my rebel friends were injured, but I'd been sprayed with shot in my leg, my arm grazed. The pain was searing, but one of the guys patched me up best he could. One of my Leicas was ruined. I dried off two of my Nikons and salvaged film from the Leica, which I hoped the lab could process. Again we walked, it seemed like days, with other days spent hiding out in the bush, knowing government troops were patrolling. I was stashed in an encampment in the hills for more than a week before we were on the run again, I hoped into the home stretch. But before I could make it out of the jungle to ship film, my leg got badly infected. It came on suddenly, with high fever. I was delirious, shaking, thought I was dying. I was left in another remote encampment, hidden in a dark tent, too sick to think or note the passage of time. It's about all I remember. I'm grateful to everyone who stood fast and saw to it that I stayed alive. I'm recuperating well and hope to be home soon.

Robert Yardley

I reread Robert's dispatch, noting the name and address of the Lisbon hospital where he was still undergoing treatment. That night I wrote several drafts of a letter, one of them eight pages long, in which I fully recounted everything about the birth of our baby and the aftermath masterminded by his aunt. I also alluded to what I knew about his own custody battle as a child. After some consideration, I mailed none of the drafts, but kept them in the same packet as the Xerox copies Stan had made of the newspaper clippings.

Instead, I ended up mailing Robert a snapshot Osgood had taken of us on the beach in St. John and a brief, rather formal note with my new address. My message read, in part:

My faith that you would return safely has been rewarded with the wonderful news you'll soon be coming home. I want to see you and it's very important that we speak as soon as you are able. Please get in touch when you can.

With love, as always,
Livvie

Chapter 28

MORNING SUN SPLASHED ACROSS THE BREAKFAST TABLE. We pushed aside our plates. Paul poured fresh coffee in both our mugs. Scattered on the table were a few snapshots of Christine and their children that he'd pulled out of a kitchen drawer. I picked up the picture of Christine again. She was standing in a field, leaning against a split-rail fence, wearing jeans and a plaid shirt, blond hair blowing across her sunlit face.

"Don't let that sweet look fool you," Paul said, smiling. "She's tough as a hound with a ham bone, but we have her to thank for finding y'all. She kept urging me to track down my birth parents and wouldn't give up. Adoption records are still closed in this state, unless voluntary mutual consent is registered. That wasn't the case, of course. All I had was the birth certificate reissued when I was adopted, but it had the correct date and place of my birth at Weymouth General. Around the time we were graduating from high school, Christine read in the newspaper that Dorah Ellerbe had died. We knew her name because my parents had mentioned that she'd arranged everything through the hospital."

"Actually, I was still in the hospital myself when she placed you with them. But the Westfeldts were never told my name?"

"No, not at all. Nor, of course, was Robert's name mentioned. My parents knew Mrs. Ellerbe only as the 'nice lady' in hospital administration. Chris was visiting Weymouth about a week after the funeral and had this crazy idea of driving by the Ellerbe house. She saw Lilah Jackson out front sweeping the porch and pulled into the driveway. As soon as she mentioned me and the adoption, Lilah put her broom down and took her inside. She didn't give anything away, mind you, but asked Chris a lot of questions. Chris just wanted to know if there was anybody around who would remember where the baby Mrs. Ellerbe placed had come from. Lilah said she might be able to find out something and asked Christine to leave her telephone number."

"And Robert?"

"His name was in the obituary as her survivor, but Lilah didn't mention him. It turned out he'd come back for the funeral, but left town again right afterward. Just after our high school graduation, Lilah called Christine and said I should stop by the Ellerbe house on Saturday morning. I rode over there and I see this guy sitting in one of the rockers on the porch." Paul sat back in his chair and made a low whistling sound. "As soon as I saw him, I had my answer."

I nodded. "You have his build, his height. I'm sure you saw the resemblance immediately."

"It was more than that. It was the look he gave me." Paul cleared his throat and sipped coffee. "I knew. It's not a moment I'm ever going to forget."

No, nor would I ever forget seeing my son for the first time. If only Paul had found me, too, years ago. *If only!* "What did he say to you?"

"Actually, I spent more time answering his questions

about me. I think I was sort of in shock. I had no idea I'd actually be meeting the man who was my birth father. I just kept staring at him. I never got around to asking the questions I should have. Lilah came out with iced tea and said hello. We didn't go inside."

"Did you ask him about me? Or anything about what happened?"

"He told me right off the bat that he knew nothing about my birth until after I'd been adopted. That didn't really surprise me because... well, that's often what happened, especially back then. He was easygoing and very nice. He let me know that things had probably worked out for the best. He asked me a lot about my parents. Told me how lucky I was. To tell you the truth, I walked away that morning feeling relieved. He was someone I could be proud of, not some ol' moonshiner up in the hills who was going to mess up my life. I figured Christine would be satisfied with that."

"But, didn't you try to get in touch with me, too? You must have asked him about me."

"Naturally, it was one of the first things I brought up. He told me your name, but I didn't know who you were back then. He said you were married and living abroad somewhere. Anyway, he mentioned that it had been a very painful time for you and that... and that maybe it was best to leave it as it was."

"As it was?" I stared at Paul, hearing words I knew Robert would have spoken. "He told you it would be better to just let things be? Not to get in touch with me?"

"I think he said it would upset you."

"No! How could he?" I sat back, my chair clattering against the wall. "Is that why you didn't try to find me?"

"I'm sorry. I'm really sorry." He reached for my hand, tugging it gently. "Please, the last thing I want to do is say something to hurt you. I don't want you angry with Rob, either."

His eyes were pleading, his face wearing the look of a little boy fearful of being caught in the middle, wanting to make things right.

I squeezed his hand. "I'm sorry, too. But you've no idea what it's like to hear this now, all these years later when it's too late."

"I know. It's hard to explain what was going through my mind back then, but I had no way of knowing how you'd feel having me show up on your doorstep, someone from another life that maybe you didn't want anyone to know about. If I'd heard there were siblings I could connect with, it might have made a difference. Or if I'd found your name on the mutual consent registry, I wouldn't have hesitated."

He wiped his hand across his face, rubbing his eyes, as though trying to clean a slate. "Look, please don't take this the wrong way, but you didn't get in touch with me, either. Your name was not on the registry. And I wasn't all that hard to find."

"I did try, but—" I started to protest, then realized I couldn't. I'd picked at the scabs of my own hurt without ever providing any means to let him know how to find me—or even to let him know I wanted to be found. "I'm sorry. I should have done more. You were in my mind so often over the years."

Silence hung between us. I stopped myself from telling him it was Robert who'd insisted I back off. How could Paul ever understand the terror wielded by the "nice lady" who arranged his adoption? More important, how could Paul and I regain some of what we'd lost over the years, or even build on what we'd shared only minutes before?

He looked at his watch. I reached over, covering the watch face with my hand.

"Please, another minute. I know it's time to go see Robert, but let's not leave it like this. There's so much more you don't know. It may not even matter to hear this now, but I did try to get you back. I didn't want to let you go."

"I know that, or at least everything Lilah told me much later on." He pushed back his chair. "We'll talk again, but we should probably head over to the hospital now."

"That's fine." I stood up, too. "I'll just clear the dishes."

"No, let me do it." He started to pick up the breakfast plates, then stopped. "You know, I was with Rob only about an hour that Saturday morning, but we hit on some rough patches, too. Things came up that were awkward between us. He was leaving the next day for Nicaragua and had a lot to do. He couldn't say when he'd be back, but he told me we'd talk again. He kept his word and we did. These things take time. A lot of time."

"Thank you for saying that." I touched his sleeve, longing to wrap my arms around him again. "I'll meet you at the door in a few minutes."

I went to Robert's room to pack a few last things in the wheelie. *Let it be. As it was.* I could hear him say those words, just as he had when I asked for his help in reclaiming our son.

He hadn't responded to the letter I mailed to him at the hospital in Lisbon. I later learned he'd never received it. When

Brígh told me she'd heard he was back in Weymouth, I called Lilah. I didn't want to risk having my call to the Ellerbe house intercepted by Dorah and lose my chance to speak with Robert.

"He's very weak," Lilah said when I reached her at home one evening. "He sleeps a good deal and still has trouble holding anything down. He's skin and bone."

"I'd like to talk to him when he's up to it. Do you think you could arrange it?"

"I don't know about that." She was quiet for a moment, then said hesitantly, "Mrs. Ellerbe's taken time off to be with him. He's got a nurse, too, so finding time to talk with him privately won't be easy."

"Lilah, I don't want to get you in trouble, you know that. Just tell me, does he have any idea what happened? Does he even know I was there or had the baby?"

"No, not at all. He's been here close on two weeks now and just not himself yet. I think you best wait to talk to him about anything like that."

"Do you mind if I call you back next week and see how he's doing?"

Lilah agreed. I hung up, feeling hope ebbing away. I knew the consent form I'd signed seventy-two hours after giving birth was irrevocable. The only possible course was to have Robert petition the court. The longer our child remained with strangers, the less chance there was that the court would even consider reversing the adoption.

I looked through the packet of clippings again that evening. I came across the news photo of Blanche Yardley, distraught, her face tear-stained, reaching for her sobbing child as he was pulled from her. I knew how she felt. If Robert saw this picture, the pain of that loss would be clear to him, too. Surely he knew how much his mother had fought to keep him and would understand.

I wrote another letter, a pared-down version of a previous draft, telling Robert what had happened and enclosing the clipping. I sealed the envelope and mailed it to Lilah's home address, attaching a note asking her to please give the letter to Robert at a time when he could read it privately.

"I got your letter in the mail," Lilah told me when I called her the following week. "I'm going to hold off a while until he's better. It might be a while. He's still pretty sickly."

"I understand, Lilah. Thank you. I really appreciate it."

Nearly three weeks passed before I heard from Robert. One day, shortly after I returned to my desk from lunch, the switchboard put a call through. I held my breath, somehow knowing I would hear Robert's voice.

"Livvie, it's me. How're you doing?"

"Robbie, I've been hoping you'd call. How are you feeling?"

"Better, but I'll be laid up for a while. They've got me on a walker, so I'm starting to get around. How's it with you?"

"I'm fine. I moved into a place of my own down near your old studio."

"Lucky you. Damn, I should never have given up my place to Norm." He chuckled. "I'd sure rather be back there than here. Along with everything else, I've got a bad case of cabin fever."

"I'll bet!" I laughed, then cupped my hand tighter around the receiver. "You know I was down there, right? In Weymouth? Lilah gave you my letter?"

"That's why I'm calling." He lowered his voice. "Listen, I

had no idea about any of this, as I guess you know. Lilah sort of filled me in. I'm really sorry you had to go through all of it on your own."

"I'm sorry I wasn't able to tell you right from the beginning. Maybe things would have gone differently, but ... anyway, as I said in my letter, your aunt had me sign a consent form giving up the baby. That's what we need to reverse."

"Lilah told me you were very ill, that you were having seizures—"

"Yes, but I'm okay now. I suspect Dorah had it in mind all along to put our baby up for adoption, but that was never my intention. Never! I wasn't even fully aware of what I was signing, so there's a legal issue involved. But whatever the situation was then, it's entirely different now. I'm well and you're alive—we could make a case. She can't stop us from fighting this."

"Wait a minute, Livvie. I'm sorry, but I can't go along with this. I've got a long way to go before I'm fully recovered. Even then ..."

"I know that. Robbie, I'm not asking any more of you than to stand by me and help petition the court. I'm working. I can support my baby and myself on my own. You can be as much a part of his life as you want to be, but I'm not expecting any sort of commitment from you. Nothing else is required. All I'm asking you to do is stick with me until I get our son back."

"Then it's an empty appeal on my part. I'm not going to fight just to take him back. Where's the sense in that?"

"Please, I can't do it alone. If we don't act now, we'll forfeit any chance we'll ever have. We can't let her rob us of our boy, our son."

"But he's not ours."

"Robbie, you saw the clipping. Look at your mother's face in that picture. That's what it feels like to have a child ripped away from you. I'm not going to let her do that to me!"

"I know what happened to my mother, but I won't be a part of tearing that boy in two. Take a look at my face in the picture. I know what it feels like to be that kid. It never leaves me. You don't own that boy's life. Nor do I."

"Listen! Whatever hell you've experienced, you do not know what it's like to give birth and be robbed of your baby. It's something that will never leave *me*—neither will the knowledge that you wouldn't stand by me."

"Sorry, Livvie. We have to make peace with this. We can't put more lives in turmoil. Where does it end?"

"That means she gets away with it."

"Dorah? She has her own pain. Don't let bitterness spoil your life like she has. It's not worth it. And, speak of the devil—sounds like she's back. I have to go. She just walked in."

"Wait, please—"

"That's it, Livvie. I know this is hard, but don't ruin that little boy's life or your own. Goodbye."

"No, please don't hang up!"

There was a click, then a persistent *beep-beep-beep* followed by a tinny female voice: "If you want to make a call, hang up and dial again." A piercing dial tone rang in my ear. I put the phone back in its cradle. I could call back, but who would answer? Dorah, probably. Did it matter? She would know soon enough that I'd been in touch with Robert.

I was about to pick up the phone when it rang. Startled, I grabbed the receiver. "Robbie? I knew you'd call back!"

"No, Olivia. It's Dorah Ellerbe. I'll thank you not to harass Robbie with your calls. He is not a well man."

"Actually, he called me. I told him everything that happened. I need to talk with him again."

"Not as far as I'm concerned. If you had an ounce of decency, you would have kept your tawdry mistake to yourself. I tried to help you and you turned on me."

"You stole our baby! I am not going to let you get away with it."

"What's done is done. Robert is not going to assist you in any little scheme you might have in mind."

"Is he hearing you say this? Let me speak to him."

"Absolutely not. I will monitor every call, every piece of mail that comes to this house. If you persist, I will be forced to make some calls of my own. I have the ear of your managing editor. As you may imagine, I am in a position to stop you at every turn in this jurisdiction. I will not hesitate to speak my mind. Do you understand?"

"I understand you're threatening me. Is this the sort of thing you did to your sister? Don't think I won't find a way to let Robbie know what you're doing."

"This only proves to me that you're the conniving woman I always knew you were, Olivia. It appears I will have to make my calls. Perhaps even a court order will be necessary. I can destroy you in more ways than you can imagine. Do I make myself clear?"

She hung up. I dropped the phone back in its cradle, my heart banging so hard I could barely breathe. Picturing her wrathful face in the news photo as she pulled Robbie from his mother, I knew I had reason to fear her. How could I fight Dorah and all her resources without Robert on my side?

With trembling fingers, I reached into my desk drawer for a bottle of pills and tipped one into my hand.

If I needed any clarification of my weak standing, it came a few days later in the form of a termination notice. My temporary job at the clip desk had been eliminated. There were no other positions available at the magazine. I had no job, no income. If Dorah had caused my abrupt dismissal, I would never know.

I never saw or spoke with Dorah again. I had no further contact with Lilah, concerned I'd be compromising her position in the Ellerbe house. While I got on with my life, I didn't fool myself that anything had been resolved, either.

For years afterward, waves of despair descended without warning. I suffered bouts of blinding rage that flared whenever I allowed myself to think about the baby stolen from me. It was Jake who brought joy back into my life.

Chapter 29

I LOOKED AROUND ROBBIE'S ROOM to make sure I'd left nothing behind. I zippered my wheelie and walked down the hall. Paul wasn't at the door yet.

I turned into the living room, which looked even more barren in daylight. Dust motes swirled in morning light filtering through muslin-draped windows, adding to the ghostly atmosphere of the stripped-down room. I pulled the sleeves of the sweater to my wrists and hugged my arms.

Once again I pictured the room as it was with Dorah's refinements and heard her sharp rebuke: *Come to your senses, for the good of the child!* Had she spoken those same words to Blanche Yardley?

I jumped at the sound of a squeaking floorboard and turned to see Paul in the doorway. "Sorry, didn't mean to startle you. I just called the hospital. Rob's doing all right, but undergoing some tests this morning."

"We've got time, then?"

"No point hanging around a waiting room." He shrugged. "So, what do you think of the place?"

"I'd say the Ellerbe house is taking on the look of a fixer-upper. What's going on here?"

"Rob just tore into the place one day, starting with this

room." Paul laughed. "It took a bit of getting used to. All DIY, as you can probably tell."

I laughed, too. "I'm betting Dorah is rolling over in her grave."

"From what Lilah told me, those two didn't get along very well. Yet she left the house to him. He kept it pretty much the way it was, until—anyway, one day he just started ripping it apart."

"So this is fairly recent? What made him do it?"

"He didn't say. I drove down here one morning and saw a dumpster in the driveway. He was hauling out some old moldings, so I gave him a hand." Paul cocked his head to the side, gazing at me. "He doesn't always give a reason, you know."

"I know." We looked at each other for a long moment. "You've got my eyes, but you look such a lot like Robert when I first met him."

"Actually, I take after my grandfather."

"How would you know? You don't look at all like my dad."

"No, Rob's father. Lloyd Ellerbe."

My breath caught, my eyes swiveling to the blank space above the mantel. I pictured the missing portrait of Lloyd—supposedly Uncle Lloyd—with his lean face and thinning hair. "My God, of course. Why didn't I think of that?"

"I didn't, either, until Rob told me when I helped him carry the paintings upstairs. I figured you knew."

"No. He always referred to Lloyd as his uncle. When did Robert find out?"

"Back in high school. Some kid showed him old photos and news clippings. Stuff came back to him that he'd overheard and it just hit him. He guessed Lloyd was his father, but kept it to himself."

"I came across some of those clippings myself. I remember Blanche Yardley refused to name the father, but admitted the man was helping her financially." Heat rose in my chest as the implications sank in. "If Robbie suspected Lloyd was his father, why wouldn't he confront him for being such a coward and not owning up?"

"He told me by the time he figured it out, his mother had been dead a long time. He just let things be. Right before he went off to college, Lloyd told him the truth. Rob said it made him sick hearing his father, a doctor, trying to justify giving his mother money instead of standing up for her. As far as Rob was concerned, Lloyd was responsible for what happened to her."

"So was Dorah. But all Lloyd had to do was keep quiet." I shook my head, my cheeks burning. "When it came time, Robbie did the same thing."

"What else could he do? He was leaving home anyway. Nothing could change what happened to his mother."

"I mean when it came to you, the apple didn't tumble far from the tree. Like father, like son. He didn't stand up for me, either."

Paul looked startled, his face flushed. "I hear what you're saying. Considering what Lilah told me, it doesn't put Rob in a good light. Maybe I shouldn't have said anything." He glanced at his watch, clearly uncomfortable. "I'm going to get more coffee. Want some?"

"Yes, please. Thank you."

"Back in a minute."

He left. I stared out the window at the rocking chairs on the veranda, anger boiling up. I smacked the back of a chair, my hand slamming the wood harder than intended. I groaned, sucking my stinging fingers to stop the throbbing. Had Paul heard me? I listened to his footsteps receding down the hallway. I could hardly blame him if he'd gone off to make coffee in order to distance himself from me.

By turns hungover, angry and weepy, I'd given him a poor impression of myself. All he knew of my role in his life was hearsay from Lilah. He'd gotten to know his father in the flesh, on Robert's own terms. Then it stuck me that Lilah hadn't got in touch with me, either. She knew my address. Had Robert told her not to let me know about Paul?

In turn, I'd kept my own secrets. My family never knew about Paul, nor would my parents ever have a chance to meet him now. Paul would never know the lake cabin of my childhood, any more than I would know about his growing-up years.

I went out on the porch and sat in a rocker. There was still a bit of morning chill, the air moist and fresh. I breathed deeply and pulled the sweater close, shivering with a wave of apprehension. Rocking back, my eyes on the spreading syca-more branches, I wondered what other secrets this house kept to itself.

Lloyd Ellerbe's feeble attempts at justification most likely prompted Robert to change his name back to Yardley. But knowing his father didn't stand up for his mother hadn't stopped Robert from doing the same to me. For that matter, if he hadn't collapsed in the post office, would I have met Paul? Even at the gallery, with photographs of both Paul and me in the exhibit, Robert chose not to tell me about our son.

The screen door snapped shut. "Is that your luggage by the door?" Paul handed me a mug. "We don't need to take it to the hospital with us, you know."

"Thank you." I clasped the mug in both hands, warming my chilled fingers. "Actually I'm booked on a flight this afternoon. I thought you could drop me at the airport after we see Robert."

"Of course, but I thought you'd stay longer." He sat in the rocker next to mine. "We'd have more time to talk."

"We can talk now." I smiled. "Is this where you sat with Robbie the first time?"

He nodded. "And quite a few other times, too. He's got some great ol' stories and loves to sit out here telling them. I once asked him how he got the scars on his arms and leg. He gave me a copy of something he wrote when he was in a hospital in Portugal. It was pretty harrowing stuff about photographing the fighting in Mozambique, Angola and... some other place over there."

"Guinea-Bissau. You were born around the time Robert was rescued. Once he got back to Weymouth, it took him a good year to recover. How much else did he tell you about that time?"

"Some, but I think I learned more from Lilah. I know it was hard on him."

"It was a painful time for both of us. By then you'd already been adopted."

"You didn't try to stay in touch with him?"

"Not much point. But years later, my husband and I ran into him in New York. Jake was teaching then, and he asked Robert to be a guest speaker."

"I remember that. He almost went."

"Jake was disappointed Robbie backed out, but I'm sure he had his reasons."

"We were going through a rough patch. I don't think Rob

felt he could leave here." Paul rocked back and sighed, his eyes shifting to his pickup parked in the driveway. "I started to say something earlier about this, but ... anyway, it's going to come up sooner or later, so may as well be now. The truth is, my mother wasn't very well at the time. Rob just couldn't leave her."

"Your mother?" A chill settled over me as his words sank in. "What about your father?"

"My dad died when I was still a kid, just after my ninth birthday."

"I'm sorry. That had to have been very hard for you."

He nodded. "And for my mom, too. The second time I came over to see Rob, I brought my mother along. Over time, he and Mom ... they—" His voice faltered and he took a breath. "I'm glad they got together. She'd been on her own for a long time. Later, when she got sick, Rob took care of her."

"Here? In this house?"

"Yes." He shifted his knees, releasing the rocker, and leaned forward. "Ever since Christine and I got married, we've lived in the old family house north of here where I grew up. My mother had already moved in here. With Rob."

"So, a long while back?" I looked at him, fierceness creeping into my voice despite my efforts to stay calm. "Look, you've told me this much. Any reason I shouldn't know the rest?"

"My mom's name was Susan. What happened between them just sort of happened. He and my mother never married, but I was happy they were together. He was very good to her. It meant a lot to me because Rob ... I really love him. I owe him a lot."

"Of course. He's your father."

"Yeah, he is. It was hard to tell you this, but I figured if Rob showed you a picture of her, you'd already guessed."

I stared at him, echoing his words. "A picture of her?"

"At the exhibit. She's in a cemetery, holding some flowers?"

I nodded, remembering the striking photo of a middle-aged woman with fair hair standing pensively among gravestones. I'd responded to the picture with empathy, thinking of the times I visited Jake's grave with flowers from our garden.

"I guess Rob wanted to keep it to himself because ... because he wasn't sure how you'd take it."

"No, he knew. Of course he knew."

"You're upset."

"Of course I am! I wonder how many times Lloyd thought about coming clean with Robert before attempting to justify what he did."

"That was different."

"Not much. Unlike Lloyd, Robert didn't slip me money and pledge me to silence. Instead, he simply refused to help me reclaim you. That's all he needed to do to stop me living my life with you."

"That's harsh." Paul stood and sloshed the remains of his coffee into the hedge.

"It's the truth. Choosing to let things be has meant keeping them secret. And I've never been offered any option in these matters. When Christine came to my book signing, you didn't want her to tell me about you because of your mother. Susan was still alive at the time, right? All of you simply made assumptions without ever giving me a choice--or even a chance of one." Trembling with emotion, I peeled off the sweater. "I shouldn't have taken this."

"It's cold. Please keep it."

"But it belonged to your mother, right?"

"And the blue robe."

"My, God, that, too?"

"Sorry, I shouldn't have said anything . . ."

"Why not?" I looked into the eyes of the man who was my son no matter who raised him, wanting desperately not to lose him again. "I'm making my own assumptions. I keep asking for truth and don't even listen when truth is spoken. When I talked about Jake, Robert said he knew what it was like to lose someone you love. Now I realize he was referring to Susan. I know how much it's meant to you having him in your life. I just want you to know how much I regret there wasn't room for me."

"I know—" His voice wavered, shifting to a lower register. "It's too bad you couldn't have known my mother because . . . she was very grateful to you. She would have wanted you to know that."

I nodded, his choked words barely audible. I started to hand him the sweater, then dropped it back across my shoulders. I touched his arm, but before I could say anything, a woman's voice rang out.

'Hey, there! Good morning! I thought I was hearing sounds over here." The neighbor I met when Robert collapsed at the post office walked toward us, cell phone in hand. "Glad I caught you, Paul. I was just coming to turn on the sprinklers. How's your father doing?"

"Hi, Marietta. Thanks so much. We're just off to see him. The doctor says he's fine."

"Oh, thank goodness." She looked to me. "I met you yesterday, remember? I believe you told me you were Mr. Yardley's wife."

"Actually, she's my mother," Paul said. "Her name's Olivia Hammond."

"Your mother?" She looked at Paul, then gaped at me. "Really? Oh, my goodness. Well, isn't that something? I thought you already had one."

"Two, actually."

"Really. Well, so nice to see you again."

"No need to turn on the sprinklers," Paul said. "I'll be staying here a while."

"Of course, of course," she said, continuing to stare at me. "Please say hello to Mr. Yardley when you see him."

"Thanks, I'll do that," Paul said. "We're off to the hospital shortly."

With another small wave, Marietta turned and headed back down the driveway, already pulling a cell phone from her purse.

"There's one in every village," Paul whispered. "Give her five minutes and it'll be all over town."

"Hope you don't mind."

"Suits me. It's not something I want to keep secret." He hesitated, then said, "You know, I wish Chris could be here now. She came home from that bookstore talking about what it would be like if we somehow all got together. She's always thinking ahead, but I couldn't help wondering how things might have been, you know, if—"

I smiled. "I think you get that from me. I always wonder 'what if,' too."

"So maybe this won't sound so funny to you, but once I knew who you were I tried to imagine what my life might have been like if things had worked out differently. If you and Rob . . . or maybe just you, or . . . I don't know. I've never been more than a hundred miles from home, even in college. You and Rob have been everywhere. I couldn't help thinking what that other life would've been like." His voice trailed off, his eyes focusing on some middle distance where the answer to an unlived past might be lurking.

I gazed at him, my own thoughts rambling. If I'd had my way, would my life have included camping trips and soccer tournaments? I would have liked that. But then, with my son to raise, would I have been with Robbie ... or Jake ... or on my own?

In the ensuing silence, our eyes met, both of us speculating on a universe of possibilities.

"So I guess we just play the hand we're dealt," Paul said, reaching for my empty mug. "I sure can't complain, yet—"

"We have time now. And more coffee."

"You got it." He smiled and pulled the screen door open. "Give me five minutes."

I strolled the length of the veranda and back again, my eyes falling on the two rockers, side by side, their arms almost touching. Then, not wanting to waste even a minute of the time I had left with my son, I opened the screen door and hurried down the hall to the kitchen and the smell of brewing coffee.

Chapter 30

JAKE. I STOOD IN THE RECEPTION ATRIUM of Woodley General thinking about Jake while waiting for Paul to park the car. What would Jake make of all this? Surely he'd been hovering nearby watching as I met my son for the first time? Or eavesdropping as I learned that I was a grandmother and that a daughter-in-law I didn't know was a fan of my books. Or standing by my side as I discovered that Robert had been living his life with my son and another woman? I felt Jake's comforting presence, his protective arm wrapped around my shoulders more snugly than Susan's white sweater. I willed him to stay with me as I stood waiting for my son to return.

If Jake was indeed lingering over my shoulder, what was he telling me to do now? Move on, of course. Hadn't he been telling me that all along whenever I got stuck, obsessed by something not going my way? He edited life with the same assurance he dealt with a page of copy, excising whatever got in the way of clarity and purpose. I tended to brood about hurts and slights, unwilling to forget and reluctant to forgive. In Robert's case, I obsessed feverishly about his betrayal and the unfairness of all that had happened, and hid it from Jake. How I wish I'd told him. He would have understood.

For that matter, perhaps together we would have tracked down my son.

I was still floundering when I met Jake, but covered it out-
wardly with a louche demeanor, becoming the embodiment
of *Cosmopolitan*'s Cosmo Girl, which was only one of several
magazines I was writing for at the time. I was brittle, sharp
edged, with a quick tongue and a cynical sense of humor that
belied my vulnerability. Like Brígh, I smoked and drank to
excess.

I was game for anything, including one-night stands in
far-flung locales, which, as a travel writer, I liked to claim was
essential to capturing the flavor of a place. An airline pilot, a
fisherman, a banker; did it matter? I wrote a jokey article
about that, too, referring to a fleeting partner in a stopover
romance not by his name, but by his drink choice, which happened to be a Moscow Mule. I nearly played the wild card
with Jake, who saw through it from the beginning.

I first laid eyes on him in London's Victoria station on a
warm April day just before we both boarded the train for a
six-hour journey to Paris. I heard his deep, rumbling laughter
first, and turned to see a hearty, good-looking man joking
with the train conductor. Wearing khakis, a well-cut blazer
and decent shoes, with a Burberry slung over his arm, I sized
him up as a London-based American businessman—and
hoped we were seated in the same compartment. We were. I
soon learned he drank single malt and was, ironically, an editor working his way up the masthead with the magazine
where I'd once worked. Over whiskeys, we discovered we
knew quite a few people in common from my days as a picture researcher, although I didn't mention Robert to him.

I told Jake I was a freelance travel writer doing a piece on La Flèche d'Or, the boat train between London and Paris, and was booked into a suite at the Hôtel de Crillon as part of my series on the great hotels of the world. By the time we arrived in Dover to cross the English Channel to Calais and board a connecting train to Gare du Nord, we'd agreed to meet for dinner. I was already both tipsy and smitten. After a talk-filled dinner and a meandering stroll to my hotel, I wasn't in the least subtle about my casual assumption we'd spend a frolicsome night together in my suite.

"But I won't respect myself in the morning," Jake said.

"What?" I laughed.

"I mean it." He didn't laugh. "I want to get to know you."

"But—"

"Before." He kissed me on the cheek and squeezed my hand. "And I'm going to get to know you very well."

We had breakfast at my hotel the following morning, without spending the night together, a shamefaced novelty for me. It was the beginning of a decades-long romance, with neither of us keen to share with the other what came before. In his case, a young wife had left him, unable to cope with his travel and long absences. I had no desire to mention the tarnished aftermath of my romance with Robert that might cloud what I was smart enough to recognize was a fresh start.

The only unexpected link to Robert came in the form of Annalisa, a translator, mother of three and the Italian wife of the deputy editor in the Rome bureau. Both were close friends of Jake's. She had also worked as a translator for Robbie years earlier—and been a friend of his, but not his girlfriend, as Dorah had implied.

How could Jake not be hovering over my shoulder now,

loving me no matter how impulsively or foolishly I behaved? He'd always distracted me from another ill-advised glass of wine, warned me off an assignment that wasn't worth my time and encouraged me to plunge in and write what I wanted to write. More importantly, I had the unconditional love of a man who acknowledged his own imperfections and seemed to exalt in mine. He was a gift I couldn't take for granted and wouldn't now.

Please, stay with me, Jake, I breathed, the words forming soundlessly on my lips as I spotted Paul entering the hospital's atrium. I waved and joined him at the elevator, my thoughts a silent plea to Jake. *You made me strong. Keep me strong.*

Robert was sipping coffee, a breakfast tray on his bed table, when Paul and I walked into his room. I led the way. I did not want to miss the look on Robert's face. He did not disappoint. Startled, his eyes widened in surprise. He grasped his cup in both hands and set it on the tray.

I smiled, my voice bright. "Good morning, Robert. You're looking very well."

"Hey, Rob, how're you doing? Look who I found," Paul said, our voices mingling.

"I see. So that's how it is." Robert regarded the two of us hovering at the foot of his bed. "Looks like you two met."

"At last," I said. "You sure know how to keep secrets. You didn't even tell Paul I'd be in Weymouth this week."

"Yeah, you shoulda," Paul said, shifting from one foot to another, "'cause we kind of bumped into each other this morning—"

"At the house, actually. You should've changed the locks."

"Where's the fun in that?" Robert said, an edge in his voice. "You never know who'll drop in."

"I'm sorry Christine couldn't be here, too, but... anyway, it's been nice to catch up with... you know." Paul waved his hand in my direction.

"Livvie," I said, realizing Paul wasn't sure what to call me.

I pulled up a chair. "We had a lot to talk about," I said to Robbie. "I like what you're doing with the house, although I never thought of it as a fixer-upper."

In the silence, Paul, leaning against a wall, looked at Robert, then at me. "This is kind of hard to believe, you know? Seeing you two together and... darn, I wish Chris could be here."

"I'm looking forward to meeting her sometime," I said. "Not just at a book signing, okay?"

"You'll come back, then?"

"I promise. I want to get to know my grandchildren." I looked at Robert. "Sounds like I have an invitation."

"Sure, why not? The door's always open," he said pointedly.

"I'm going to drop Livvie at the airport later," Paul said, "but meanwhile, I've got to make some calls, so I'll leave you to catch up on your own. Rob, you want me to bring you anything? A malt? Burger?"

"A ham sandwich. Mustard, no cheese. Thanks."

"Okay, back in a while." He left, his athletic shoes squeaking noisily on the linoleum as he moved down the hall.

"Good kid," Robert said.

"Damn good kid," I answered. "I'm taking full credit."

"Hell you are!" He chuckled. "Wait until you meet his wife. She's something special."

"I'm looking forward to it. I wish it could have been

sooner." I pulled my chair closer to the bed. "Why didn't you tell me about them before?"

"There was never a time that seemed right."

"And you're going to say it's because you didn't want to upset me?"

"That, too. You really want to get into this?"

"If not now, when? How could you keep something like that to yourself all those years?"

"You never told Jake."

"By the time we married, children weren't an option for us. But why wouldn't you tell me about Paul?"

"You'd have to deal with it again. It would have—"

"Stop telling me what would upset me! What upsets me is that another woman was living my life. He was my child and I wasn't a part of his life."

"Let it go, Livvie."

"Tell me about Susan, since you didn't when I saw her picture in your exhibit."

"She's dead."

"Why did you never marry?"

"Susan?"

"Anyone."

"It worked out that way, Livvie. Don't do this to yourself."

"Just curious. I'm not saying it wasn't a shock to hear about her. But it's worse knowing Paul didn't get in touch with me because you were with Susan. Why did you tell him to leave things be and not reach out to me?"

"You had Jake."

"I know what I had! But that doesn't make it fair. I had no opportunity to know Paul and his wife, or our grandchildren, in the way you have."

"You made a choice that wasn't my doing."

"You made your choice by not standing up for me."

Robbie turned his head away. "Fine, blame me. But you've had a good life, a whole lot better than anything I could've given you. I know I let you down back then, but I couldn't be that man. I'm glad you had Jake. You deserved him. At least I didn't mess that up for you."

"That's nice to hear, Robbie, but this isn't about happily ever after with you. I got over that some time ago. I even managed to hate you, but I didn't get over losing my son. Now I've found him, no thanks to you."

He sighed, his eyes grave as he looked at me. "I don't want to see things spoiled for him. I was going to tell him you were coming. I thought it was time. But the closer your visit was coming up... I just couldn't do it. It's too tangled, Livvie. Let it be now."

"He's a grown man. He has a right to know who his parents are and what happened. Let him untangle things for himself. You can't deny him the truth, or deny me the right to know my son. How dare you?"

"I just wanted to spare him, Livvie." His voice was barely a whisper. "To be pulled apart like I was as a kid wrecks you. Just empties you out. You're no good to anybody. It haunts me every day that I was the cause of so much pain for my mother. I never wanted to be responsible for it again. But then it happened. I couldn't let Paul go through what I did. And... I didn't want this for you, either, but I couldn't see what to do except stand back, leave it be. I'm sorry."

I stared at Robert. I heard desolation in his voice, saw it in his eyes. I tried to comprehend his little-boy thinking, a view of life not so easily demolished as plaster covering brick walls. His was a world seen more safely through a viewfinder, a parade of events and a kaleidoscope of people passing through, left untouched, distant enough to not touch him, but which had tugged him in, anyway. I knew what it was like to be pulled apart, but not as a child in the sad way Robbie had experienced.

Reading "we" on the postcard had spurred me to call Robert after leaving Norm's place that evening. Finding the ring in the Mulligan's matchbook only confirmed my need to see him again. The "we" turned out to be my son and the woman who'd raised him instead of me, but what had Susan's life been like? She'd hung a blue robe in Dorah's bathroom and hadn't had to keep her toiletries in a shoebox under the bed, but I was certain she, too, had lived with the crippling aftermath of Robbie's terrible custody battle.

Shifting my gaze, I looked out the window at the ridge-line of trees miles in the distance, the autumn hues blurring in the sheen dampening my eyes. I felt Jake's guiding hand on my shoulder, encouraging me to stop dwelling on regrets and loss and embrace a future that looked rosier than it had yesterday. I'd be back for my grandson's science fair. Perhaps I'd share holidays with a family I had yet to get to know. Someday, perhaps they'd even visit Willow Creek.

It was time to forgive and be grateful for my life as it was. I plucked a tissue from the box on the bed table and dabbed my cheeks. Without thinking, I picked up Robert's coffee cup.

"You're going to drink a sick man's coffee? They'll bring you fresh."

"I don't think high blood pressure is catchy." I sipped coffee and put the cup back down. "Besides, I already have it— and I remember to take my pills," I added pointedly. "How are you feeling?"

"Okay, no need to worry, except . . ."

"What?"

"I don't know how much time I've got left on my meter."

"No one does." I patted his knee, feeling the boniness through the bed linens.

"Let's make peace, okay?" He slid his hand across the bedcover, turning his palm up. "Can't turn the clock back to fix things. If I could, I would have."

"I know that." I reached into my shoulder bag for the matchbook. "It occurred to me that Christine might like to have your mother's ring. What do you think?"

"Good idea. You keep it for now. We'll give it to her when you come back." His eyes flickered with emotion, his voice hoarse. "You are coming back, aren't you?"

"I'll be back again, Robbie. Don't worry. Everything's going to be fine."

I slipped my hand in my pocket, folding my fingers around the heart-shaped stone I'd found on the beach, holding it tightly for a moment, feeling its warmth. I sensed Jake's presence again, and this time, I knew exactly what he was telling me: That leaving the past "as it was" didn't always mean ignoring it; sometimes it meant embracing that life had worked out the way it was supposed to, even if it wasn't the way you would have chosen.

"Here's something for you."

I dropped the stone into Robbie's palm, wrapping my hand around his.

"Let's make peace."

TO BE NOTIFIED WHEN KATHRYN'S BOOKS
ARE AVAILABLE FOR PREORDER AND/OR
SALE, FOLLOW HER AT:

AMAZON
https://amazon.com/author/kathrynleighscott.com

BOOKBUB
https://www.bookbub.com/profile/kathryn-leigh-scott

GOODREADS
https://www.goodreads.com/KathrynLeighScott

FACEBOOK
https://www.facebook.com/kathrynleighscottauthor

TWITTER
https://twitter.com/kathleighscott

Reading

Group

Guide

TO INVITE KATHRYN LEIGH SCOTT TO SPEAK WITH
YOUR BOOK CLUB VIA SKYPE, E-MAIL:

CUMBERLANDPRESSBOOKS@GMAIL.COM

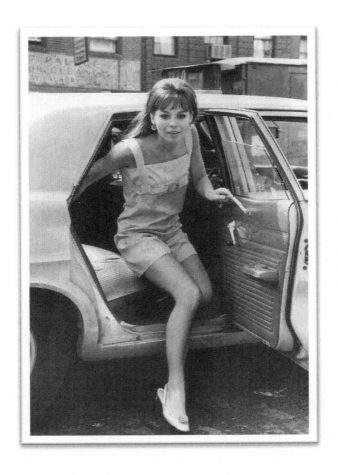

Kathryn Leigh Scott in New York City in 1966

The Story Behind the Story:
The Inspiration for September Girl

KATHRYN LEIGH SCOTT

Another woman was living my life is a line in my novel, *September Girl*, that alludes to a secret at the heart of the story. An old friend said something similar to me over lunch years ago and her words became the inspiration for the book.

I hadn't seen my friend for a while. I asked her if she ever ran into a former classmate of ours, a man she'd married shortly after high school graduation. They'd had two children together and a seemingly happy eight-year marriage, until her husband abruptly left her for another woman. My friend, a beautiful, vibrant and successful fashion designer, had not remarried. I knew their divorce some thirty years earlier had been a bitter jolt for her, but I was startled when she responded, "Yes, I see him at family weddings and funerals, but he's always with this other woman who's living my life."

I realized my friend had never accepted that her former husband had remarried and started a new family. Decades later, she still considered his wife the "other woman" living what should have been her life with him.

Yet, if my friend, who has since passed away, were to read my novel, she'd hardly imagine that her comment motivated me to write this novel. But then, it isn't her story. Instead, her words over lunch prompted me to weave an entirely different scenario in which my protagonist learns, by chance, that another woman really did "live her life," and that a shocking betrayal in her youth robbed her of something she'd once fought for and held dear. Although she was able to move on from this profound loss, enjoying a happy marriage and fulfilling career, discovering long-held secrets spurs her to face a terrible truth and reevaluate the consequences of a life not lived. In the end, she finds redemption that I suspect my friend never could.

Discussion Questions

Early in the novel, Livvie makes a discovery that prompts her to revisit her past. Would you have reached out to Robbie in her position? Or do you subscribe more to Robbie's philosophy of leaving the past "as it was"?

Livvie never told her husband, Jake, about her history with Robbie. Why do you think that was? Based on what she reveals about Jake, how do you think he would have reacted? Do you think their lives would have been very different if she'd shared her secret, and in a good way or a bad way?

Do you think Livvie always felt there was something missing from her life, or do you think she was content? She tells Paul that she resents that her choice was taken away from her. Do you think it's ever better not to know something, or should a person always have a choice?

What do you think Dorah Ellerbe's intentions were regarding Livvie? Regarding Robbie? Knowing what prompted the custody battle with Blanche, do you feel sympathy for Dorah?

In chapter twenty-seven, Livvie learns about a pivotal event in Robbie's childhood. Did knowing about this experience change your opinion of his behavior? Why or why not? How do you think he felt about his mother? Why do you think he remained loyal to his aunt?

If you were in Paul's shoes when he learned about Livvie, what would you have done?

Near the beginning of the novel, Livvie flees her house in Connecticut, then spends much of the novel trying to reach the house in Weymouth. Why do you think the Weymouth house is such a powerful lure for her? How does the theme of *home* relate to her character's internal journey?

When Robbie returns from Angola, he refuses to help Livvie. Did you agree with his decision? Why or why not?

What do you think Robbie intended to do with the ring? What do you think changed his mind?

The present-day scenes in *September Girl* take place in the year 2000. People had cell phones but not smartphones, and very little social media existed. (Facebook, for example, wasn't founded until 2004.) Do you think this story would have unfolded differently if it had taken place in the year 2019?

When you learned about Robbie and Susan, how did you feel?

The novel ends on a note that suggests that Livvie and Robbie's story will continue forward, off the page. What do you think happens next?

Acknowledgments

My deep gratitude to my literary agent, Cynthia Manson, for her wisdom and unflagging support, and to Caitlin Alexander for her masterful editorial guidance and publishing expertise. These two remarkable women made this book happen— thank you, my friends!

Many thanks to friends and colleagues who offered encouragement with "first reads" and assisted with their professional knowledge, foremost among them Nicolette Caliente Harlan-Haq and Ben Martin. As always, Patrick Oster, Heide Wickes, Jo-an Jenkins, Pamela Osowski, Brian Kellow, Steven Sorrentino, Harry Hennig, Michelle Kletti, and my brothers, Orlyn and David . . . when I need a word of advice, a bit of information, another "quick read" or just an ear to bend, you're always there for me.

About the Author

© Jonsar Studios

Author/actress Kathryn Leigh Scott grew up in Robbinsdale, Minnesota, and now lives in Beverly Hills and New York City. She continues to work as an actress and is writing her next novel.

Please visit her website at kathrynleighscott.com.

Made in the USA
Columbia, SC
23 September 2019